DEATH OF A THREAT

A BARBARA O'GRADY MYSTERY

SHARON ROWSE

THREE CEDARS PRESS

Death of a Threat
A Barbara O'Grady Mystery
By Sharon Rowse

Book cover designed by Sharon Rowse & Three Cedars Press
Published by Three Cedars Press
www.threecedarspress.com

ISBN: 978-1-988037-16-5

ALSO BY SHARON ROWSE

The Barbara O'Grady Series: (in order)

Death of a Secret

Death of a Threat

Death of a Promise

Death of a Shadow

Death of a Lie

Death of a Dream

Death of a Chance

The John Granville & Emily Turner Historical Mystery Series: (in order)

The Silk Train Murder

The Lost Mine Murders

The Missing Heir Murders

The Terminal City Murders

The Cannery Row Murders

The Hidden City Murders

The Dockside Murders

*For my friends, each and every wonderful one of you.
You enrich my life.*

CHAPTER ONE

"Barbara, I need your help," my best friend said. "I'm scared of Jake. I want him out."

She was perched on a stool in the window of our favorite coffee shop, a chocolate croissant in one hand and a latte steaming gently in front of her. I'd just taken a sip of my double cappuccino, and I nearly choked on it.

Andrea Fisher and I have been friends since elementary school, and I can usually read her pretty well. But when she'd suggested we grab a coffee, she hadn't given the slightest hint that she planned to drop this little bombshell.

"What? Jake-your-tenant? That Jake?" I asked.

She nodded.

"You're kidding me."

"I wish I was."

Jake Scott has been living in Andrea's basement suite since before she bought her turn-of-the-century house. In fact, it was the 'mortgage helper' suite complete with long-term tenant that convinced the bank to lend her the ridiculous amount of money she needed to buy the place. She'd never so much as complained about Jake before, and now she was scared of him?

"So what's changed?" I asked.

"I don't know," she said. "I really don't. Jake's always been pretty laid back, but lately he gets mad at the least little thing. And not just garden-variety pissed off. This is major blowup angry. I don't even recognize the old Jake in this new version."

"Angry how?"

"You know the renovations I'm doing?"

I nodded. I've heard about little else for months now. Good thing I don't have to live with it, that's all I can say.

"Well, yesterday Jake started swearing at the carpet layer" Andrea said. "He said the guy was making too much noise. This was the middle of the day. It's not like they're working late or starting early or anything."

How to phrase this diplomatically? Not that diplomacy has ever been my strong suit. "I can see where living with someone else's renovations could be annoying…"

"We're not talking annoyed," she said. We're talking making physical threats. That carpet layer is a big guy, but he refused to leave my place while Jake was anywhere around."

"Maybe he was using it as an excuse to spend more time with you," I said.

It was possible. Andrea is a vibrant blue-eyed blonde who's been garnering male attention all her life. To her credit, she mostly ignores her effect on men.

"Definitely not. He's gay," Andrea said. "And you're not taking me seriously here."

It was hard to take her complaint too seriously. For one thing, she and Jake always got along just fine. My mind flipped to the last time I'd seen Jake Scott. He'd been mowing Andrea's lawn, looking pretty good in jeans and a tight T-shirt.

Jake is quite a flirt, attractive in that slightly shaggy but rugged way a lot of women find appealing, but he's more guy next door than bad boy. Just doesn't have that threatening aura. Nope, not scary.

Andrea didn't smile, and she'd abandoned the croissant, which meant I'd better start taking her seriously. It takes a lot to get between Andrea and her croissants. She allots herself two a week, and she seriously enjoys them.

"Look, he's gone from making suggestions about the yard to yelling at anyone who tries to set foot on the property," Andrea said. "He got into an argument with some poor soul doing a survey on parking bylaws who made the mistake of coming up on the porch. Jake got so loud and threatening I had to call the police."

"What did they do?"

"Warned him to clean up his act. But they told me there wasn't much else they could do." She gave a tiny shrug. "It's made him worse. He's always swearing at something, usually me."

"Has he done anything physical?"

"Not yet."

OK, that was good. "So maybe he'll settle down once the reno's finished."

She didn't look convinced.

"There's more," she said, her voice not quite steady.

Over Andrea's shoulder, the kaleidoscope of color and style that confirm Robson's status as Vancouver's trendiest street whirled by unaffected. A shaft of sunlight highlighted her taut features. I've drawn my best friend so often, I know every line and hollow of her expressive face, and I'd never seen her look so strained.

She was scared. Really scared.

"Go on," I said, bracing myself.

"Jake lived in LA before he moved here," Andrea said. "He came home one afternoon—Barbara, his apartment was broken into and his girlfriend murdered. He says it was random, and that he moved north to get away from the memories and the violence, but I'm starting to wonder. At very least he's got reason to be paranoid. And with that rash of gang shootings and the way he's been acting…"

Her voice trailed off and she spread her hands in a gesture of helplessness.

Metro Vancouver's gangs have been growing and diversifying over the last ten years or so, mostly driven by drug money, with crack cocaine and crystal meth being the front runners. Now fentanyl has joined the mix. Not too long ago gang wars created a rash of targeted hits, taking our murder statistics into the double digits.

The violence that underlies any port city seemed to be moving from back alleys and the drug-ridden Downtown East Side to everyone's neighborhood. Suddenly drive-by shootings were taking place in parking lots outside bowling alleys and mom n' pop groceries as well as outside the homes of known gang members in upscale suburban neighborhoods.

Like Andrea's. And Jake lived in her basement suite.

I wasn't liking any of this.

"Jake's got a new tattoo," Andrea added. "And I'm pretty sure he has a gun. I'm afraid he'll use it."

Tattoos were hardly an indicator. Maybe she was over-reacting?

But if she wasn't... "You're thinking he might be associated with a gang?"

She shrugged one shoulder, then nodded.

The possibility fried my brain cells into something resembling curry. "You really think he could be that dangerous?"

"Yes."

I tried for rational. "Because he's swearing more? He could just be losing it with all the renovations."

"This feels worse, Barbara. And he's been getting worse."

OK, then. "Where's the tattoo?"

"Right bicep."

"Of what?"

She glanced at me, turned over her napkin and held out her hand. I reached into my purse, handed her the soft '3H' pencil I always carry.

She drew a wobbly blotch that looked something like a dagger with a rose twined around it, a drop of blood falling from the tip.

I watched the lines form, feeling none of the amusement that her drawings usually spark in me.

"It's done entirely in black, except for the blood," she said, handing it to me. "And he's just got a new bike, too. A big one."

I'd forgotten he rode a motorcycle. But again, that didn't mean much. I know of several former CEO's who bought Harleys when they retired. Boomers all.

"Doesn't mean he's in a gang."

"It means he could be."

"Then evict him, so you don't have to deal with this. It sounds like you have enough issues. Have you talked to a lawyer?"

"Yes, I talked to Claire."

I've worked with Claire Chan in the past, and she's good. I breathed a sigh of relief. "OK, then. What did Claire say?"

"She said I might have enough evidence to get him evicted."

"Well, that sounds…"

"But that I'd have to file an application, and it would probably take a couple of weeks for an appointment. It could take months to get him out. And it can get really messy if the tenant doesn't want to leave."

She met my eyes. "Jake isn't going to want to leave. And with his moods lately—I'm afraid of what he might do."

I could understand that. "Can't the police help?"

Andrea got an odd expression on her face and shook her head. Something was up. But her next words drove the thought out of my mind.

"Barbara, I want to hire you to get that gun away from Jake, get him out of my place," Andrea said. "Whatever it takes."

My response was automatic. "Andrea, I'm a private investigator, not a police detective. I'm the one who spends her life following suspected insurance defrauders and wandering husbands. I can find out if he has a gun registered. I can talk to the police about your concerns. But there isn't much more I can do."

Especially not if he really was involved with a gang.

She wasn't listening. "I need your help, Barbara. I don't know where else to turn."

Well, that was it, of course. I was hired. And completely out of my depth.

———

HALF AN HOUR later I was sitting in my cramped office staring at the sketch Andrea had drawn, questioning my own sanity.

I'm a private investigator. As I'd tried to tell Andrea, I excel at stakeouts, at tracking down missing relatives and checking out deadbeat dads and potential boyfriends. Potentially homicidal gang members, not so much.

Still, here I was. Taking a deep breath, I fired up Google.

Twenty-three searches and forty-seven web pages later I sat back, relieved.

It always amazes me what you can find online, even if some of it is suspect. In addition to various news reports, I'd found a database some enterprising citizen had started on local gang members— anyone who'd been arrested or profiled in the papers, which included a number of gang tattoos.

I'd peered closely at each and every one of those photos. And I'd found no imagery combining roses, daggers and blood drops. Jake's tattoo didn't seem related to the Hells Angels or any of their alleged puppet clubs. And from what I'd found, the Red Scorpions, UN and Independent Soldiers gangs mostly used initials, sometimes combined with images.

I picked up the phone.

"Trusted Temps, Andrea Fisher speaking."

"Andrea, it's me. Jake's tattoo. Did it have any writing or initials on it?"

She didn't hesitate. "No. Nothing like that."

"You're sure?"

"Yes. Is it important?"

"I think so." I paused. "I read somewhere that digital SLR cameras can use non-digital lenses. Have you still got your old long-range lenses?"

"Have you ever known me to throw anything out?"

She had a point. Organize and label it, yes. Throw it out, no.

"Think you can use the old lenses and your fancy new camera to get a photo of that tattoo? Without him noticing you?"

She was silent for a moment. "I think so. I've got some lenses that will give me a real close-up. And any time it's sunny, Jake's out working on that bike. I should be able to get something."

"OK, but be careful." As if I had to tell her that. "E-mail it to me as soon as you have it, okay?"

"Will do. Barbara?" She hesitated. "Any news on whether Jake has a gun?" The words came too fast, nearly running together.

"No, nothing yet."

"You'll call me?"

"I promise."

I disconnected, considered the ridiculously bad drawing in front of me. If Andrea had captured something even vaguely resembling the real tattoo, the likelihood that Jake belonged to a gang seemed pretty slim.

And the man sold insurance, for heaven's sake.

I blew out the breath I hadn't realized I was holding. Probably there was no gang connection. Probably.

But he didn't exactly sound stable, and if it turned out he had a gun? Not good.

How do I get myself into these things, anyway?

Guns and Barbara O'Grady are a bad combination. Plus there's that working for friends thing. Yet here I was.

Not just working for my best friend, but taking on a case that starts with the premise that someone might be armed and dangerous.

The last time I'd gotten too close to a gunman, I found myself staring down the barrel of a loaded pistol into the cold eyes of a man who'd already murdered three people, a man who had nothing to lose.

I still relive that moment. The utter disbelief that it's really happening mixed with the awful realization of what it means to be mortal.

Once the shock—not to mention being shot—wore off, I started questioning whether I was really cut out to be a P. I. I might have eaten a lot of beans in my painting days, but at least no-one was trying to kill me.

While my arm healed, I took some time off and traveled, toyed with the idea of getting a good bean cookbook.

In the end I came back, but I've been very careful to take only routine cases. Ones where I wasn't going to get shot at.

Until now.

But there was no way I could have said no to Andrea.

And there was no proof Jake actually had a gun. Maybe all the renovations were getting to Andrea too, and she was getting paranoid.

That didn't sound like my level-headed friend, though. And she'd asked for my help.

Resigning myself to the inevitable, I started with a call to my buddy Jerry Hawald. Now that he's risen to the rank of detective, Jerry isn't usually too pleased to hear from me when I'm working on a case. But maybe he'd have some good news for me on Jake's possible gun.

"You've reached the voice mail of…"

"Never fails," I muttered. "Jerry, it's Barbara. I need to talk to you urgently. Call me."

I'd barely disconnected when the phone rang. I glanced at the number, but it was blocked. Not Jerry. Now what?

"O'Grady Investigations. Barbara O'Grady speaking."

"Ms. O'Grady? I'd like to hire you," a voice I didn't recognize said in a hoarse half-whisper.

My favorite words. But what was with the voice? "And your name?"

"No names. I just want you to find some information for me."

"I'm sorry, I can't accept a case from an anonymous client."

"You'll be well paid."

"I'm afraid not."

"Check your mailbox," he said, and disconnected.

"Stupid caller." He didn't deserve it, but I was too intrigued to ignore the call.

My overactive curiosity keeps getting me in trouble. Probably why I became a P. I., come to think of it.

I headed down the echoing stairwell to the lobby. I'm doing pretty well as an investigator, but not well enough to afford a flashy office in a new building, or one on the west side of downtown.

Still, my building has character, which is a nice way of saying it's old. It was built in 1907, which makes it a heritage building in this town. Vancouver doesn't have a lot of what any eastern city would consider history.

The lobby retains some flavor of the building's former elegance with marble floors and much scuffed paneled walls. The mailboxes are the old fashioned scrolled kind, with the contents partially visible even before the box is opened.

There was a sealed nine by twelve manila envelope in my box. No postmark, so it had been hand delivered.

Swearing under my breath, I checked the lock on the mailbox. There was no obvious sign of tampering, but these mailboxes are original to the building, which means that they look great, but aren't all that secure.

The building is locked at night, but during the day people come and go. My caller must have been watching the lobby and seized his opportunity.

"Amateur hour! I do not need this," I muttered to myself, and took the stairs two at a time all the way back up to the seventh floor landing.

CHAPTER TWO

B ack in my office I slit the envelope, dumping three crumpled twenties, two tens and a note on the desk. I stared at them for a moment, then unfolded the note. Which told me the money was my retainer to investigate the murder of one James Forrester. I'd be contacted with further details.

There was no signature, no return address, no way to contact or even identify the sender of the note.

Why me? Why had this sender decided that I was his investigator of choice? Some incurably curious part of my nature wanted to know what was going on. The rest of me wanted nothing to do with this one.

I examined the contents of the envelope again and thought about the incongruity of the crumpled bills and the crisp, laser printed note. The phone rang.

"Look, whoever you are," I said. "I don't want anything to do with your case, and an eighty dollar retainer is not about to change my mind."

"Morning, O'Grady. Problems with your clients?" Jerry's voice asked.

Of course. It would be Jerry. They way my day was going, how could it possibly have been anyone else?

And Jerry would be insufferably amused by my would-be client. "Morning, Jerry."

"So what is it now, O'Grady?"

"It's about Andrea."

"What about her?"

There was an odd note in his voice. Was that a nervous edge I was hearing? "Apparently she wants to hire me."

"Why?"

"No need to bark at me. It's her tenant. She's afraid he's got a gun, and that he might use it. She's scared, Jerry."

"Yeah?" There was a pause, and I could hear keys clicking. "It's Jake Scott, right?"

"Right."

"I'll look into it, get back to you."

"Jerry, before you go… Do you have a contact on the gang task force? Someone who'd recognize a gang tattoo, know what it means?"

Set up a few years back, the Integrated Gang Task Force is a collaborative effort between the local Royal Canadian Mounted Police, or RCMP, and various Metro Vancouver police forces. Jerry had never talked about it, but surely he'd know someone.

"Why?"

"Same reason. I doubt it's related, but I'm just being careful." I hoped.

"I'll let you know," he said. And disconnected.

Jerry wasn't usually so cooperative.

Where were the "serves you right, you're the one who wanted to be a P. I." comments? And what was that odd note when I'd mentioned Andrea? Could there be something going on between Jerry and Andrea?

Jerry, Andrea and I have been friends forever, and there's never been anything between the two of them, anything sexual, I mean.

But lately there's been a hint of electricity in the air, just a touch of sizzle. And now this.

Or was I imagining it?

And if I wasn't? How did I feel about the prospect of two of my best friends hooking up?

It wasn't like there was anything between Jerry and me. I think of him more like a brother. Plus there was Alessandro, the man whose open-hearted enjoyment of life, and of me, had almost convinced me to move to Venice and live on pasta instead of beans.

Even after I came home, I seriously considered moving. Then I discovered exactly how much Alessandro travels, and decided I'd see as much of him living in Vancouver as I would have living in Venice.

Which has proven true. Mostly.

So why was I finding the thought of Jerry and Andrea together unsettling?

Granted, I don't much like change. Except when it's my idea, of course. But their relationship wouldn't affect my friendship with either of them.

Probably I'm just antsy because I haven't seen Alessandro in three weeks. His last few trips through Vancouver were re-routed. I miss him, that's all.

Nothing to do with Jerry and Andrea.

With a sigh, I got up and brewed a cup of Viennese Roast. Mug in hand, I stared at the phone, daring it to ring again. I wanted it clear to the author of that note that I wasn't going to investigate his murder case for him.

He could go to the police. They were equipped to handle murder. I wasn't. Especially not for an eighty dollar retainer.

I took a mouthful of coffee, grimaced and put it down. More caffeine wasn't going to help. Running away might.

———

FIFTEEN MINUTES later I was well into my run. I'd parked my car near Second Beach because it's convenient for the Stanley Park Seawall. Since they've put pay parking in all the lots, I've learned to carry plenty of toonies, as our two dollar coin is affectionately called, and I've speeded up my run so I always make it back before my meter expires.

A parking fine is just one more hassle I don't need. Still, running the Seawall is worth any price.

They say a city's parks define its character—New York has Central Park, San Francisco has Golden Gate. Vancouver has Stanley Park, minutes from downtown, a thousand acres of green framed by English Bay.

Where else in the world would you find rush hour traffic, winding through the park towards the narrow Lion's Gate Bridge and tony West Vancouver, politely stopping to let a family of Canada Geese toddle across the road? With not even a horn blaring to protest the delay?

The Seawall winds around the perimeter of the park, along the shoreline. You have the ocean on one side with a vista of mountains beyond it, and the beauty of forest, lakes and gardens on the other side.

Freighters anchor in the bay, and tugs chuff steadily upstream pulling their cargo of logs. The fresh salt air and the beauty all around me, combined with the exertion of my run, never fails to clear my mind and calm my soul.

I was breathing deeply and evenly, concentrating on keeping each stride clean and strong, when a voice spoke from behind me.

"Morning, Barbara," it said, as a magnificent pair of shoulders pulled into my line of vision.

Nicholas Markham. Tall, wavy brown hair falling over one eye, angular features. I smiled.

Nick rents the office down the far end of the hall from mine. Our landlord, Mr. Chang, introduced us when Nick first rented the space, but I see him most often on the Seawall. He's some kind of insurance agent, I think, though Mr. Chang wasn't very specific and Nick has never volunteered any information.

I guess I could check him out, but it feels wrong to pry into people's lives unless it's part of a case. Plus it would mean admitting I'm interested in him. And there's Alessandro, after all.

The currently missing-in-action Alessandro.

Nick fell into step with me, and we ran in silence, except for the sounds of our breathing. Despite the difference in our heights, I have long legs, so our steps matched pretty well.

I slanted a look at him. He looked absorbed, deep in thought. We ran on.

The Lion's Gate Bridge was in sight when he finally spoke.

"D'you know your office is being watched?" he asked, spacing the words out so as not to interfere with his breathing.

"What?" I gasped, having slightly more trouble than Nick in talking while running at this pace.

"Uh huh." It was almost a grunt. "I've spotted this little guy lurking around. Kinda short, thin, tow hair—looks like he might be a teenager. Couple times, I've seen him near your office. Scuttles off when he sees me."

A teenager? My nephew was the right age, but he had dark hair. I ran through my current client list, which didn't take long. None of them had children the right age and coloring. So who was this kid?

"Thanks. I don't know who he is, but I'll keep an eye out."

He nodded, and we ran on in silence, well past the spot where I usually turn around.

"Time to head back," I said eventually, spacing my words carefully so I wouldn't sound winded. "Join me for coffee?"

"Thanks, but I'm running the whole thing today. I'll take a rain check, though," he said with a flash of white teeth. He wasn't even breathing hard and his smile nearly stopped my breath. It wasn't fair.

I smiled weakly in return, then headed back the other way.

As I retraced my steps, I shifted my thoughts with an effort from Nick to the kid. Nick's teenager. Why was he hanging around outside my door? I flashed on the crumpled bills I'd found in my mailbox.

Oh no. Please tell me my would-be client wasn't a teenager. But it all fit. And if it did, it meant I had a second client I didn't want.

No way I could turn down a kid in trouble.

Just like I couldn't turn down Andrea.

My thoughts were starting back into the same pointless circle the run was supposed to get them out of. Muttering to myself, I went back to concentrating on my breathing and counting each step.

When I finally got back to my aging Civic, sweating heavily and breathing hard, I felt more relaxed. I headed back to my place for a quick shower, picked up a fresh set of running gear, and went back to the office.

Within minutes of sitting down at my computer, the clarity I'd gained from my run was lost under a pile of paperwork. Then the phone rang. I glared at it.

That phone was what had got me into this mess. First it had been Andrea, then the would-be client. They say bad luck comes in threes. If there was another case like those two on the other end of that phone, I didn't want to answer it.

I nearly let it go to voice mail, but by the third ring I couldn't just leave it. "O'Grady Investigations."

"Jake Scott has a gun permit," Jerry said. "He owns a .32."

Oh no. "You're sure?"

"Yeah. I double-checked everything."

"Then Andrea could be in real danger from Jake?"

"Not necessarily." He paused, as if hoping I'd say something. For a change, I couldn't think of a single thing to say. "I checked the report, though. From when Andrea called us."

His tone gave me a cold twisting in my gut. "And?"

"You'll keep this confidential?"

How could he even ask? "Of course. What is it, Jerry?"

"Jake Scott's sworn out a couple of complaints against Andrea."

"What?"

"She didn't tell you?"

"No." What else hadn't she told me? And what was going on? "What did he complain about?"

"Says she's stalking him."

"Andrea. Stalking Jake?"

"Yeah."

"Not a chance." There was no doubt in my mind.

"I know. But it's officially on record. We can't ignore it."

"I can."

"Yeah. I know."

"So has Andrea sworn out a complaint against Jake?"

"Uh huh. The last incident."

"And?"

"Report says he was pretty belligerent."

"Damn."

"Yeah." A pause. "But according to the report, so was Andrea."

As an attempt to lighten the moment, it failed. A small silence feel between us. It wasn't a comfortable one. "Is there anything you can do?"

"No. Unless he makes a move, our hands are tied."

"She's pretty scared, Jerry."

"I know." His voice sounded tired.

"There must be something you can do."

"Andrea could file another complaint, put it on record. But even then we'd be pretty much limited to a restraining order, forbidding him to be within a certain distance of her. Not much help when they live on the same property."

He sounded like he was reciting facts, like it didn't matter to him. Jerry never did deal with emotion very well. "That's it? Jerry, there's got to be more."

"Unless he actually hurts her, we can't step in. Especially with his complaints on file too."

Oh, terrific. "Thanks a lot, Jerry. Nice to know the cops are on the job."

I drew a deep breath and tried to calm down. This wasn't Jerry's fault. "So what's she supposed to do? Sit and wait for him to lose it one day and attack her?"

"I don't like it any better than you do, O'Grady."

"I know, I know. But Andrea needs help, Jerry."

"Isn't that why she's hiring you?"

That stopped me cold. He wasn't kidding. "Me?"

Was that a squeak in my voice? I took another deep breath and nearly choked. Some part of me had been hoping still that she wasn't really hiring me. Or rather, that she didn't really need to.

I didn't want to recognize how scared I was for Andrea, much less admit it to Jerry. "What happened to telling me not to get into dangerous situations?"

It didn't fool him for a minute. Even over the phone lines his sigh was audible. "Officially, there's nothing I can do. Unofficially, you're probably her best hope. And O'Grady?"

"What?" I was still digesting his previous remark, the one about me being her best hope. I didn't like the sound of that, not one bit. Jerry's next words didn't make me feel any better.

"The guy you need to talk to about gang tats? Stuart Ng." He gave me the number.

I took it down numbly.

"Call me if anything changes."

What, if it got worse? Now, there was a comforting thought. "Yeah. I'll call you. Jerry, is there anything you can do about the gun?"

"Nope. Not one damn thing."

There was a long silence. Neither of us seemed to know what to say. Finally Jerry spoke. "Can she kick the bastard out?"

"She's working on it. It may take a while, though."

"No special provisions?"

"Apparently not. Pathetic, isn't it? Andrea owns the house. She's a single woman, living alone. Her tenant is armed and abusive and she still has to go through all the proper channels."

"This is when I hate being a cop. You've seen it before, you know what's coming, and there's not a damn thing you can do about it."

That pretty much said it all. "I'll be in touch, Jerry."

Then sat staring at the phone for a long moment. I wasn't dealing with a case that might have an element of danger, I was dealing with a possible maniac with a confirmed gun.

Who might be getting ready to kill my best friend.

And I was supposed to do something about it.

CHAPTER THREE

I started a cup of French Roast brewing and paced from desk to window and back while I waited for it to drip through. I could feel a headache starting just behind my eyes, the kind that end up with my head pounding and my neck and shoulder muscles tied in knots.

So much for the benefit of the run. When my head gets really bad, I can't concentrate, much less think. My doctor tells me it's stress, and I should try to relax more. Easy for her to say—she's the one with the ulcer.

Pouring myself a cup of fresh coffee, I retrieved the bottle of extra strength painkillers from the top drawer and took two.

Five minutes later, I was still pacing, waiting for the drugs to kick in.

I debated calling Jerry's gang squad contact, but without a better picture of the tattoo it wasn't likely to be helpful. I could follow up on that new motorbike, though. I poured more coffee, punched in another set of numbers.

"Zabel."

"Rob? Barbara O'Grady. Have you got a minute?"

"B! For you, always."

"Even though I still owe you that steak dinner from the last case?"

"So I'll order a bigger steak. What can I do for you?"

"Andrea's got a problem with her tenant and she's asked for help. I need to know what he drives."

"Not serious, is it?"

"I hope not."

"Hmmm. You know I can't give out private information on … what's the guys name?"

"Yeah, I know. It's Jake Scott."

"Same address as Andrea, right?"

I sipped my coffee while keys clicked madly over the line, then Rob's voice came back. "Well, I can't tell you he owns a Harley. Big one, last year's model." And he gave me the plate number.

A Harley? I keyed it in, my mind racing. "Anything else you can't tell me?"

More clicking. "Nope. Not a thing."

"OK, thanks Rod. And we'll have that steak, I promise. Next time I'm in Victoria. Or you're over here."

"You're good for it, B. But you should plan to come over, take a break once in a while."

"I know, I know. Maybe when I've sorted out this situation with Andrea." Yeah, right. There'd be another urgent case right behind this one. It was the nature of the business.

"I'll hold you to it. But I gotta run. Later, B."

"Later." I disconnected, stared at the notes I'd taken.

The Harley changed things. Maybe. It did raise a few questions, though.

How had Jake afforded it, for starters? He did live in Andrea's basement, after all. Even if it was a pretty upscale basement suite, it still didn't fit with a Harley.

And the Hells Angels and their affiliates were inordinately fond of them.

I pictured Jake as I'd last seen him, giving me a smile and a wink over some joke he'd made. I just couldn't see him with gang connections. He had no edge of danger to him, not that I'd ever seen, anyway.

But Andrea was afraid of him. And he had a gun.

I needed to talk to Jake Scott, and soon.

The phone rang. Great. Shutting out the pain throbbing behind my temples, I answered.

"Did you get the package, Miss O'Grady?"

It was my would-be client. Just what this day needed.

"It's Ms. O'Grady," I corrected automatically. "Now look…"

"Good," he broke in, as though I'd said yes. "First, I want you to look up all of Forrester's friends. Then, find out what he did that last week."

I was amazed to note that although he was still whispering, there was now a commanding sound to the whisper. Could this be the teenager Nick has spotted? It was possible, but I couldn't tell. The hoarse whisper was a pretty good disguise.

"Slow down," I said. "I'm not sure I can take your case."

"You're not?" Now there was a shocked note in that hoarse voice. "But why not? You've got the retainer, and your instructions."

Oh, great. I was dealing with someone who had seen too many detective movies, and probably old movies at that.

"Look, I have too many cases on the go already, and I don't investigate murders. That's for the police."

"But they think it was suicide. And he would never—I mean it had to be murder. There's no other explanation." He'd forgotten to whisper, and his voice was light and shaky. And young? Oh, hell.

I still wasn't sure. But he sounded so sad, I couldn't keep pushing him away.

"Look, I can check the facts for you. But that's all I can do. If there's anything to suggest it was murder, I'll turn whatever I've found over to the police, and they can take it from there."

"Oh," he said. There was a short silence. "Well, I guess that would be okay." Another silence. "You're sure you couldn't just solve it yourself?"

Now he sounded hopeful.

"I'm sure," I said, keeping my tone as firm as I could. I had the feeling if I wavered even slightly on this one, I'd be sunk. "How'd you get my name, anyway?"

"Googled you. I read those articles where they convicted that guy who killed the Senator and they talk about you."

It figured. Doug Matthews had done me proud in reporting that case. And ever since, I'd been discovering what people meant when they say publicity can be a two-edged sword.

It seemed my current caller was yet another reminder of that little fact.

"That was a murder case," he said, sounding aggrieved. "You solved that one. Why won't you solve mine?"

"It's a long story." And not one I was eager to talk about—no way I wanted to admit that I'd solved that case mostly by mistake. Oh, I'd exposed the murderer all right, I just hadn't intended to nearly get killed in the process. I wouldn't be making that mistake again.

"But if I'm to take your case, I'll need some information. Your name and phone number would be a good start. And you'll need to come in to sign a contract."

"No names. Just find Forrester's killer," he said. And disconnected.

I shook my head in disbelief. It was definitely not my day.

At least my headache was gone. I'd been so involved in my conversation with my newest client I hadn't even noticed when the pain departed. I didn't hear the footsteps in the hallway, either.

The office door creaked. I jumped a mile.

"Does Jake have a gun, Barbara?" Andrea asked as she stepped into the office, looking as chicly pulled together as ever. Everything coordinated, except the darkness in her eyes.

It's probably the only time in my life I haven't been happy to see her. "Yes, Andrea. He does."

"Oh. My. God." She'd gone white as a freshly primed canvas. "What am I going to do? What can I do, Barb?"

"I don't know what to tell you, Andrea," I said. And felt like a complete failure.

She sank into one of my vintage leather guest chairs and just looked at me. For a moment I was afraid she was going to faint, then she drew in a shuddering breath.

It took everything I had to keep from telling her that I was nearly as panicked as she was.

Finally she spoke. "You'll do what you can, won't you, Barbara? There must be something you can do? Please."

I couldn't imagine what it must be like to be afraid of someone who lived in your own home, beneath the floorboards of your kitchen, your living room. To hear him every day, fearing he was dangerous, knowing he was armed.

To have to tell her that there was nothing she or anyone could do about him—nothing but wait until the day he actually did something violent—was unthinkable.

"I'll find something, Andrea. There has to be a way to deal with Jake, and I'll find it for you."

Good thing she didn't ask for details. I hadn't the foggiest clue what I was going to do.

"Thanks, Barbara," she said, sounding a little calmer. "I'm counting on you."

That's what I was afraid of. But Andrea didn't need to hear about my fears. She had enough of her own. "So how's Jake been behaving himself?" I asked, striving for lightness. "Any run-ins?"

She matched my tone with an effort that I could almost feel. "No, nothing since the carpets went in."

"Well, that's a good sign," I said, adding 'I hope' silently to myself. Until I had something concrete, I wasn't about to add to Andrea's fears.

"In fact, he's been nearly invisible lately," she said in good imitation of calm. "He paces the floor a lot though. And come to think of it, he must be stomping fairly hard for me to hear him."

"A little stomping never hurt anyone."

"No. No, it hasn't." Her voice caught on a sob. "But I don't think he'll stop there. Barbara, what am I going to do?"

I'd been thinking fast, and this time I had an answer. "You're going get that photo for me. And you're going to gather all the information you have on Jake. Anything you know, anything you've heard, anything at all. And I need it sorted, indexed and collated."

Andrea choked on a laugh. It's a running joke between us. I think her mania for organizing everything in sight verges on obsession. She thinks I'm a slob.

"I can do that," she said, looking a little more like herself.

"And you'll need to include every detail, no matter how small. You'd be surprised what ends up being useful." And I'd rather she was busy than sitting worrying.

She pulled out her iPad and made a few quick notes. I had no doubt that in a day or two I could expect a detailed report, properly formatted, that laid out everything she knew about her tenant. "OK, I've got it. Is there anything else you need?"

Here it comes. "There is one thing I need to know. I hear that Jake took out a complaint against you. For stalking?"

She went white. "And you believe him?"

"Of course not. But I need to know everything about him, especially anything that's out of character, anything that might give me a clue as to why he's acting the way he is."

"Oh," she said, but she looked suspiciously watery. "I couldn't stand it if you didn't believe me."

"Of course I believe you. You're my best friend. It's in the contract."

She laughed a little. "Right."

"But I really do need to know what happened."

"OK." A pause. "Well, this was nearly a month ago. Before he got worse. I'd already been hearing complaints about Jake being belligerent, from the neighbors, y'know? And since he's my tenant, they expected me to fix it.

So I came home in the middle of the day a few times, to see for myself. I came up behind him in the yard one day when he was arguing with Carol, you know her? The gray house? Anyway, I joined in the argument and it seemed to upset him. That's when he complained about me."

It sounded reasonable. But I've known Andrea a long time. There was something she was avoiding saying. "And?"

She looked sheepish. "Well, when I was arguing with him, I kinda followed him into his suite."

"Andrea, you didn't."

She wouldn't meet my eyes. "Not very far, you know, just inside the back door. He'd thrown some insult at me and gone storming inside, leaving the door open. I couldn't let it stop there. I followed him. I still hadn't made my points."

I sighed. "Andrea, you're his landlord. And you've just made my job harder."

"I know. I know. I was too ashamed to tell you. I didn't even tell Claire, when I was asking about evicting him."

Oh, Andrea. No wonder she didn't want to go through the eviction process. "Was it afterwards that Jake's temper seemed to get worse?"

"You know, it wasn't. In fact, after that, he seemed to be calmer for a couple of weeks. The complaints stopped, both from him and about him. I was just thinking maybe it was going to be okay, when the incident with the carpet-layer seemed to set everything off again. And he's been getting steadily worse."

I jotted down a few quick notes. There was a pattern here, I just wasn't sure yet what it meant. "Anything else I should know?"

She gave me a look. "No."

OK, then.

We talked a little longer, then she left. I took another deep breath, trying to ease the tension I could feel creeping back into my neck muscles. I was out of my depth on this one.

I looked from the stack of papers on my desk to the notes I'd taken while I talked with the kid to the notes I'd made talking to Andrea. I needed to focus all my energy on doing something about Jake. Time to clear everything else off my desk.

I called Doug. His story had brought me my would-be client, it seemed only fitting that he help dig up the facts on James Forrester's death.

"Yeah?"

"Are you so polite to all your potential leads?"

"Who is this?"

"Very funny."

"Look, Barbara, I'm on deadline. I've got a story to finish in the next hour. I don't have time to chat."

"I thought you'd be interested in another story."

"Not right now I'm not," he said, and disconnected.

So much for clearing the case off my desk. I fired him an e-mail, setting up a meeting for the following afternoon. I'd hand him the case then. In the meantime, I needed to clear my schedule for the next few days.

With a sigh, I pulled up a couple of case files that were complete except for the final reports and started typing.

Hours later I finally typed the last period. I yawned hugely and stretched out my aching back muscles, gazing absently out the window as I did so.

It had been one of those hot, sunny days Vancouver gets in early fall, when everyone and his dog is outside—sunning on the beach, sailing on the Bay, sipping margaritas or designer beer in a sidewalk cafe. A perfect day, and I'd been trapped inside.

The sun was low in the sky now, and the light held that golden quality it gets just before sunset. Suddenly I realized how late it was, and how tired I was. It was time to go home.

I'd finished three reports and there was nothing I could do about Jake tonight. Maybe I'd even accomplish more in the morning, with a fresh point of view.

CHAPTER FOUR

The following morning my point of view might have been fresh, but nothing else was. Yesterday's sunshine had been replaced by drenching rain and I got soaked dashing from car to office. I'd overslept, my head hurt and my eyes felt like somebody had glued them shut then pried them open with a crowbar. Plus the vision in one eye kept fuzzing out.

Problem was, it had been such a beautiful evening and I'd been starving, so I stopped at Guido's on the way home. I only intended to stay for a quick bite, maybe a glass or two of wine. Yeah, right. I'd just found a seat on the patio when Guido, bless him, brought out a plate of chicken wings along with my glass of Merlot.

"Barbara, you must try these wings and tell me what you think. They are a new flavor I am trying out," he said.

"They're great, Guido," I said, when my mouth had recovered enough to talk. "You might want to back up a little on the peppers, though."

I finished all the wings he'd brought out, though, washed down with a couple of glasses of wine. When it started to get chilly, I moved inside and ordered yet more wings. And more wine.

The jazz trio was terrific, so it was about two in the morning before I actually got home. Luckily Guido's is only a five minute walk from my place, because I was in no shape to drive.

So now I felt like death warmed over and I still didn't know how to begin dealing with a maniac with a gun. Moving in slow motion, I put on a pot of Viennese Blend and slumped down in my vintage burgundy leather swivel chair while I waited for it to brew.

Groaning, I turned on my computer and loaded Andrea's file. Looking at the information I'd compiled the previous day, I couldn't think of a single constructive thing to do with it.

What was needed here was action of some sort. The welcome burbling of a completed coffee cycle interrupted that thought. I got up, poured a cup and sank down again.

After a restorative couple of mouthfuls, my brain was actually starting to function. I picked up the phone and dialed Sid Fluxgold's number. He'd been back from his cruise for three months. Pre-retirement, Sid had been a tenacious investigator and a generous mentor. Despite the frequency with which he'd wished for retirement, I just couldn't picture him taking it easy now.

"Fluxgold."

"Sid? It's Barbara. Listen, can I buy you lunch? I want to bounce some ideas off of you."

"I'd have to say no to lunch, Barbara."

Until I felt my heart hit my toes, I hadn't realized how much I was counting on Sid's insights.

"Brunch, though, brunch I would say yes to."

"Don't tell me you just got up!"

"So I won't tell you."

"Retirement certainly must be agreeing with you."

"Do you want to keep insulting me, or do you want to buy me brunch?"

"Brunch it is. I'll meet you at Beans in an hour?"

"Make it an hour and a half. I will see you there, Barbara. And bring your questions."

"Thanks, Sid."

"Hey, you're buying. I'm happy to come."

———

BEAN'S IS a one of my favorite coffee shops. Wood paneled, long and narrow with ever-changing original art on the walls—for sale, of course—it manages to be cozy and current at the same time. I still haven't figured out how they manage it. They have great coffee and a narrow but tasty menu. And they serve brunch all day. What's not to like?

Once Sid and I were seated at a small table near the back and had placed our orders, he listened intently while I explained about Andrea and Jake. I didn't tell him how worried I was, but Sid's pretty good at hearing what isn't said.

"I can see why this one's got you going," he commented when I finished, his bushy eyebrows drawing together.

He swallowed a mouthful of coffee, while I waited for him to say something insightful. And waited. Growing impatient, I glared at him. He got that twinkle in his eye, the one that always annoys me.

"You're enjoying this," I said.

"No. Just waiting for you to tell me where you're taking it from here."

I sat back, feeling like an idiot. Deep down, I'd been looking to for some advice from him. That isn't my style, nor Sid's. Never has been.

And it told me exactly how messed up I was over this case. Just in case last night's exploration of the inside of a wine bottle hadn't already made it clear.

Trust Sid to call me on it. He'd undoubtedly noted the bloodshot eyes, too. He hadn't been my teacher and mentor for three and a half years for nothing.

"I'm scrambling on this one, Sid. This idiot's living in Andrea's house, threatening her, and he's got a gun."

Sid forked up a mouthful of eggs and bacon, and chewed slowly. I waited. When he'd finished, he gave me his patented 'what is wrong with you' look.

"Did I teach you nothing?" he said. "Here you are interrupting my brunch with your worries, and you have no facts. Who is this Jake? What does he do? What does he care about? Why does he have a gun? Those are facts. You have nothing but fears. So get some facts."

By now I was grinning, partly at his humor, mostly at my own stupidity. Sid was right, as usual. First I needed to find out who Jake is.

I had to know him as well as if he'd sat for a portrait, know every expression, every flaw. If Sid had taught me nothing else, he'd taught me that.

Andrea's fear was contagious, and I was reacting as a panicked friend rather than as a professional. It was an unsettling realization. It was the first time since I set up my own shop that my emotions had got in the way of my ability to do my job, and I didn't like it.

Of course, it was also the first time my best friend had hired me to save her from a potentially life threatening situation. Maybe a little panic was to be expected.

I looked at Sid, still calmly drinking his coffee. "Thanks, Sid."

He nodded as he signaled the waitress for another coffee. "You're good at what you do, Barbara. All thanks to me, of course. Just don't forget it. And don't think you can control events and outcomes. It doesn't matter how good you are, you can't do that."

It was good advice. I didn't realize how good until much later

I took a deep breath and felt some of the tension draining from between my shoulder blades. Sid got out some photos from his cruise. He looked like he was enjoying himself, which wasn't surprising, seeing as in every photo he was with a different woman.

"Sid, you dog. And here I thought you'd gone on a rest cruise."

"I did," he said with a sly grin. "See how rested I look. See the tan?"

"She's gorgeous. Are you seeing her again?"

"No, she's from Florida. But I am considering another cruise, real soon."

"I'll just bet you are." It was good to see him again, and to see how relaxed he looked. Maybe retirement was going to agree with him, after all. "Look Sid, I've got to run, I have another appointment. But keep in touch, you hear?"

"And you take it easy, Barbara," he said, serious for once. "Don't be so hard on yourself."

Easy for him to say.

———

IT WAS NEARLY two when I arrived at the Palm Court. I was running late, and Doug was already sitting at a palm-shaded table in the back with a pint of dark beer in front of him. We don't get enough sun in Vancouver for palm trees, even under glass, but that never stops anyone from trying.

As I made my way between the straggly trunks, I caught the bartender's eye and gave him a nod. My glass of wine reached the table the same time I did. Associating with Doug has given me some bad habits.

I told Doug what was going on with Andrea, then began to fill him in on "the Forrester problem." I'd guessed right, he was amused, particularly by the part his stories had played. Partway through my recitation of the facts, he began to frown.

"Forrester," he said thoughtfully. "With two r's?"

I nodded. "James Forrester."

"There was a James Forrester involved in building the mall that collapsed last year. The one that injured half a dozen people and killed three."

"Wait a minute, I remember that one. And they were all there to celebrate the grand opening of the mall, weren't they? I don't remember the name, but I remember the story. It seemed such a tragic irony."

Doug wasn't much interested in irony, tragic or otherwise. "If this is the same guy, he committed suicide several months later. Or at least the official verdict was suicide, apparently stemming from remorse over the deaths. Supposedly the collapse was due to negligence on his part, but I don't think the investigation is final yet."

We looked at each other, recognizing the same thought. It was Doug who voiced it. "If it wasn't suicide, if it was murder, then it's no wonder your client doesn't want to give a name."

Especially if my suspicion is right and it's a kid I'm dealing with. "And no wonder he chose me based on the conviction of the Senator's murderer. If Forrester was murdered, it could be a cover-up for something much bigger. Meaning some pretty powerful people would be involved."

"I want to work with you on this."

"I'm not sure how far I can take it. For one thing, my client can't afford me, and for another, murder is police business. And I don't have time."

Doug was nodding impatiently. He'd heard it all before, and we both knew I'd just been hooked into this case. "But how does your whisperer fit in? What does he know and why can't he convince the police?"

"You sound like a reporter. Why don't you find out what you can about the mall collapse and any legal action. I'll try to arrange a meeting with the client."

"I want to be there."

"I don't know if I can manage that. He's pretty cautious. But I'll do what I can, just as soon as I've sorted Andrea's problem out. You ever hear of a Jake Scott?"

"Nope."

Knowing Doug's memory for news, that means he hasn't done anything major. At least not yet. "OK. I'll be in touch."

"Good luck, Barbara," he said, lifting his mug in a toast. "Andrea's lucky to have you."

I wished I was sure of that.

CHAPTER FIVE

I was dreaming something was chasing me through thick undergrowth in the pouring rain when the frantic ringing of the phone woke me. 4 a.m. I kicked myself free of tangled sheets and leapt to answer.

"Babs, I need you. Here. To come here, I mean."

"Andrea, what is it? Where are you?" For a moment all I could hear was my own heartbeat, far too loud.

"Home, I'm home. And it's Jake. I think he's gone over the edge. I'm scared to be here alone, and I'm scared to leave. He'll hear me."

"I'll be right there," I said, the fear in her voice snapping me wide awake. "Don't move. Lock your doors."

Keen grasp of the obvious, Barbara, I berated myself.

Driving through the quiet tree-lined streets of Kitsilano, I barely noticed the mix of new condos and Victorian style duplexes and town homes crowding that trendy area, darkened windows indicating that their inhabitants were still asleep. There was no traffic. I put my foot down, covering the thirty blocks between my place and Andrea's in seven minutes flat.

I parked half a block down, arriving at her front gate in a cold sweat.

There was no sign anything was wrong. On the main floor, there was a light shining through from the kitchen. Jake's suite appeared to be in darkness.

I crept along the walk that led around the house, fending off the overgrown yew hedge that bordered it. At the back, I could see a light on in Jake's kitchen as well as the one in Andrea's kitchen.

I climbed the worn stairs and tapped on the French doors.

Andrea froze, her shoulders tense, then saw it was me and hurried to let me in. Her face was haggard, frown lines etching between her brows. She gave me a hug, and I could feel the tension in her.

"What's going on?" I whispered.

She put a finger to her lips, handed me a cup of fresh coffee—bless her—and beckoned me into the living room. She turned on a halogen lamp and we seated ourselves in the two Danish modern chairs in the far corner. I could see her fighting to hold back tears.

"It's okay," I said, gripping her hand. "I'm here. Cry if you need to."

She half-smiled, and gulped a couple of times. "I won't cry. I'm determined not to cry. It's bad enough I can't get him out of my house. I won't let him make me cry."

"What's going on?" I asked again.

Andrea took a deep breath, and then another. When she was sure she could speak without sobbing, she answered. "A noise woke me. I was asleep upstairs, and I heard a loud bang."

Andrea's house is on three levels. On the first level is Jake's self-contained suite, which has a private entrance. On the main floor are the kitchen, bathroom, living room, den and guest room. The third floor is all one room, which Andrea has turned into a very private bedroom/retreat. For a noise from Jake's suite to waken her, it must have been really loud.

"What did you do?"

"After sitting bolt upright in bed?" she asked with a shaky attempt at humor. Andrea's sense of humor, even in a crisis, is one of the things I value most in my friend. In fact, without it, I doubt she'd have been able to put up with my own rather warped sense of humor for this long.

"I pulled on a robe and snuck down to the kitchen. It was really quiet. You know that eerie quiet it gets when there's none of the usual traffic noise. I couldn't even hear the pigeons. Nothing. I started to think I'd dreamed the first sound, but then there was another bang. I thought my heart would stop."

She paused and sucked in a deep breath.

"It came from Jake's suite. And I could hear him cursing. Steadily. It went on for quite a while, and he must have been yelling, because it was clear right through the floorboards. Then he stopped, and it was quiet again.

It went really quiet for a long time, and I was heading back to bed when he started hitting his ceiling with something heavy and swearing. I didn't know what to do. So I called you."

I drank some coffee. She took another deep breath.

"He went quiet again just before you got here," she said. "I can't stand this, on top of everything else! The man really must be nuts. No normal person is going to be thumping on my floor and cursing in the middle of the night."

I had to agree with that.

"So what do I do?" And she looked at me.

It was my turn to take a deep breath. "You could call the police. They probably wouldn't be able to do a lot, but they could at least give him a warning about disturbing the peace."

I was thinking about that complaint Jake had made against Andrea, though, and wondering effective yet another complaint would be. If Andrea hadn't already decided against evicting Jake, it would be worth finding out.

"It might shake Jake up," I told her. "Make him think twice before he disturbs you again. On the other hand, it might make things worse. It depends what's triggering these rages of his."

"So you don't think I should call the cops," she interpreted. "Not even Jerry?"

I shook my head. "No. Until we have a chance to figure out

what's going on here, I think you want to avoid any kind of confrontation with Jake."

"Maybe. But it's horrible, being woken up in the middle of the night, feeling trapped by a maniac."

"For now, you can't do much about being woken up—except maybe invest in a good set of earplugs?"

Andrea made a face at me. At least it lightened the moment a little.

"But you don't have to stay here feeling trapped. Come home with me, go visit your grandmother. Whatever works. Just don't confront him, don't add to his emotion, whatever it is. From what you've said, it sounds to me like a combination of rage and paranoia."

"Based on his previous behavior, I'd say that's pretty accurate," she began, only to be interrupted by a loud bang coming from the back of the house. She looked at me.

"See what I mean?"

"Jake?"

Andrea nodded. "That's the noise he's been making on and off for the last hour or so."

I stood up and headed for the kitchen, Andrea right behind me. I stopped near the table and listened. Jake was banging on his ceiling with what sounded like a large mallet. I could also hear a steady stream of cursing, punctuated with the occasional phrase. He didn't sound sane.

"Any idea what set him off?"

"None. I haven't even seen him for two days."

"You haven't increased his rent or anything, have you?"

She grinned weakly, shook her head. "I've gone out of my way in the last month or so not to set him off. I've been as considerate and careful as I know how to be."

I listened to the banging and cursing still coming from the floor below. "Obviously there isn't anything you can do or not do that will help this situation. How long does he go on like this?"

"It seems like forever."

I didn't say anything.

"But it's probably only five minutes or so."

"Any idea what he's hitting the ceiling with?"

"No. I just hope it doesn't have a sharp edge. That ceiling is going to be a major pain to fix."

"True. But if he's causing damage to the suite, it might help to evict him faster. The hard part will be getting in there to prove it."

Then a nasty thought occurred to me. "Andrea, how thick is that floor? Is there any possibility he could break through his ceiling and your floor?"

Now she was reassuring me. "No. This is an old house, and they built to last back then. There's about a foot of solid wood between where he is and where we are. He'd have to be hacking at the ceiling for a lot longer than he has been if he wanted to break through.

I think he's taking his rage out on the ceiling to make my life as miserable as he can. I don't think he's trying to get at me through the floor."

She paused for a moment, glanced around. "After all, it would be so much easier for him just to break through the French doors at the back. With the trees I've got, no-one would see or hear anything until far too late."

I looked out through those French doors. It was true. Andrea's backyard was surrounded by large, mature shade trees that had to be fifty or sixty years old. They made her backyard into a private green oasis, but they also meant that any disturbance at her back door would not be noticed. By anyone.

"I think you need to start packing," I said. "Maybe even get out of town for a few days."

As if to prove my point, at that moment Jake hit the ceiling again with a particularly loud bang. I'm sure I felt the floor shudder beneath my feet.

"Work's pretty busy. I can't leave town right now," she said.

"Then come over to my place for a few days, while I try to figure out some options for dealing with him."

"I'm not leaving my place to him. Who knows what he'd do."

Which seemed like a pretty good argument for leaving, but nothing I said would convince Andrea. She'd only agree to going to her office for now, so I waited while she had a shower and dressed.

Then I went back to my place, showered and headed for the office. It was barely six, but I was motivated.

I put on a pot of Sumatran coffee and sat down to think through the problem of Jake. What I'd seen very clearly this morning was that the most urgent problem might not be Jake's gun or potential gang connections, but rather his newly violent behavior. And if I couldn't convince Andrea to move out temporarily, she could be in real danger.

So why was Jake suddenly acting out? And what was I going to do about it?

———

A KNOCK on the door nearly had me spilling my coffee. Through the frosted glass, I could make out a large shadow. I glanced at the clock, which read seven-thirteen. Pretty early for clients.

Telling myself not to be a fool, I opened the door. To my surprise, Nick Markham stood on the other side, looking very presentable indeed in a tailored gray suit.

Waving him in, I offered coffee, which he accepted. Even at this hour, he looked good. Sitting across from him, drinking coffee, I tried not to stare.

"Good coffee, Barbara."

"Thanks, Nick," I said after a slight pause, which I hope he hadn't noticed. I was short of sleep, after all.

Not that being short of sleep is any excuse, not when I was on my third cup of coffee. If I wasn't awake by now, I never would be. "What's up?"

"I saw the kid again yesterday, hanging around your door. You see him yet?"

"No, not even a sign of him."

He nodded. "I figured you hadn't buzzed him in. Security in this building not being the greatest."

I grinned at his irony. Security in our building consists of a front door buzzer that might be effective if the door latch actually worked consistently.

"You said he was thin. This kid seem like he's looking for drug money?"

I hated to ask it about a teenager, but it's a reality, especially in this end of town. And if this kid was my would-be client and he did have a drug problem? Bad news, any way you looked at it.

He shook his head. "No, I wasn't thinking about drugs. This kid seems more sad than dangerous. And maybe frightened."

"Frightened?"

"Yeah. Kinda furtive, like he's trying not be noticed. I've never got a good look at him. He jumps and scuttles off when he hears me coming. Like a too-thin rabbit."

Now the light was dawning. "You're concerned about him. For him, I mean."

"Yeah."

He grinned, and I nearly fell off my chair. I'm not usually attracted by a well-built physique, though I will admit to admiration. But a man with a great smile, well, that'll get me every time. And Nick's grin, full force, was truly something. I tried to bring Alessandro's face and also spectacular smile into focus, but for some reason it wasn't working.

I needed more coffee.

Nick was still talking. I wrenched my attention from my suddenly wide-awake libido back to what he was saying.

"I get the feeling something's not right. So, if I can help out in some way, let me know."

"Thanks. I think the kid's been phoning me, and you're right about him being scared. He won't give me a name, doesn't want to meet with me. And maybe with good reason, based on what little he's told me so far. I'm not sure how to get him to trust me, never mind someone else. But I do appreciate the offer."

"Any time," Nick said, and drained his mug. "Thanks for the coffee, Barbara. I have to run. I've got meetings stacked up all morning."

I saw him out, then cleared his coffee mug in a bemused way. It was a relief when the phone rang.

"Hello. I mean, O'Grady Investigations, Barbara speaking."

"Barbara, what's wrong?" Andrea asked.

"Aside from being worried about you, you mean?"

"I'm fine. And I know that note in your voice. It has nothing to do with your investigations."

"What note?" I said, hoping to throw her off. Knowing it wouldn't work. She knows me too well.

"The one I only hear when a relationship's going sour. What's going on?"

I was not going to tell her about Nick. I needed a distraction. "It's nothing, Just that I haven't heard from Alessandro in three weeks."

"Why didn't you tell me?"

"He travels a lot. I'm sure I'll hear soon."

Even in my own ears, it didn't ring true. What worried me more was that I didn't seem to care. When had that happened?

"He's married." There was a note of finality in her voice.

"No, he's not. What makes you say that?"

"I've been pretty sure all along, given his behavior. This just clinches it. It's exactly like Jayson."

No way I was letting that one by. I'd be in an on-again, off-again relationship with Jayson Ho for nearly five years. A fellow artist, Jayson was completely caught up in his growing fame.

Still is, from what I hear of him. He didn't think much of my art when I was painting, nor of my becoming a P. I.. He was pretty vocal about both.

"Alessandro couldn't be more different from Jayson. He's not all wrapped up in himself, and he doesn't think my place is at home, waiting for him."

"Because he has someone else at home. Besides, he does have you waiting for him. Every time he comes to town."

Huh. She was right, in a funny way. I had a sudden, unwelcome thought. Maybe part of Alessandro's appeal was that he lived three thousand miles away and so couldn't have much impact on my life?

My mind flipped back to that final night with Jayson. I could just see the shocked look on his face as I told him we were done. Picturing it, I suddenly realized that part of what drew me to Alessandro was that I didn't feel for him the kind of attraction I'd felt for Jayson.

The same attraction I didn't want to admit I might feel for Nick.

Oh boy. I needed a change of subject. And fast. "Never mind your speculations about my love life. Why did you call, Andrea?"

"I almost forgot. I managed to get a few good shots of Jake's tattoo yesterday evening. He was out working on his bike, and he didn't notice me. I just e-mailed them to you."

I checked. "Got them. Thanks. I'll let you know what I find out."

"See that you do. And Barbara? We're not done talking about Alessandro."

Oh yes we were.

I loaded Andrea's photos. She was right, she had got some good shots. And the tattoo bore at least a passing resemblance to the one Andrea had drawn for me, which was pretty good for an Andrea drawing.

While I had the file open, I enlarged the best of the photos, then did a split screen comparison with the ones I'd pulled off the gang-related websites on Monday. Jake's tattoo still didn't have enough of the gang elements to worry me.

But what did I know? This was Andrea's life. I wasn't about to trust a web-based source and an amateur opinion, even if that amateur was me.

It was still too early to call Stuart Ng. I e-mailed the tattoo photos to him, explaining the urgency of the situation. If I didn't hear by nine, I'd call.

I wasn't feeling patient. I didn't have time for patience.

But there wasn't much I could do at this hour, either.

CHAPTER SIX

So I went for a run. The Seawall was empty. I'd caught it at a time when the early birds had already left for work and late risers hadn't risen. There's an amazing sense of freedom in running with all that space, all that scenery to myself.

It was still early enough that the air was cool, crisp with the scent of salt and autumn leaves. It would be hot later. I didn't want to think about anything except how my muscles felt as they stretched and limbered, and getting my breathing slow and even.

Sometimes when I run, I get into a state that's almost meditative, when all I'm aware of is the flow of my breathing and the feel of my feet hitting the pavement. This wasn't one of those mornings.

I couldn't stop thinking about Andrea. There was no telling what Jake would do next, or how much danger she was in. The pounding of my feet just seemed to jar more worries free. I ran harder.

Forty-five minutes later I got back to my office to a ringing phone, managing to get the door open just as before voice mail cut in. I expected it to be Jerry, but it was Doug's voice I heard. And he sounded more excited than I'd heard him in quite a while.

"It was Forrester," he began, almost before I'd said hello.

"What was Forrester?" I was too emotionally wrapped up in

what was going on with Andrea. I couldn't change gears that quickly.

"James Forrester was the architect responsible for that shopping mall. There were rumors that he might be found criminally negligent, but when he committed suicide the case was basically buried."

"You found out more than that." I've come to know Doug well enough to know that there is no way he'd sound so excited about the information he'd given me so far.

"Forrester had a junior partner, one Cliff Walters."

"So?"

"So Walters now has a big job at a big salary with Crendall and Barton."

"The developers?" Even I knew who they were. Now he had my full attention.

"Yup. And guess who was developing the shopping center site?"

"Crendall and Barton." I didn't even have to guess. "So were they implicated in the lawsuit?"

"Yeah. It hasn't settled yet, though, not while the investigation is still open. It's looking like there will be a couple of hefty settlements. But it's also looking like most of the blame will fall on Forrester and his company."

"What about his junior partner, Walters? Wouldn't he have been equally liable?"

"Nope. Only the company were named in the suit, though a couple of the plaintiffs are still trying to go after Forrester as well," Doug said. "With Forrester's death, his company's already folded, and it looks like their insurer, Crestlife Insurance, will be paying the bulk of it. They're still fighting it, of course, though from what I can see they're doing a remarkable ineffective job of it."

"Interesting."

"Uh huh. Usually in these things the suits and countersuits tie up any possible settlement for years. Crestlife are dragging it out some, but it's pretty much a done deal that most of the liability will rest with Forrester's company. Especially with him and his company both gone."

"Which could strengthen the case for murder. Or it could have driven Forrester to suicide. Might be interesting to know the story on his insurance company, though."

"Yeah, I'm on it. Have you met your client yet?" Doug didn't miss a beat.

"I'm not sure he is my client. He hasn't contacted me again, and I have no way of contacting him. But an office neighbor of mine tells me he's seen a teenager lurking around. I'm just hoping it isn't my would-be client."

"Huh." A pause. "Who is this guy? And what does he do?"

"My neighbor? Or the would-be client?"

"Funny. Your neighbor, of course."

"His name's Nick Markham. And I don't know exactly what he does, some kind of insurance I think. Just that he has the office down the hall from me, and that he's a runner." And that he's gorgeous, I added silently, but I wasn't about to mention that one to Doug.

"Could he be involved?"

That was a new thought, but I doubted it. Doug's just naturally suspicious. Forty years of journalism will do that to a person. "He's concerned. No big deal."

"Umm," was all Doug said.

I tried to hide my irritation. I had enough suspicious characters around without adding Nick to the list. Doug means well, but he's a bulldog when he gets hold of something he thinks will be a good story. "I'm up to my ears with Andrea's case, here. Jake's showing signs of turning violent, and I'm worried about her. I can't focus on the Forrester case right now. I don't even have a client."

"You've got a retainer."

"Yeah, right."

"Sorry, couldn't resist. Look, if there's anything I can do… About Andrea, I mean."

"Thanks, but I don't think there's anything anyone can do. Until Jake actually does something, our hands are tied."

"Let me know," Doug said, and I could hear the concern in his quiet voice.

"Thanks, Doug. And about Forrester. You're going to keep following it up?"

"Yeah. Think I'll do a little research into Crendall and Barton. See what I can dig out. You'll let me know when your client gets in touch?"

I said I would, and we disconnected. I sat and contemplated the opposite wall for a moment, then got up and walked to the window. I felt restless, overloaded, confused. If I hadn't just got back from a run, I'd have gone running to shake the feeling. Instead, I looked out over my part of the city.

One of the best things about my office, apart from the cheap rent, is the view. Unlike most downtown offices, the higher floors don't command higher rent. There's a reason for that, of course.

It's an old building, and despite sporadic efforts at sprucing it up over the years, shows its age. And the higher the floor, the more that impact shows. Which was why I was looking out over the eastern edge of downtown Vancouver. In addition to a close-up view into the multistory parkade across the street , I had a partial view of Gastown, the rail yards and the harbor beyond. Today even that couldn't distract me.

The phone rang.

This time it was Stuart Ng. I thanked him for calling me back so promptly. "Have you had a chance to look at the photos?"

"I have indeed. Very interesting tat you've got there. It isn't a gang tat, though."

"You're sure?"

"Yes. No doubt about it."

It felt as if something tight inside me had just released. Okay, maybe I was still worried that Jake could have a gang connection.

Stuart Ng was still talking. "A tattoo's typically one of the most dynamic indicators of gang affiliation. In the gangs we're aware of, they all use specific tattoo elements to symbolize membership. The tat you sent me doesn't include any elements that I recognize. And I think I know them all."

"What about affiliated groups? I've heard them called "feeder groups" for the gangs?"

"We track those, too. Still no matches with the photo you sent me."

"That's great news. Thank you."

He chuckled. "Nice to be able to give good news for a change. Let me know if I can help further."

"Thank you, I will."

Whew. One problem down.

I clicked off and the phone rang again. This time it was Jerry.

"How's Andrea doing?" he asked.

Oh, right. Gangs were the least of my worries.

"Not great. She called me early this morning. Jake was banging on his ceiling. She ended up going into the office early."

"What kind of advice are you giving Andrea, anyway? She can't go on living in that house, with that maniac in the basement."

I had to hold the phone away from my ear. When Jerry's upset, his voice gets louder.

"Look Jerry," I said, resisting the impulse to yell back. "It's Andrea's decision, and it's her home. She's a grown woman. I've told her she needs to get out for a while, offered to let her stay with me. That's all I can do."

"She hired you to protect her, O'Grady. Doesn't sound like you're doing much of a job."

That was a low blow. And why was Jerry sounding more like a distraught husband than a rational officer of the peace? "Is there something you're not telling me?"

"Like what?"

"Are you two seeing each other?"

"Hardly. We've had dinner a couple of times, but we're just good friends."

Sure they were. "Well, if you're such good friends, why don't you talk her into staying somewhere else?"

"I tried. I even wanted her to move in with me." He stopped abruptly.

Caught. Jerry must be really upset to have admitted that. He's pretty reticent about his private life. Even with me.

I'd guessed there was something between them, but neither of them had let on that it had gone so far. For him, anyway.

I still wasn't sure what Andrea's feelings were, since she hadn't told me any of this. The sneak. And then she'd had the nerve to interrogate me about Alessandro.

"Maybe after this morning's episode you can convince Andrea that she can't keep living at her place while Jake's acting like this," I said. "I think it's getting serious, and she's not listening to me."

"It's worth a try. Anything's better than worrying about her and that maniac."

I couldn't argue with that one. Maybe he'd say the right thing, for a change. Before I could over-think that one, the phone rang again.

It was my mother.

"Barbara, I haven't seen much of you lately. Why don't you come for dinner on Sunday? Bring anyone you like. I'm trying the 100 Mile Diet, and everything's local and fresh. If this weather holds, we'll have a party out back. Susanna and Godfrey and their kids will be there."

Oh, terrific. "I doubt I can make it. I'm in the middle of a pretty urgent case."

"All your cases are urgent. You'll still get the bills paid if you have time for a life too."

"Mom…"

"If you really want to work this hard, Barbara, then get a real job, one that pays real money. I still have contacts downtown, you know."

Here we go again. "I have a life. But this case isn't about paying the bills. It's for Andrea."

"So bring her to dinner, too."

I gave up. "Fine, we'll make it if we can."

"How is Andrea? Now she's in a business that makes sense."

Which to my mother means anything corporate. Given how hard she'd found that rat race as a single mom, I've never understood why she thinks I should join it. "Andrea's okay, but she's having some problems with her tenant, and it looks like the situation is turning violent."

"Then she should evict him."

"It's not that simple."

"I don't see why not." A pause. "You're not going to get yourself shot again, are you?"

"Not if I can help it."

"Well, see that you don't. And why aren't the police involved, in any case? What can you do that they can't do better?"

A vote of confidence is always nice. I could feel a headache beginning behind my right eye. "I'm doing some background checks on the tenant."

"Well, be careful. And I do hope you can make it on Sunday. If not, as soon as this mess gets cleared up, you'll both have to come to dinner."

I wished it was as easy as she made it sound. "We'll do that."

"Good. See that you do. I'll cook something interesting."

Oh, yum. Not. After she disconnected, I put my mother's contradictions out of my mind and made a pot of French Roast.

When my coffee was ready, I swallowed a couple of aspirin and went back to the problem of what to do about Jake.

CHAPTER SEVEN

In dreams I was slashing thick red strokes across a white canvas when an insistent ringing woke me. Switching on the bedside lamp I peered blearily at the clock, which read two-thirty a.m. Then the phone rang again, and I scrambled to retrieve it from under a scatter of newspapers before it went to voice mail.

I hate it when the phone rings in the middle of the night—I'm always certain that it's bad news. This time I was right.

"Hello?" My voice sounded nearly as disoriented as I felt.

"Babs, it's me" said a strained voice I had trouble recognizing as Andrea's. "I need you."

"Where are you?"

"The police station. They've arrested me for killing Jake."

Jake was dead?

I didn't waste time on details. "Which station?"

"The new one."

"I'll be right there. Have you called a lawyer yet?"

"No. No, I just wanted to call you." There was an edge of desperation in her voice. "I told them I wanted a lawyer. Would you call someone for me?"

"Claire?"

"Claire's good. You're coming then?"

"I'll be there as soon as I can. Just hang on till I get there."

"I don't think I have much choice," said Andrea with a wavery laugh.

At least she still had her sense of humor.

I called Claire, filled her in, then scrambled into jeans and a sweater and checked that none of yesterday's mascara had ended up under my eyes. Even at that hour, it wouldn't help Andrea's credibility if I showed up looking like a raccoon. Wishing I had time to make coffee, I grabbed a jacket and my bag and ran for the door.

I shivered in the damp chill air, but at least it wasn't raining. The streets were nearly deserted, and the streetlights glimmered oddly against the pinkish glow of city lights reflecting from the low clouds. I drove on autopilot, reviewing what I knew of the situation, trying to understand how things had reached this point.

Obviously Jerry hadn't been determined enough. If he'd succeeded in persuading Andrea to move, I wouldn't have been driving to the police station at two-thirty a.m. to find out why she'd been arrested for murder.

Arresting her made no sense. Jake had been harassing her, and the police knew it. Or wait—they didn't know it. He said she'd been harassing him.

I hated this case.

All I knew for sure was that Andrea needed me. I had no idea where or how Jake had been killed. And I desperately needed coffee.

When I got to the police station, Claire hadn't arrived yet, so I'd have to wait. Claire lives on the North Shore and it would probably take her a while even at this hour. I had time to find coffee.

I was working on the dregs of a triple espresso by the time Claire showed up and got me in to see Andrea.

My best friend looked awful, pale and shaky. She was dressed in black jeans and an old sweatshirt, with no makeup, her hair barely combed. I hadn't seen her look this disheveled since she was twelve and discovered makeup. It hurt to see her so stricken.

"Andrea, what happened?" I blurted out.

"Jake's dead."

"Yes, I know. What happened, Andrea?"

"He's dead, Barbara. Someone shot him. There was blood."

"Who shot him, Andrea?"

I glanced at Claire, but she seemed content to let me take the lead, at least for now. Maybe because Andrea was becoming more coherent as she answered me.

"I don't know. He was dead. They think it was me."

"Who found the body?"

The question seemed to help her focus. "I did."

"Who called the police?"

"I did."

"Was the gun still there?"

"Yes. I think it was Jake's. It was hot."

Oh no. "You picked it up?"

"Yes. I think so. Yes. I wanted… I don't remember."

I wanted desperately to ask if she'd shot him, but I couldn't afford to know. That was between her and her lawyer. Though from the way the officers were treating Andrea, I had the distinct impression they expected this to be proven to be self-defense.

Especially if the murder weapon turned out to be Jake's gun.

And I knew Andrea didn't own a gun.

Problem was, I wasn't buying the self-defense argument. I didn't have a better explanation, but I couldn't see Andrea pulling the trigger of a gun under any circumstances. She won't even kill spiders, just traps them under water glasses and releases them outside.

And she hates guns, can't even bring herself to touch one.

Unfortunately for her defense, she seemed to have managed to touch Jake's gun.

"I think Andrea and I need some time now," Claire said.

"You'll get me out of here, won't you?" Andrea asked me, her eyes too wide.

"Yes, Andrea. We'll get you out of here," I promised. Just as soon as we could get bail posted.

I left the two of them together and went in search of another cup of coffee. I found Jerry instead. If he'd looked worried before, that was nothing compared to how he was looking now.

"O'Grady. I need to talk to you."

"I could really use a cup of coffee, Jerry."

He nodded and snagged a cup of crankcase oil masquerading as coffee for me, then headed for his office. "What's going on, Jerry?"

He stared at me for a moment, his eyes flat. "It isn't my case, so I can tell you a little. Andrea's fingerprints are all over the murder weapon. She says she found him dead. She can't explain why she picked up the gun."

"Ouch." Despite all those mystery novels whose plots turn on the innocent victim picking up the gun after the murder has been committed, in reality most people don't do that.

"Yeah. It also doesn't help that when we showed up, she was standing over the body, still holding the gun. In his kitchen."

"In his kitchen? What was Andrea doing in Jake's kitchen at that time of night?"

"Exactly. It looks bad."

"How did Jake die? Can you tell me?"

"Might as well. There's no disputing the facts, and we've got our suspect."

I winced at his bluntness.

"Basically, Jake was killed by a single bullet through the heart, probably between one-thirty and two a.m. A call came into 911 just before two a.m., and an almost hysterical female voice said that there had been a murder and gave the address. It was Andrea. When we arrived, the body was still faintly warm."

It sounded bad for Andrea. "What did Andrea say?"

"That she was awakened by a loud noise coming from the basement suite. Seeing Jake's kitchen light reflecting into the yard, she went down to investigate."

"That sounds like Andrea."

He grimaced. "It gets worse. She says she peered in the window and saw an out flung hand. She raced in, saw Jake on the floor in a pool of blood, the gun lying beside him. She says she checked his pulse, picked up the gun, checked the apartment, then called us."

I took a long swallow of coffee. Then regretted it. "I hear huge holes in that story, and I'm biased in Andrea's favor."

Jerry ran a hand across his brow. "Yeah. It's possible things happened as Andrea said, it's just not plausible."

I didn't need Jerry to tell me that when it comes to murder cases, the police are definitely looking for plausible explanations.

———

I DROVE to Andrea's house, expecting but still surprised by the number of flashing lights, the coroner's car, the ambulance and the yellow crime scene tape everywhere. They'd cordoned off the whole yard, and a small, hastily dressed crowd had gathered at the edge of the sidewalk.

I mingled with the crowd and worked my way to the front. In the eerie light from the red and blue flashers, the yard and the front of the house looked undisturbed.

Jake was killed with his own gun. Had he surprised an intruder and lost control of the gun in a struggle? Had he known his killer, invited him in? Or was Andrea lying?

None of the options felt right, but nothing else fit the facts I had either. I looked at the normal seeming yard. If the killer had been a stranger to Jake, there should be signs somewhere of forced entry, or at least something to indicate a break-in.

And it wasn't likely to be at the front of the house, in plain sight of the street.

Andrea's house backs onto a lane, but you have to know the neighborhood well to realize it. The lane doesn't extend the full length of the street, but breaks off abruptly two houses down from Andrea's. The only entrance is located one house in from the other end of the block, and the trees in Andrea's back yard screen the lane from the house.

If I was going to get into the backyard without the police stopping me, it would be from the lane. Which was also the logical way for an intruder to break into the house.

I worked my way back through the crowd and walked briskly down the street. No-one seemed to have noticed me. Good. Grabbing my digital camera from the car, I cut through the next yard and into the alley.

Keeping to the deepest patches of shadow, I walked quickly up the alley towards Andrea's, keeping my footsteps as silent as I could. The last thing I needed was to be spotted lurking behind a murder scene.

It was an odd feeling, skulking through an alley at three-thirty a.m. The whole evening had a surreal feel to it. I still couldn't quite believe that my best friend was arrested for killing her tenant.

Reaching the back of Andrea's yard, I eased between the apple trees that border the yard and onto the back lawn. I could see shapes moving inside the house, particularly in the suite. The yard itself was deserted. Moving cautiously around the perimeter, I worked my way towards the house.

In the light from the house, everything looked normal. There was no sign of a break-in. Jake's motorcycle stood on the small deck just outside his front door. Andrea's flower beds and neat garden hadn't been trampled, except where the sidewalk narrowed at the corner of the house and turned towards the street.

I made a mental note to check the area later, but my guess was that the trampling had been done by the police.

I set the camera for low light and took photos of the house and yard from all angles. Patches of shadow dotting the yard looked deep enough to touch, but you never know what will show up when you enlarge a photo and play with the contrast.

A hint of white on one edge of the lawn caught my eye and I moved quickly towards it, keeping a careful eye on the movements behind the lit windows. It was a scrap of paper, a receipt of some kind. Probably nothing. I took a couple of close up photos anyway, made sure they were legible. The receipt I left for the police to find.

I made one last survey of the house and yard, then turned to go.

A sound behind me froze me where I stood. Two police officers were coming out the door of the suite, straight towards me. I tried to shrink deeper into the shadows without actually making a movement that might draw their eyes.

They were too focused on something that the taller of the two held in a small plastic bag dangling from her hand to notice me.

"This will help tie things up," she was saying.

"She wasn't worried about being subtle," the other replied.

I couldn't see what it was they were discussing, but it didn't sound good for Andrea. I'd have to pry the information out of Jerry later. At that moment, it was enough that they had passed me and gone towards the front of the house without noticing me.

Drawing a deep breath, which I noted with annoyance was slightly shaky, I eased my way towards the back of the lot. Reaching the alley, I sprinted back the way I'd come and took the long way to where I'd parked my car.

I'd done all I could for one night—it was time to seek my warm bed and any sleep I could steal from what was left of the night. I'd start looking for a killer tomorrow.

CHAPTER EIGHT

Later that same morning, I woke feeling disoriented and apprehensive. The events of the previous night had assumed a nightmarish quality. For a cowardly moment, I was tempted to roll over and sink back into oblivion. Before I could do so, something large and heavy landed on my midsection.

"Oof," I said. "Get off me, you big lug."

Cat purred and settled in.

I opened one eye, to find him staring back at me, amber eyes unblinking. If I hadn't known better, I'd have sworn he looked sympathetic.

"That's it, I'm losing it," I told him. Cat twitched his tail and purred. "Where did you come from, anyway? I haven't seen you for a few days."

He butted his head against my stomach.

Rolling to my side I tipped him off, then swung my legs out and headed for the shower. When I emerged, more awake if not actually more cheerful, Cat was waiting for me.

"I suppose you think you'd like breakfast?"

"Rrrowrr."

"I don't know why I bother," I said as I set out a saucer of milk for him. Cat purred loudly as he drank, pink tongue darting in and out.

Shaking my head, whether at him or myself I wasn't sure, I put on a pot of French Roast and threw a bagel in the toaster oven. Cat was right. Breakfast did help.

By the time I reached my office, I was sort of ready to face what lay ahead. In one sense, my worst fear had been removed.

Andrea was no longer likely to end up dead. Jake wasn't a threat to her now. To put it in its ugliest terms—someone had taken care of the problem for her.

Whoever that someone was, they had killed Jake. But unless the police had found new evidence last night, they weren't looking for that someone. Why would they, when they had Andrea?

I had a nasty suspicion that unless I wanted my best friend to spend the next ten or so years in jail, it was going to be up to me to find that someone, and prove that he or she had killed Jake. Unless Andrea really had killed him?

I'd always known that having a friend for a client was a bad idea. When that friend is accused of murder, it's a really bad idea.

I'm a professional. I consider the facts, and only the facts. That's what I'm paid for. Only this time, I wasn't sure I could do that.

On that unsettling thought, I checked my voice mail. There were two hang-ups and a message from Claire, Andrea's lawyer. She'd called to advise me that Andrea had been formally charged with killing Jake, and that she, Claire, would like to retain my services to investigate this case.

She'd also like the three of us to meet, but since Andrea wouldn't be released on bail until later in the day, that would have to be postponed. I called Claire back, and arranged to meet her at her office in an hour to take care of the paperwork.

Sometimes I wonder why I bother to rent an office at all, given that I usually meet my clients somewhere else. The alternative would be working from home, though, and I need the discipline of leaving the apartment and going to the office in the morning.

Besides, my image of a private investigator is someone who works out of an office in a seedy, low rent district.

The seedy part isn't quite true, though the low-rent part fits. In any case, I wouldn't feel like a real P. I. working from home, and if I can't convince myself, I certainly won't make the right impression on my clients.

And my office rent is low enough that even in the really slow periods I can usually pay all my bills.

I glanced at the clock, then dealt with the mail I'd picked up on my way in. There wasn't much of it—a couple of flyers which I threw out, a couple of bills that I put aside to pay later and a blank, slightly grimy envelope.

"Uh oh." I turned it over and pried up the flap. Sure enough, it was another communication from my whispering client, who seemed determined to remain anonymous. The letter was unsigned.

This guy was beginning to annoy me. Enough with all the mystery, already. I had more important things to do. I glanced through the letter, which held basic information about one Cliff Walters, and directed me to investigate him.

Walters? That was Forrester's former partner, wasn't it? The one who was now working for a developer? I briefly wondered what the kid knew about him, then shrugged and sent a quick e-mail to Doug along with a scanned copy of the letter.

By ten after ten, I was sitting in Claire's very zen office, having signed on as her official investigator. As I listened to her outline the facts of the case as she knew them so far, I could feel my shoulders tensing up.

"They are charging Andrea with manslaughter, though I rather think they expect her to plead self-defense."

"If she'd killed Jake, why would she call 911?"

Claire lifted delicate shoulders in the most elegant shrug I'd ever seen. "That could be explained. Perhaps she panicked? It if was self-defense, events might simply have moved too quickly for her."

"You don't believe that?"

"At the moment what matters is what the police are able to prove."

"True enough. So why are they charging her on so little evidence?"

"The victim had sworn out a complaint against her. She was found standing over his body, in his apartment. There was no sign of forced entry. Her prints are all over the murder weapon. That constitutes fairly substantial evidence."

"Except that she didn't do it."

"So she says."

"Do you believe her?"

"My client says she's innocent."

It wasn't an answer. "Exactly what did Andrea tell you?"

"She says she woke up because she thought she heard the same loud banging she'd heard the previous night. When she went down to the kitchen to investigate, the banging had stopped. She thought she heard Jake talking to himself, but since he wasn't yelling, she couldn't be sure."

"Any possibility he was talking to someone else?"

"The police obviously didn't think so."

"They know about this?"

"Yes. Andrea made a statement. It didn't seem to make any difference."

"Oh."

"Exactly. Anyway, Andrea says she went back up to bed, and the banging didn't resume. She says she had a hard time falling back to sleep."

"Understandable."

"She says she had just fallen asleep when a noise woke her. A loud, sharp sound, is how she described it. I don't know if she suspected it was a gunshot or not. I think she's not sure herself. In any case, the sound was enough to send her down to the kitchen again."

"Obviously she didn't stay in the kitchen. Is it too much to hope that she called the police then, from the phone in her kitchen?"

"I'm afraid so," Claire said. "According to Andrea, everything was too quiet."

"With all the noise she'd had to put up with lately, I'd have thought she'd be dancing a jig. But I suppose she went to investigate," I said, knowing her too well.

"Yes, and unfortunately she grabbed the spare set of keys to Jake's flat before she went. Apparently she kept them in…"

"A plastic bag in the bottom of the flour canister," I said. "It only needed that. So the cops found not only the murder weapon at the scene, they also found a spare set of keys. With Andrea's fingerprints all over them."

"You can see my problem."

"Did Andrea at least have an explanation for taking the keys?"

"She says that it was spur of the moment, and that she wasn't awake enough to be thinking clearly."

Knowing how slowly Andrea wakes up, it didn't surprise me in the least that she could dig a set of keys from the bottom of the flour canister without being fully conscious. In fact, I'd personally seen some of the results of her half-awake actions.

Anytime Andrea's been staying with me, I expect to find the sugar canister in the fridge, the milk in the cupboard, and Cat in my closet. And that's after she's taken her shower and partly woken up.

But in a murder investigation, that kind of behavior is going to be held against you.

"Andrea also says she didn't need the keys," Claire said after a moment.

"What?"

"She says the suite door was already unlocked when she went in."

"Did she see anything? Hear anything?"

"She says not."

"Obviously the police didn't believe she found the door unlocked," I said.

"Would you?"

She had a point. Not knowing Andrea, and with the evidence they had, including the knowledge that Jake had been hassling

Andrea and that he'd claimed she was stalking him, she was a pretty neat fit as a suspect. Barring any evidence to the contrary, I could see why they'd charged Andrea. Which reminded me.

"I went to the scene last night, after I left the station. I saw two officers leave Jake's suite examining or discussing something that one of them held in her hand. Do you have any idea what that was?"

"Not yet. Whatever it was, it clearly wasn't anything that would change their minds about Andrea."

"What if Andrea were to plead self-defense?"

"My client," said Claire in measured tones, "refuses to even discuss the possibility. She says she didn't have anything to do with his death, and that's the end of it."

"I see."

"Exactly," said Claire with a dry smile. "Now, fill me in on the situation with Jake and Andrea."

I wasn't sure if Claire knew about the supposed stalking yet, and I couldn't tell her without breaking Jerry's confidences. I briefed her on everything else right up until the day of the murder, with heavy emphasis on the tension between Andrea and Jake as well as the odd behavior I'd witnessed the previous night.

Claire listened without comment, taking copious notes. Her game face was too good for me to judge what she made of the information.

"Are you free to give this case your full attention?" she asked.

"Yes." The letter I'd just received on the Forrester case crossed my mind, but I dismissed it. Doug could deal with that. Andrea came first.

"Good. Then let's meet again at ten tomorrow morning. Andrea should be out today, and the three of us need to strategize."

"I'll be here."

Back in my office, I reviewed my notes, highlighting the pertinent information. Given what I knew now, it seemed likely that Jake had been killed by someone he knew, someone he'd been entertaining in his apartment that night. That would be my starting point, anyway.

And the only way to find this probable someone was through Jake himself.

Which meant I was back to learning everything I could about Jake—who he had been, who he had associated with, what had made him tick. I was going to know him better now that he was dead than I ever had when he was alive.

But at least now I wasn't racing the clock trying to find answers before he hurt Andrea. Now I was just racing the clock trying to keep her out of jail.

I shook my head over the irony of it, then called Jerry. He wasn't in. And I couldn't just sit here.

I grabbed my jacket and camera and headed for the murder scene.

———

I PARKED a few doors down from Andrea's. The street was deserted and except for the yellow crime scene barriers, there was no sign anything had happened here the previous night.

It was another sunny day and every leaf and blade of grass stood out clear and perfect. I shot off another dozen or so pictures showing the yard and the front of the house from various angles, then went down the side of the house, taking pictures as I went.

Around back, everything seemed normal, even what I could see of the suite through the kitchen window. I finished taking daylight pictures of the yard, the door, Jake's motorbike, even the sidewalk.

As I took the last shot, I suddenly remembered the piece of paper I'd photographed on the lawn the previous night. It was gone now. I hoped it hadn't just blown away.

I flipped through the photos on my camera until I found the right shot. I peered closer. Just a gas receipt. Someone, presumably either Jake or Andrea, had paid cash for fifteen liters of gas. But what if it hadn't been them?

The receipt was from a gas station in West Vancouver, dated the previous day at ten twenty-five p.m., just a few hours before the murder. It takes a good half hour to get to Andrea's from just about anywhere on the North Shore, even at that time of night. It takes even longer if there's any kind of traffic on the Lion's Gate Bridge, and if there's an accident on the bridge, you might as well forget it.

I'd double check, but I was fairly sure Andrea had been home all evening. In any case I doubted she'd gas up that far away unless she were on her way back from Whistler or from the ferry terminal at Horseshoe Bay.

I knew for a fact that Andrea hadn't been to Whistler in a couple of months, because she'd been lamenting that fact just the other day. We'd talked about scheduling a get-away-to-Whistler weekend, as a matter of fact. I didn't think she'd taken any ferries lately, either.

It was probably Jake's receipt. I wondered where he'd been last night, and what time he'd actually got home. Making a mental note to ask Jerry about it, I turned my attention to the suite and peered in the window. I couldn't see much.

Technically Jake's suite was still a crime scene. I shouldn't be going in. But the scene had already been processed for trace evidence. Andrea had been charged. The police wouldn't likely be back. And I knew where Andrea kept her keys.

I wrestled with my conscience for a moment. My conscience lost.

Using the key Andrea gave me years ago, I let myself into her place. In addition to the set of keys in the flour canister, Andrea kept another backup set of keys locked in her desk. I headed for the den.

Moments later I was standing outside Jake's suite, listening hard. No sounds. Nothing. I let myself in.

Someone had mopped up the blood and the body was gone, but otherwise it was unchanged. Newspapers lay open on the table, dirty dishes moldered in the sink, empty beer bottles and old pizza boxes cluttered the counter. Gray fingerprint powder lay thickly over everything.

The smell of blood and death hung in the air.

Trying not to breathe too deeply, I pulled on a pair of plastic gloves, took out my notebook and camera, and went back into the small kitchen.

A half-empty bottle of wine on the counter caught my attention. It was a Bin 945 Shiraz, not a bad wine. There were no wine glasses, but there was one juice glass on the counter that looked like it had held red wine. I leaned closer, gave it the sniff test. Yup, red wine.

I didn't see a second glass, but there was quite a collection of empty beer bottles, all Granville Island Pale Ale.

Flipping back through my notes, I found what I'd half-remembered. Andrea had said Jake didn't drink wine. So who had been drinking it? It was the first discrepancy that might validate Andrea's story. I took a couple of photos.

Moving further into the kitchen, I stepped carefully around the spot where the body had been. On the table I saw Tuesday's *Province*, a crumpled package of Player's Light, a copy of last month's *PC Magazine* with coffee rings on it, a tattered copy of this month's *Hot Bikes* magazine and what looked like insurance rate sheets and actuarial tables, also covered with coffee rings.

From the kitchen I moved down the hall to the bedroom. The mess continued. Clothes were strewn from one side of the room to the other, the bed was unmade, and from the look of the stuff hanging in the closet, Jake didn't own an iron. Another fact—Jake was a slob.

I checked the dresser top, and, with some reluctance, the drawers. At least everything seemed to be clean. Black T-shirts and jeans had been Jake's preferred style, but that was about all I learned. There were no papers left in the bottom of the drawers, nothing hidden. I checked the closet and found a couple of black jackets but not much else.

The bottom of the closet yielded the usual collection of worn footwear. At the back of the top shelf, a padded black nylon case held a fairly new laptop, also covered in fingerprint powder. Probably the police had copied the contents, then left the computer. I proceeded to do the same, then headed for the living room.

At first glance it looked like it had been tossed. A closer look revealed that the mess had probably been Jake's chosen environment. Old newspapers were stacked on one end of the sofa and had slid off to the floor. There were used potato chip bags under the chairs, flyers and an impressive collection of bar coasters on the coffee table and an empty thirty gallon aquarium on its own stand, stuffed with more paper.

The furniture was battered late nineties. A thin coating of dust covered everything, overlaid with more gray powder.

The aquarium looked like the most interesting prospect. It seemed to contain business papers, filed in something resembling a geological strata system. By getting down on my hands and knees and peering upward, I could make out some of the documents on the bottom of that stack, dating back three years or so.

The stuff on the top was several months old—the police had probably taken the most current forms. Probably his bills as well, since I couldn't see any of them, and Jake didn't have a study or even a desk.

I shuffled through the top inch or so of paper. Basically, it looked like Jake used the old tank to file his client information. I took photos of the top dozen or so forms. Maybe some of his clients could tell me a bit more about Jake.

That only left one room to check. The bathroom was as much of a mess as the rest of the place, which was no surprise. The tub was turning green and the grout between the tiles was black. Moldy smelling towels were strewn everywhere and the mirror was almost too dirty to see into.

The medicine cabinet yielded nothing but a razor, toothpaste, toothbrush, Band-Aids, some very strong headache tablets and more fingerprint powder. I wasn't sure what I was looking for—the police would have removed anything suspicious.

I looked anyway, just in case. After all, they thought Andrea had done it. I didn't.

The contents of the cupboard under the sink were similarly utilitarian, notable only for the lack of cleaning supplies. Had the man never heard of cleaning services? I hoped Andrea decided to hire one to clear out this mess.

Disgusted, I started to put everything back before I realized there was a medium-sized dark plastic jar in the furthest corner. Stretching half my body into the confined space, I managed to pull it out. It was full of a granular white powder, and seemed strangely free of fingerprint powder.

Could it be?

———

I DROPPED the powder off with a chemist that I've known for years, first swearing her to secrecy. Caryn works the same ridiculous hours I do, and she promised to call me as soon as she'd had a chance to run a few tests.

Safely back in my office, I loaded the thumb drive holding the files I'd copied from Jake's computer and scanned the main directory.

There were no subdirectories. All of the documents in the main directory had dates as filenames, one document per week. A weekly report?

The spreadsheet files had names that looked like either acronyms or contractions, none of which made any sense to me. Checking the file information, I saw that they seemed to have been created at a rate of one a week as well.

I opened the most recent document. As I'd guessed, it seemed to be a weekly report, detailing the clients and prospects contacted and the policies and funds he'd sold. I reviewed several months worth of these reports, looking for a pattern as well as for information.

For a man who had lived in the kind of mess I'd seen in his apartment, Jake was surprisingly well-organized and detailed in his business life. He'd kept in contact with a long list of people, and he seemed to be selling policies and funds on a fairly consistent basis, with no major increases or decreases in his level of activity. I couldn't tell from the reports what kind of money he'd been making.

That information turned out to be contained in the spreadsheets. Jake's cash flow was steady, and he'd been making enough to afford his rent plus a moderate lifestyle. And from what Andrea had told me, a moderate lifestyle was exactly what Jake had.

Except for that motorcycle.

I couldn't see anything that explained the money for that extravagant purchase. Even going back a year in the spreadsheets, I didn't see enough variation in Jake's income to explain it.

I checked the creation dates on the spreadsheets against the dates on the reports. All but one of them matched, so I loaded the odd one, which proved to be Jake's year-to-date income and expenditure statement. His income was steady, with money flowing in at about the same rate each month.

The only exception was the fifteenth of February, when he'd recorded a payment of thirty thousand dollars. The explanation against the sum said, "Expected payment". The expenditure statement showed that he'd spent thirty-one thousand dollars on "bike" two days later.

Other than that, the expenditure sheet was as predictable as the income sheet. I examined the list of expenses, but there was nothing that seemed to offer any explanations. He'd listed "rent, hydro, phone, cable, food, gym, entertainment-business and entertainment-self". I tried to reconcile the personality that would create a list like this with the man who'd been harassing Andrea, and couldn't.

I looked again at that thirty thousand dollar entry, and thought about the white powder I'd found. Had Jake been dealing? I wouldn't know until I heard from Caryn.

I was re-reading my notes when the phone rang. Not bad. Caryn doesn't usually get to my requests that quickly.

Except that it wasn't Caryn, it was my whisperer. The kid. Perfect. Just perfect.

"Ms. O'Grady. Did you get my letter?"

"Yes, I got your letter."

"And?"

"I'm in the middle of an urgent case. I'm afraid I won't be free to do much on your case until that one is cleared. Maybe you need to think about hiring another investigator."

I felt bad saying it, but I just didn't have time. Not the kind of time the case would probably require. Not with Andrea in so much trouble.

"But I want you."

Terrific. "If you're really sure it's me you want, then I'll work with you on the terms we discussed. I've sent your information on Cliff Walters to one of my associates, who's looking into it. But it may be a week or two before I can get back to you."

"That'll be too late," he said, and the despair in that whispering voice stopped me cold.

I remembered Nick's obvious concern over "the little guy" and began to see what might have prompted it. I wasn't sure what I was dealing with here, but I needed to figure it out. Fast.

"Look," I said as gently as my impatience to be helping Andrea would allow. "If you need help that badly, I'll do what I can. But you'll have to level with me. I can't do my best for a client when I don't know who my client is. You'll have to meet with me."

There was a long pause. I didn't attempt to break the silence.

"OK. I'll meet with you."

"I'm free in half an hour," I said, half-expecting him to change his mind. "Where do you want to meet?"

"I'll come to your office," he said, surprising me again. I expected him to choose neutral ground. "I'll see you in half an hour."

"I'll be here."

While I waited for my mysterious client, I reviewed what little I knew of the Forrester case so far. My biggest questions were about him, the kid, if kid he was. What was his relationship to Forrester? How did he know about the case? And what did he know about the case?

I glared at the few facts on the screen. There was so little to go on.

Since I hadn't heard from Doug, I was guessing he hadn't come up with anything new. The phone rang.

Caryn?

But it was Jerry's voice on the other end. He sounded distraught. "What's going on with Andrea?"

"Shouldn't I be asking you that?"

"I'm not part of the case, I'm too close. So you have to get her to plead self-defense."

I took a deep breath and released it slowly before answering. I knew Andrea's arrest had put Jerry in an impossible situation, so I restrained my normal tendency to bite his head off when he tries to order me around.

"I haven't talked to Andrea yet. But I'll be working with Claire on her defense."

Jerry has seen Claire in action on various cases, and I know he has a great deal of respect for her abilities.

"Damn, I'm sorry, Barbara. I hate that I can't help Andrea now."

I could hear it in his voice. "I know. Look, why don't we meet later. I have a few questions."

We agreed to meet later that afternoon at the coffee shop close to his office, which boasts an eccentric decor and great coffee. The phone rang again.

"O'Grady Investigations."

"Barbara, your suspicious white powder?"

Caryn. "That was quick. What about it?"

"It was Vitamin C."

So much for that lead. "Vitamin C? What was he doing with that much Vitamin C?"

"Maybe he was a fitness nut. Anyway, just thought you'd like to know."

"Stop chortling. And thanks, Caryn."

"Don't mention it. Your requests are always so amusing." And she disconnected.

Amusing.

Somehow that was not the image I'd imagined for myself when I hung out my shingle.

Shaking my head, I went back to my notes. So Jake wasn't dealing. It was probably too obvious anyway. I crossed it off my list.

There was a soft knock at the door. It had to be my elusive client.

CHAPTER NINE

"Come in," I called out.

The door swung open, and a short, slight figure walked into my office. He was wearing baggy jeans, a faded red T-shirt with an indecipherable logo and dirty sneakers. Pale hair straggling from beneath a baseball cap worn backwards and oversized dark glasses completed the look.

It was obviously Nick's teenager in person, and it was equally obvious he was nervous. I gestured him towards a chair.

As he sat down, he reached up a shaky hand and removed both hat and glasses. He was about twelve years old.

No wonder Nick had been concerned.

And no wonder the bills making up my retainer had been so crumpled. It must have taken him months to earn it. The whispering had been an attempt to disguise his age.

We sat and looked at each other wordlessly for a moment. He had direct gray eyes and there was an odd stillness about him. He looked like every twelve-year old I'd ever met, and yet there was maturity in the set of his thin shoulders and the way he held his head.

I could also see the vulnerability that had concerned Nick.

It worried me. I didn't have time for this case right now, and I especially didn't have time to worry about a kid who looked like he had the weight of the world on his shoulders. And was struggling valiantly to carry it.

"Why don't you start," I said.

He looked at me in silence a moment longer, then seemed to come to a decision.

"James Forrester was my dad," he said. "He and Mom were never married, so I never lived with him. About four years ago he found out about me, and he worked it out so he could see me. He was a great guy."

He stopped for a moment, swallowed a couple of times, then continued. "He was supposed to meet me that day. The day his body was found, I mean. We were going cycling on the Seawall."

His voice faded, then got stronger. "We only saw each other every two weeks or so. If he were going to commit..." His voice broke, and he swallowed, hard. "To commit suicide, he never would have done it right before he'd arranged to meet me. That's not the kind of guy he was. He'd never've not met me like that."

Those big, gray eyes met mine.

"You've got to believe me, Ms. O'Grady"

"Call me Barbara."

The eyes widened, then he looked pleased.

"Barbara. Even if my Dad was... was suicidal, he wouldn't have done that to me. And he wasn't suicidal. He wasn't."

My heart ached for him. "That's not what the police said. Did you talk to them?"

His eyes dropped to his hands, which were gripped tightly together in his lap.

"They wouldn't believe me. They said I didn't understand it, the pressures he was under, that he wouldn't have hurt me on purpose, but that he felt he had no choice. They even had me talk to some stupid doctor."

He looked up, and his eyes met mine. "But I did understand, Barbara. I did," he said. "My Dad explained it to me. And he was upset, and he was sad for those people who died. But he wasn't hurting like that, not bad enough to do that. He wasn't."

"And Cliff Walters?"

"He worked for my dad. Dad trusted him, but I don't. And he avoided us at the funeral."

Not exactly proof of anything. "What does your mother say about your Dad?"

"She's still mad at Dad for stuff from before I was born. She wasn't going to stop me seeing him, but she wasn't going to forgive him either. She's trying to protect me as much as she can, but she thinks he killed himself. She thinks he was responsible for that building falling, for those deaths, and that he couldn't take it and… and killed himself."

I looked at the boy sitting across from me, and I knew that this case wasn't going to wait until I 'had time'. I knew that if there was any way I could help this particular kid, I was going to do it.

And as I met his eyes I had the feeling he knew it too. He grinned, and suddenly looked like an average twelve-year-old, bent on mischief. In another ten years, he was going to break more than his fair share of hearts with that smile.

"So, what exactly do you want me to do?"

"I want you to believe me."

I wanted to give him a hug, but I was pretty sure that would embarrass both of us. "Even if I believe you, it doesn't mean I can prove that your father didn't commit suicide."

"I know. And if you can't prove it, that's okay. I just need to know somebody tried."

This kid was going to break my heart. "I can promise you that. I'll do the best I can for you on this case. You'll know that you tried, and that I did too."

He nodded. "OK."

I reached into a drawer, and pulled out a form. "This authorizes me to investigate the case on your behalf. It's my standard contract, and it says you're my client, and states the terms. You've already given me a retainer, so there isn't any more money involved."

"I know what I sent was nowhere near enough," he said, surprising me again. "You probably make more than that in a day."

He had that right.

"I'm not—this isn't a charity case. If you can prove my Dad didn't commit suicide, then I can pay you. If you're willing to work on contingency?" He looked at me expectantly. "That's what the lawyers call it, isn't it? Contingency? Where you get paid only if you prove your case?"

"Yes, that's what they call it. But how does that apply in this case?"

"My Dad had a life insurance policy, a big one. And I'm his beneficiary," he said, stumbling slightly over the word. "If he committed suicide, the insurance company won't pay up. If he didn't, they will. I'll sign the policy over to you, so if you can prove he didn't commit suicide, you get paid."

"Who's the insurance company?"

"I don't know but I can find out if you need to know."

"I'll need the name. And how old are you?"

"I don't see that it matters."

"If you're under age, which in this province is nineteen, then you can't legally sign anything over to me. It's probably in trust, and you'd need your guardian, your mother to sign it for you."

"That's not a problem. She thinks he committed suicide, anyway, so I'm not giving anything up. She'd sign it, because she knows I'm still worrying about it, and she'd hope that this would make me feel better."

How old was this kid, anyway? "How much is the policy for? Do you know?"

"Uh huh. It's for three million dollars."

"Three million? There is no way you can sign that kind of money over to me. Are you serious?" But I could see that he was.

I sighed, then plunged in. "OK, this is what we'll do. I'll take your case on a contingency basis. If I do prove your father didn't commit suicide and you collect on his insurance, I'll bill you at my regular rate, plus expenses."

"Plus a bonus."

"OK, plus a five percent bonus."

"Twenty percent."

"Ten percent, and that's my final offer. And only if your Mom signs the agreement I'll draw up." What was this? I was bargaining my own rate down, instead of up. But I couldn't overcharge a kid, especially this kid.

"She'll sign it."

"Okay. But I do need to know how old you are, so that I can draw up the papers correctly," I said, stretching the truth by quite a bit.

From the look he gave me, I didn't think he was buying my story. But he told me anyway. "I'm thirteen. Well, almost."

Right. "Then we shake on it."

I stood up and extended my hand. His grip was firm despite hands that were still the hands of a child. I filled out the forms for him to take away and have his mother sign.

And that was it. I had a new client, one Christopher Clinton Forrester, Chris to his friends.

———

WHEN CHRIS HAD LEFT, I put on a pot of French Roast, contemplated a swath of sunlight on the wall while it brewed. Then I phoned Doug.

"I've met my newest client," I said when he answered.

"Hello to you, too."

"Hi, Doug it's Barbara. How are you today? I thought you wanted to know who my client on the Forrester case was."

"Oh, that client. Yes, I do want to know who your newest client is."

"After that response, I'm not sure you deserve to know."

"Barbara."

I grinned. "Okay, okay. My newest client, the whisperer, is none other than Forrester's twelve-year old kid."

"Huh. Twelve, you say?" A pause. "And he's the one who sent you the letter on Cliff Walters?"

"Uh huh."

"So what else does the kid know?"

"Not a lot, from what he's told me so far. Basically, Forrester was supposed to go cycling with Chris, that's the kid, the same day his body was found. Chris is convinced that his dad would never have killed himself just before he'd arranged something like that."

"Interesting. Not that Forrester wouldn't have killed himself, just that he wouldn't have done it when he had a prior arrangement with his kid."

"I picked that up too. This kid is surprisingly mature, and he's convinced that Forrester didn't kill himself. Apparently they'd talked about the disaster. Chris says Forrester was upset, but not guilty."

"You think Forrester would let his twelve-year-old kid see him suicidal? And there's no other evidence that it was murder? Come on, Barbara. You're not usually susceptible to dewy-eyed innocence."

I took a sip of my coffee, which was still pretty hot, and a deep breath. Sometimes Doug's abrasive nature is a little hard to take. "Chris isn't exactly an innocent. I'm not quite sure what he is. But he's convincing enough that I'm prepared to look into it. Besides, I thought you were excited by what you'd found out on Walters. And apparently Chris doesn't like or trust Walters either. That's why he sent that info on him."

"If the only indication we have of murder is the word of a kid, the stuff I was finding out starts to look pretty circumstantial."

"I gather that's what the police thought too. And the insurance company."

"Insurance company?" Now there was a note of interest in Doug's voice. "Forrester had a personal policy as well as the one through his company?"

Doug's sharp, I'll give him that. I've never met anyone who can take a small piece of information and correctly fit it into the overall picture more quickly. That's why I like working with him so much.

"Yup. Apparently the kid's the beneficiary. If his father didn't commit suicide, that is."

"So what'd he do? Offer you a contingency?"

He doesn't miss a beat. "Uh huh."

"You're right, this isn't a typical twelve-year old." Another pause, and I heard the distant crackle of the phone line.

I had to grit my teeth. No matter how often I yell at the phone company, they can't seem to get my lines clear.

"Is he smart enough just to be after the money?" Doug was asking.

I considered it. I'd believed Chris, but I've met my share of believable con men in my time, and it wasn't impossible that a kid could be trying to work a con. Especially for three million dollars.

"I don't think so. My gut says he's honest. If it's a con, I don't see how it would work. We'd have to find a murderer before the insurance company would pay up. There's no way he accidentally fell off that bridge. And unless I'm missing something, I think Chris really believes his father was murdered."

"Poor kid."

I didn't say anything. What was there to say?

"It'd be interesting to know who Forrester's insurance company was."

Doug sounded like he was thinking out loud. I could picture him, pencil tapping against his forehead, expression grim. He was on the scent of a story. There would be no stopping him now.

"I'll know in a couple of days. You're thinking about a connection between the insurance company and one of the construction companies?"

"You have to admit it would be interesting."

"It's a good thing you're a news hound. You're too suspicious for your own good."

"Speaking of which, what's the story with your friend?"

"Andrea?"

"You have other friends who've been arrested for murder?"

It was no surprise that Doug had already heard about her arrest. "Not at the moment."

"So?"

"So she's been arrested for a killing she didn't do. I'm going to be working with her lawyer. At the moment, that's all I've got."

"You're going to try to get her off? Isn't your investigation likely to be a little biased?"

"Give me a break. I deal in facts." I picked up my mug, swallowed a mouthful of coffee. He was kidding, but it was a sore spot all the same. I had to treat this like any other case, if I was going to be any use to Andrea at all.

"And what facts are you dealing with so far?"

I probably didn't need to ask, but this was Andrea's life. "This is off the record, right?"

"Of course."

Yup, he sounded offended. But I'd had to make sure we were clear.

"Okay. So far, I know that the circumstances allow for the possibility of self-defense," I said, thinking out my position as I spoke. "And that the police aren't going charge her on no evidence, so they must think they've got something. But based on her character, I don't think she killed him, so I'll be looking for evidence of the real killer. That's all I've got at the moment."

"How can you be sure she didn't kill him? Do you honestly believe anyone is incapable of killing, given the right circumstances?"

Exactly what I'd been trying not to think about.

Because I wasn't sure. Not entirely. I didn't believe Andrea could kill anyone, but I wasn't certain that she hadn't killed Jake, especially given how afraid she'd been of him.

"She says she didn't."

"Like you believe everything a client tells you."

He was right again, damn it. If I believed what my clients told me without question, I'd be out of business in a hurry. "What's your point, Doug?"

"You're in a tough spot, Barbara. I'm just trying to point out that you'll have to keep an emotional distance if you're going to stay sane on this one," he said. "Just remember, you've got my number."

I could hear the sincerity in his gruff voice. "Thanks."

"And if there's anything newsworthy, you'll keep me in mind?"

I laughed. Trust Doug to inject a little humor.

"Right. As long as it doesn't injure my client or her case."

"Yeah, yeah. Seriously, Barbara, if there's anything I can do..."

"Thanks, Doug." I was touched, because it's an offer he wouldn't make unless he meant it.

"At the moment, you could help me the most by following up on Forrester," I said. "My heart really goes out to that kid, but I can't give him much time right now. And too much time has passed already. It's going to be difficult to find anything the police might have missed after this long. Assuming that the kid's right and they did miss something, that is."

"I'll look into the insurance company for starters, as soon as you can get me their name. I'll also look for anyone who might have benefited from the disaster."

"That's an ugly thought."

"It happens, and you know it."

"Sure. But I don't have to like it. Anytime I can expose someone who cold-bloodedly benefits from someone else's misfortune, it makes a case worthwhile."

"Plus it makes a hell of a story."

"Cynic."

Doug just laughed. I suddenly remembered the note the kid had sent about Cliff Walters, and told Doug I'd send it to him.

We ended the conversation, and I sent the note off, then printed off copies of the photos I'd taken at Andrea's place, both last night and this morning. They didn't tell me much.

CHAPTER TEN

When I reached Claire's office, Andrea and Claire were sitting at the small meeting table, looking anxious. I checked the clock on the wall behind Claire. I was early.

Andrea was not looking her usual energetic self.

In the sunlight streaming through the window to the left, her face looked drawn and tense and there were dark smudges under her eyes. Claire is always calm and pulled together, but today even her straight, perfectly cut hair had developed spikes.

I poured a cup of green tea from the pot that Claire keeps going at the side of the room, and sat down. It was the signal she'd been waiting for.

She handed us typed copies of the statement Andrea had made. I read it through intently, looking for anything that might give us a clue as to how Jake had really died. There was nothing.

I read it again, more slowly. Then I glanced at Claire, who gave me a nod, and turned to Andrea. "I can see why they arrested you," I said. "I'm your best friend, and even I don't believe this statement."

Andrea burst into tears. That wasn't the reaction I'd had in mind —I'd kind of been hoping for an explanation. I felt awful.

I started again, hoping I could get her to focus that detail oriented mind of hers. "Andrea, if you didn't kill Jake, then either he killed himself, or someone else killed him."

I reached for her hand and gave it a squeeze. "Given the trajectory of the bullet, it's almost impossible for him to have killed himself, so we have to assume he was killed by someone else. The police found no evidence of someone else, so there won't be much to go on. I'm going to need anything you might have seen or heard, no matter how small or insignificant, if I'm going to clear you."

Andrea drew a shaky breath, which caught on a half-sob. "Sorry, Babs. I don't think I know anything. Except that I didn't kill him. And nobody believes that," she said with a half-laugh that sounded way too close to tears.

"It's okay, Andy," I said. In the stress of the moment, I reverted to her childhood nickname, just as she had mine, completely ignoring Doug's advice. "I know you didn't. You told me that already."

"Oh, yeah, right." It was a fair approximation of her usual cheery tones, and I gave her full points for it. "That's right, just after they'd arrested me. It slipped my mind for a moment there."

"Can't imagine why it should have," I responded, deadpan.

That earned me a shaky smile, then Andrea's expression turned serious again. She met my eyes, and the expression in hers made me wince. "Claire says she's hired you. I'm glad, because if she hadn't, I would have. I know you'll find a way to get me out of this mess I'm in. But I really don't think I know anything that'll help."

"You may not know that you know. Something you heard without being aware of it, something you saw." I shrugged. "It could be anything. Probably it'll be something that didn't seem important at the time, that you noticed without realizing it because something didn't fit."

"If I don't know I know it, how am I supposed to remember it?"

I grinned, relieved to see my friend bouncing back. "That's the key, you don't. Just sit back, close your eyes, and listen to my voice."

Andrea had begun to do as I'd asked, but at the last words she'd straightened and stared at me accusingly. "Are you going to hypnotize me? Because if that's what you're thinking, you've got another think coming. I've never been hypnotized, the very idea scares me silly, as you well know, and I'm not about to start now."

Claire, who has come to know both of us rather well over the last few years, was sitting back in her chair, a slight smile on her face, clearly choosing the role of spectator. I noticed that she had pen and paper poised.

"I've never learned hypnotism, Andy. You know that. I do know some of the theory behind it, though, and I use it to help people remember things they didn't consciously notice. When you're telling someone what you remember, you tend to tell it in a certain order, covering all the things you've chosen to remember. But you're aware of a lot of things that you don't include, and it's those things I try to get at. Are you willing to try?"

"I suppose so." She settled back in her chair, then met my eyes. "As long as you just deal with that night."

It was an order.

————

I'VE KNOWN for a long time that Andrea is afraid of things like psychics and hypnotists, and that she thinks therapists are a great idea for somebody else. All of us have our dark demons, and we deal with them as best we can. Despite how long we've been friends, I'm not sure what all of Andrea's are.

I've suspected for a long time that there's something she's buried deep and is determined never to get even a glimpse of, and as her friend I respect that. Who am I to judge someone else's coping mechanisms? I have enough trouble with my own, especially now that I don't paint much anymore.

All I could do for Andrea was to try to find Jake's killer, without increasing her worries. I started with the easy stuff, like what had woken her up, deliberately asking questions out of order to keep the answers spontaneous.

As we talked, I could see Andrea relaxing. Claire was busy taking notes. The information Andrea was giving us was pretty much what she'd said before—she woke up because of the banging, she'd gone back to bed then heard a loud noise. Now it was time to see if there was more.

"Okay," I said, pitching my voice low. "You're in your bedroom. You've been half-asleep, and a loud sound has woken you. Before you do anything, take a long moment to look around you. What do you see?"

Andrea's voice came slowly. She had relaxed and was fully participating in this exercise. "The bedroom is dark, but there's a faint glow from the streetlight outside. There are no lights from the main floor."

"Can you see your clock?"

She nodded. "It's just a few minutes after one."

"Good. Now what do you do?"

"I put my robe on and go down the stairs."

"And do you see anything as you go down the stairs?"

"No, I'm watching my footing because the kitchen is dark."

"You don't turn on your bedroom light?"

"No."

"Do you know why not?"

"I think I don't want anyone to know I'm awake. It seems important to be very quiet."

I let that go for the moment, though I checked to be sure Claire had taken note of it. "Do you see anything else?"

"As I descend, I can see out the kitchen window. There's a patch of light reflecting off the lawn and the trees at the back. It must come from Jake's suite."

"Can you tell which windows it's coming from?"

"When I first see it, it seems to be right across the yard, but as I come further down the stairs I see it's only on part of the yard, where it would be if Jake's kitchen light was on."

Realizing that Andrea had nearly confronted a murderer tied my stomach up in tight knots.

I shot a look at Claire. She'd caught the significance of what Andrea had just said too. Andrea was too caught up in remembering to notice, which was good. I took a deep breath, then probed further.

"As you come towards the window, what do you see in the yard?"

"Just the light across the lawn, and the deep shadows in the trees. And there must be a breeze, because the shadows are moving."

"Where are the shadows moving, Andrea?"

"In the bushes along the alley."

Those bushes are taller than I am, and would easily hide a person from sight, even if there was enough light to see them otherwise. It sounded as though someone had turned off a light in the suite and run across the yard in the time it had taken Andrea to descend the stairs. So now I knew the probable time of the murder and at least the first part of the escape route the murderer had taken.

"What do you do next?"

"I look out the window for a moment, but I can't see anything, so I go down the back stairs and around the patio to Jake's door."

"When you go out, are the shadows still moving?"

"No," she said in some surprise. "And there's no wind. I guess it died down."

"Do you see anything?"

"The light is on in Jake's kitchen but there's no movement. All the other lights are out. I knock on Jake's door, but there's no answer."

"Do you see anything in the yard?"

Her brow wrinkled. "No," she said slowly.

"Think, Andrea."

"Wait, there's something. It's silly, but I nearly tripped over the hose. I hadn't left it out, so I put it away."

"You put the hose away at one in the morning, after hearing what you thought was a gunshot?" I couldn't believe what I was hearing.

"It's a habit, almost a reflex," she said. "I really hate things lying about, and I tripped on a hose once and broke my arm. So I just automatically put it away."

"Hmmm." I glanced over to make sure Claire had that one too.

She did. And judging by the expression on her face, she was having as much trouble with it as I was. "Anything else?"

"No."

"Do you hear anything?"

"There's a noise like an engine starting, somewhere down the alley, then it fades into the distance. After that, everything is quiet."

"Can you tell what kind of engine?" I asked, knowing how hopeless Andrea is with anything mechanical.

"It wasn't that loud, but it sounded like a lawn mower or something. But there was something wrong with it."

Terrific. A lawn mower at one a.m.

Which meant it probably wasn't a car, or at least it was a small car. I wondered if Andrea could tell the difference between a lawn mower and a Kia. Still, it was better than no information at all.

"Okay, you knock on the door. Then what?"

"There's no answer, and when I look through the window I can see a hand on the kitchen floor, as though someone is lying there, so I go in."

"Wait a minute. Is the door locked?"

"Oh. No, it isn't. I just turn the knob and go in, but I've got the keys anyway."

"You had your keys with you?" According to Claire, it was one of the main pieces of evidence against her.

"Yes, of course."

"Why?"

"Well, I didn't want to lock myself out." She opened her eyes at that, giving me that look, the one that says I should be more practical.

"Wait a minute. You told the police you had the keys to Jake's suite with you. You mean had your own keys as well?"

She nodded, looking surprised at the question.

She'd got me again.

"So what you're telling me is that you not only dug the spare keys out of the flour canister, you took your key ring too? And then you locked your door behind you? At one in the morning? You went out in your robe, at one in the morning, and locked the door behind you?"

Unfortunately, both she and I knew that it was just the kind of thing she would do. The downside of all that amazing efficiency is that she's a little compulsive about some things. Locking her door behind her in these circumstances is typical Andrea behavior. But I doubt you'd ever get a jury to believe it.

"Okay," I said. "You took your keys because you didn't want to be locked out. Makes perfect sense. Why did you take Jake's keys?"

"Well, obviously if there was a problem I was going to need to get into his suite," Andrea said.

And this was the man she was afraid of. Sometimes I just don't understand how Andrea's mind works. I didn't say anything for a moment, just took a deep breath.

"Right," I said. "Okay, sit back, close your eyes, and let's continue."

At that point I made the mistake of looking at Claire, who obviously wasn't aware of some of Andrea's little quirks. At the look on her face, I almost lost it.

She looked absolutely dumbfounded, as if she'd just run head-first into a brick wall. And given some of the clients I've seen her handle over the years, it takes a lot to make her look like that. I took a deep breath, swallowed a strong desire to giggle, and turned back to Andrea.

"You've opened the door to the suite. What do you see?"

"The hallway is dark, except where the light from the kitchen shows at the end."

"What do you do?"

"I walk down the hall. I'm holding my keys as a weapon."

"Do you hear anything?"

"No. It's really quiet in the suite.

"Then what?"

"I go into the kitchen." Her voice broke off.

At the look of remembered horror on her face, I prompted her gently. "It's over, Andrea. But we need to know what you saw."

"Jake was lying on the floor, on his back. He—he—" She couldn't go on.

"Okay. Don't look at Jake. Do you notice anything else in the room?"

"There's a gun on the floor. By Jake's hand. I pick it up. It's heavy."

"Before you pick up the gun, Andrea. Do you notice anything else? What does the room look like?"

"Messy," she said. "As usual. There are dishes in the sink and unwashed pans on the stove. The table's stacked with newspapers and dirty glasses. He hasn't even re-corked the wine."

"What kind of wine?"

"Red wine. I can't see the label. That's odd."

"What's odd?"

"I never saw Jake drink anything except beer."

I looked over at Claire. She was scribbling furiously.

"What about wine glasses?"

"No, I don't see any wine glasses. Just tumblers and beer mugs. One of the glasses on the table is half full of what looks like red wine, though."

"How close is Jake to the table?"

"He's lying right beside it."

"And the gun?"

"Between him and the table."

"Do you notice anything else?"

"The expression on his face. He looks so—angry."

I didn't yet know whether Jake had died instantly, but the description was unexpected, creating a vivid mental image. I could almost see it as a painting—the jarring shock of bright blood against the gray linoleum, the disordered kitchen, the darkened face set in angry lines, resisting death to the last second.

I wrenched my mind back to the task at hand. "Do you see anything else?"

Andrea shook her head, then opened her eyes. "I don't think I can take any more of this, Babs. I'm sorry."

"It's okay. You did great."

"I did?" She looked puzzled.

"You did. Just a couple more questions, then I'll explain. Did you smell anything in the suite?"

At this question Andrea turned quite green. "Blood. I'd always read it had a metallic smell, but it didn't really mean anything. But it's not a smell you ever forget."

I nodded. I knew what she meant. "Nothing else?" I prodded gently.

She shook her head wordlessly.

"Okay. Last question. Did you notice the time when you woke up the first time?"

"When I heard the banging, you mean? It was twelve thirty-two."

"You're sure?"

She nodded. "I was furious. Well, scared and furious. When the noise woke me, I looked at the clock. It was after midnight, so I was planning on calling the cops, reporting him as a noise violation, or whatever you call it. But it stopped before I could call, so eventually I went back to sleep."

I nodded, then looked at Claire. "Did you get it all?"

"Oh, I think so," she said.

Andrea looked from one to the other of us. "Will somebody please tell me what's going on?"

I looked at Claire, then back at Andrea. "You nearly walked in on a killer."

CHAPTER ELEVEN

"I what?" Andrea said. It was almost a shriek.

"Well, where did you think the murderer was in all of this?" I asked her.

It was clear Andrea hadn't thought about it, if the look on her face was anything to go by. To be fair, I could see where being arrested for murder might interfere with normal logic. But the risks that Andrea had unknowingly taken, the knowledge of what had so nearly happened to her, made my heart stop.

The fact that she was so sublimely unaware of what she'd done just made it worse. I glanced at Claire, but her expression was unreadable.

"When you were coming down the stairs from your bedroom, you probably did see more light from the top of the stairs," I said. "Most likely the killer turned off the light in the hall, which is what you'd have seen on the lawn. Either that, or the opening of the suite door allowed enough light out that you could see a difference."

Andrea showed no signs of interrupting, so I continued. "The 'breeze' you saw in the shadows was most likely the murderer leaving. If you'd been a few seconds faster…" I shrugged, leaving her to finish that thought. "But it's a very good thing you decided not to turn on any lights."

Andrea sat silent for quite a few moments. She had turned that interesting shade of green again.

I let her digest it, hoping that another time, my fearless friend would think things through before she rushed off to investigate a shot in the night.

"It was stupid," Andrea finally said. "I hadn't realized how stupid. " She paused, then sat straighter in her chair. "But at least it's clear I'm not the murderer."

"It may be clear to us. But there's no evidence there was anyone else in the suite." I tapped the copy of her statement, lying on the desk between us.

"And the police are not going to believe what you've told us. It's too convenient an explanation, and you didn't tell them initially. You've had enough time to invent an explanation, and quite frankly, that's exactly what this would sound like to them."

"But it's the truth."

"Doesn't matter. The evidence is against you."

"Which is why we've hired Barbara," Claire said. "To prove your innocence."

That was easy for her to say. From where I sat, it looked like there was nothing to prove that innocence. The only way we were going to get Andrea off was to find the real murderer.

And I knew exactly who was going to find herself responsible for that little task. Me.

Already Andrea and Claire were looking at me expectantly. They both had that expression people get when they're waiting for the magician to pull the rabbit out of the hat. I hated to disappoint them, but this was not going to be a one-woman show.

"What? Surely you're not expecting me to just go out there and find the killer?" Both faces wore identical expressions of surprise. It was clear that's exactly what they were expecting. "It's not quite that simple, folks. It's going to take all three of us to get Andrea out of this little mess."

I turned to Andrea. "Have you done that report on Jake I asked for?"

"It's at the office, but it isn't quite finished. Now that Jake is dead, why do you need it?"

"Because I'm going to start by assuming Jake knew his killer. He was killed in his own home, after midnight, and the police found no signs of forced entry. Which is why they're looking at you. But if the killer was a friend or an acquaintance of Jake's, he would have let them in. And if Jake did know his killer, then maybe Jake can lead me to him or her."

"That makes sense."

Claire looked thoughtful, and scribbled something on her legal pad.

I pulled out the photos I'd taken, and spread them out on Claire's desk.

"These are photos I took at your place that night and later that morning, Andrea. I want you to look at them, and see if anything looks wrong, different, or out of place."

Andrea moved closer to the desk to get a better look. She surveyed all the photos for a few minutes, going carefully from one to the other.

Finally she picked up a shot of the backyard I'd taken the night of that murder, one that showed the back of the house, the patio and part of the shrubbery. She looked at it intently for a moment, then handed it to me.

Claire came around her desk to have a look over my shoulder.

"There's something not quite right with this shot. I'm not sure what it is, but something feels wrong."

Claire and I both looked intently at the photo. Whatever Andrea was picking up was not obvious. Neither of us could see anything different or out of place.

"Don't worry about it," I told Andrea, handing her the second set of prints. "It'll come to you. Just don't try too hard to remember. Keep the photos, glance through them now and then. If you figure out what it is, or if you see anything else, let me know."

I gathered up the other set and put them back in my bag, with the one Andrea had singled out on top.

"One other thing, Andrea. You said you heard an engine of some kind in the alley. I need you to listen for something similar, then find out what it is."

My guess was that she'd heard a motorbike. If she could narrow it down, that would help. But I wasn't holding my breath. Andrea is totally uninterested in any kind of motorized vehicle, though if you want to know about mountain bikes, she's your person.

She nodded. Then we got down to business.

Claire briefed us on when the preliminary hearing was to be. I made a note of that, then made notes of what Andrea had said, checking my memory against the notes that Claire had been taking. Claire and Andrea went through her defense, and I made a note of the holes in the case.

There were a lot of holes.

Part of my job would be to fill in as many of them as possible.

Basically, though, I either needed to find the killer or to find enough evidence that it wasn't Andrea to convince the police to investigate further. I'd have preferred the latter, but I had a funny feeling that I'd have more luck finding a killer than convincing the police that it wasn't Andrea. Especially given the complaints Jake had filed against her.

We set a follow-up meeting in two days, and Andrea promised to get me her report on Jake the next day. By the time I left, Andrea was looking more her usual self. And I was ten minutes late for my meeting with Jerry.

REACHING Java Joe's slightly out of breath—I couldn't find close parking, and it was a warm day—I could see Jerry's dark hair over the top of the back corner booth. He must really have wanted to talk to me. It isn't like him to be on time.

As I slid into the red vinyl upholstered booth, he nodded at the waitress, and she brought a second cup of coffee, strong and hot in a thick white pottery mug.

"I figured you'd need this," was his greeting.

I'd grabbed it, taken that first sustaining mouthful before I spoke. "You're right. It's been a hell of a day already, and there's no end in sight."

"How's Andrea?"

As Jerry spoke, the little muscle beside his right eye began twitching madly. Not a good sign. He has to be under an awful lot of stress before that reaction shows up.

"Surviving. It's tough on her, but she's holding her end up. Claire's a good lawyer."

"She'll have to be." He paused, took a swig of his coffee, looked undecided. "Look, just between us—did she do it?"

I could hear the fear in his voice, but it was a tough question to answer. Conflict of interest is that much harder when the parties involved are friends.

The more involved I get with this case, the more convinced I am that my usual policy of not working for friends is the only way to go. Still, Andrea had nothing to hide, and maybe something to gain if I answered Jerry's question. So I did.

"She says she didn't do it. And I believe her." As I said the words, I realized that I meant it. That last lingering doubt about whether Andrea might actually have killed Jake was gone. Good to know.

From the look on his face, Jerry hadn't expected my response.

"You believe her?"

No wonder his eye was twitching.

Despite having known her for years, despite the growing relationship between them, Jerry must have been convinced, or at least mostly convinced, that Andrea had killed Jake. Maybe killed him in self-defense, but killed him all the same.

How would I have been feeling if I'd been convinced she'd done it?

I'd known all along that it was possible she'd killed him, but I'd kept shoving that possibility to the far corners of my mind. The idea that someone you care about might be a killer is mind-boggling. It was easier to imagine myself killing someone than Andrea doing so.

Maybe we're just more aware of our own dark sides than we are of our loved ones'.

Personally, I believe that everyone has it in them to kill another person, given the right set of circumstances. But then I also believe that for most people the right set of circumstances is pretty extraordinary.

Would I kill to save myself? To save someone I loved? Maybe.

I just don't know.

The only time I've been face-to-face with someone trying to kill me, I wasn't armed, at least not with anything lethal, so I've never had to face that decision, and I hope I never do.

Knowing Andrea as I do, though, knowing the situation with Jake, I hadn't really let myself consider the possibility that she'd shot him. Even knowing that investigating the murder meant I was going to have to fully consider that possibility, I'd avoided facing it. And after talking to Andrea, I was now convinced she was innocent.

But Jerry wasn't.

He must have been trying to reconcile everything he knew about Andrea with his belief that she'd killed Jake. Being involved with her on top of the history we have together would have confused his feelings even further, and the fact that he was a cop would just make it worse. Accepting that people kill other people just doesn't seem to apply to someone we care about.

No wonder he looked so awful.

"Yeah. From what Andrea remembers, I think the killer left just as she came down from her bedroom."

Jerry knows that house as well as I do. I could see him picturing it. The twitching beside his eye stopped as he weighed possibilities.

"You got anything to go on?" It was the logical, 'just the facts, ma'am' tone that he uses when he's analyzing a case. Good. At least he was considering other interpretations of what he knew.

"Nope. Not yet, anyway. But it seems likely it was someone Jake knew."

"No forced entry."

I nodded. Might as well begin the campaign to convince the police to look for another killer now.

"So you're going to be looking for evidence of a killer?"

"Yes." It didn't seem to be the time to tell him that I'd actually be looking for the killer. Jerry gets a little unreasonable if he thinks I'm stepping too far into what he considers police business. And what he doesn't know won't hurt him.

The trick would be making sure it didn't hurt me.

"If there's anything I can do…"

From his hopeless expression, he didn't think there was. "There is one thing."

"What?"

"When I went back to the house that night, I saw two officers leaving the suite holding something small. Any chance you can tell me what it was?"

I'd put him on the spot, and I knew it. I also knew that to clear Andrea, I was going to need every break I could find. So I focused on my coffee, let the silence stretch out between us.

It was Jerry who finally broke it. "They found Andrea's pen, that fountain pen she's so proud of, the one with her initials? Found it lying beneath the body."

"Andrea's pen? Beneath Jake's body?" This was not good news. "No wonder you charged her. If she killed him, everything fits together. But if she didn't kill him, then nothing makes any sense."

"That's about it," he said. He didn't look happy about it.

"Do you know for sure the pen was Andrea's?"

"We showed it to her later that night. She claimed it as hers and wanted to know why we had it."

"And did you tell her where you'd found it?"

"No."

I nodded. That made sense, but it didn't help my investigation any.

"I'm starting from the premise that she didn't kill him," I said.

"And that there's a third, unknown party involved. The pen just doesn't fit."

I dug into my purse, pulled out the photo of the receipt I'd found the previous day and passed it to Jerry. "I went back to the house the next day, and found this on the back lawn."

He gave me that look.

"It was outside the crime scene tape. But I thought it might be important."

Especially now I knew the murderer had probably left the property through the yard, but this somehow didn't feel like the time to tell Jerry that. "Do you know if anyone's looked into it?"

He scanned it, his expression skeptical.

"Huh. I'll ask, but it could have blown there from anywhere." He took a mouthful of coffee, looked at me hard. "You really don't think she killed him?"

"No, I don't. I believe Andrea's telling the truth. "

Jerry nodded slowly. "I hope you're right, for all our sakes. And I hope you can prove it in time."

He'd just done a great job of expressing my own fears, and in a tone that doubted my ability to do any such thing. Looking at his tired face, I forgave him for the lack of support.

Right then, Jerry didn't look like he had the ability to believe in much of anything.

CHAPTER TWELVE

Back in my office, I reviewed my notes and added a couple of points. I didn't see a pattern. What I did see was too few facts.

I sat back with a sigh, and noticed the voice mail icon on my phone. The light wasn't blinking, though. I'd have to get that fixed. Again.

Muttering under my breath, I grabbed a pen. One message.

It was Chris, sounding breathless and excited. "Miss O'Gr… I mean Barbara? I think I might know who killed my Dad. I'm going to follow him and I'll call you back."

Now what?

If Chris was right about his Dad's death, these men were dangerous. And the call had come in nearly two hours ago. There was no second call. And there was nothing I could do about it until he called me back.

All I could do was compartmentalize.

With a sigh, I went through my notes again, focusing on what I knew and what I assumed. I knew that Jake had been killed between twelve-thirty and one a.m., that he was killed by a single bullet to the heart, fired from his own gun and that a pen Andrea claimed as hers was found under his body.

I was assuming Jake knew his killer and had let him or her into his suite and that the killer had left via the back yard and then in a vehicle he'd left in the alley. Not much to solve a murder with. The phone rang.

Chris?

"O'Grady Investigations. Barbara speaking."

"Barbara, do you have a minute?"

It was my sister. If I'd known it was her, I wouldn't have answered—I'd about had it with the distractions. Cash flowed be-damned, next week I was upgrading to call display. And maybe call waiting.

On the other hand, Susanna doesn't usually call me at work. The last time she'd done so, her husband had just left her. They seemed to be fine now, but who knew what really went on inside another's marriage. "What's up?"

"Have you talked to Mom lately?"

Not what I'd expected to hear. "Sure, she called to invite me to dinner a couple of days ago. Is something wrong?"

A hesitation. "I'm not sure. What did you talk about?"

"Dinner on Sunday. The Hundred Mile diet. The fact that I'm in the wrong career and need to get a life. You know, the usual."

She laughed a little, but you could tell her heart wasn't in it. "Barbara, she means well. You just make too much of everything she says."

Which was probably why Susanna got along with her so much better than I did. That and the fact that she wasn't critical of Susanna's lifestyle. "Maybe. Why are you asking, Susanna?"

"How did she seem?"

"Like always."

"She seemed her normal self? She didn't seem… off?"

Off? "No, she seemed fine. Maybe she just had a bad day."

A sigh. "Maybe. It's more than one day, though. I'm worried about her. I think something's wrong."

"I didn't notice anything."

"That's because you don't really talk to her."

Maybe I'd upgrade to call display today. "Yes, I do. We talk every week. Or so."

"About what?"

"Whatever she wants to talk about. Usually what's wrong with my life."

"She's not that bad, Barbara."

I grinned, glad she couldn't see me. "Yes, she is."

Her voice lightened a little. "You never change. No, what I meant was, what do *you* talk about? With her?"

"She talks. I listen. It works better that way."

"See what I mean?"

"Yeah, yeah. Look, Susanna, I'm in the middle of a case and I have a deadline. If you've got a point here, I'd appreciate hearing it."

"Oh Barbara, I heard about Andrea. I'm so sorry. I know you'll get her off."

Easy for her to say. Though the vote of confidence was nice, if a little unexpected. I hadn't known my sister knew much about what I did.

"Thanks. But it's going to take everything I've got. So unless there's something specifically wrong with Mom…"

"I know, I know. Just the facts."

I laughed. "Not quite that cut and dried. She's more likely to be stewing about something we haven't done than about something actually wrong. Look, I'm not discounting your feelings, but I'm sure she'll tell us if there's something really wrong. She's not much for keeping secrets."

Truth at all costs, that's my mother. Sometimes it's a good thing. Sometimes.

"Okay, you've got a point. But Barbara? I have a bad feeling about this. Pay attention next time you talk to her, all right?"

I gave a mock sigh. "Do I have to?"

"Yes." This time there was no humor in her voice.

"I'll let you know how it goes."

"Good. And good luck with Andrea."

"Thanks. I'm going to need it."

I disconnected, then began wondering about Jake's family. Did he have a mother? A sister? Other loved ones? Who would mourn him?

I made a note to ask Andrea, then turned to the crime scene photos. What had Andrea noticed, anyway? I couldn't spot anything. I separated out the photo she had picked and examined it. It was one from the night of the murder, showing the area around Jake's suite. It didn't raise any questions for me at all.

I brought the photo up on screen and zoomed in, but nothing caught my eye. I compared it to a couple of similar photos, one taken that same night and one taken the following morning. Still nothing.

So I e-mailed all three shots to my favorite photo shop, asking for 8 x 10's. They can develop detail that my lowly inkjet printer just can't find—sometimes something jumps out at me.

I'd pick the prints up in the morning.

———

I WAS JUST ABOUT to make another pot of coffee when the phone rang. Maybe this would be Chris.

It was Nick, he of the broad shoulders and the gorgeous smile. Now why was he phoning rather than just dropping by?

"Have you heard from the kid recently?" he asked.

Oh no. "He left a message earlier, but he hasn't called back yet. Why?"

Please, don't let it be bad news.

"He's got himself into a situation," Nick said. "And I need your help to get him out of it. Can you meet me at the Seabus Terminal in North Van?"

Questions could wait. "Yes. Where?"

"In front of Starbucks, on the Quay."

"I'll be there in half an hour."

All the way across town, I worried about Chris, and about what Nick's involvement in the Forrester case might be. Maybe it was time I did a little investigation of my too attractive neighbor. Scruples are well and good, but enough is enough.

Traffic across the Second Narrows Bridge was horrific, and It was nearly four-thirty by the time I managed to find a parking spot off First Avenue.

I raced to the meeting spot, arriving disheveled and out of breath. Nick's tall form was easy to spot despite the homeward-bound commuters from downtown thronging Lonsdale Quay.

"I'm here. What's up?"

He handed me a coffee. "Come on. I'll fill you in as we go."

Well, at least Chris must not be in immediate danger. I accepted the coffee with a feeling of relief.

As we passed the overcrowded loading area, I could see another distinctively flat-topped Seabus arriving from downtown. No sign of Chris, though. "What's going on?"

"I overheard Chris leave you that message. I was worried about him, so I followed him here."

I gave him a questioning look.

"Bus," he said with a grimace.

I bit back a grin at the mental picture of tall Nick trying to be inconspicuous while tailing a twelve-year old on a bus. I'd bet dollars to donuts that Chris had spotted him.

Unless Chris was too worried about whatever it was he was up to himself.

"The kid seemed to know where he was going. He headed straight for that blue and white office tower just outside the quay and hung around the doorway for a while. He did a pretty good job, too. He had some kind of video game with him, and he managed to look like a kid who was waiting for his Mom, and pretty bored by the whole thing."

He grinned. "I had a harder time trying to blend in."

I'd just bet he had.

"Chris didn't even bother going inside. He checked his watch, and headed for that little park. When I left him, he was lying in the sun, playing whatever. Way I figure it, whoever he's waiting for must work in that building and he's planning to pick him up again after work—maybe five, five-thirty."

That explained part of his urgent call to me. "So why exactly am I here?"

"He knows you. And he already called you about this, so he won't hesitate to involve you further."

Okay, I'd buy that, at least for now. I wondered just how much of Chris's story Nick knew.

Before I could ask him, I spotted Chris in the crowd just ahead of us, energy drink in hand. I tapped Nick on the arm and pointed.

Chris was moving slowly and casually along the walk in front of the building, looking like a kid who had all the time in the world. I wondered how he'd learned to look so aimless, then remembered all those long, empty summers of my childhood.

As I watched, Chris spotted one of the men coming out of the office buildings. If I hadn't been looking for it, I don't think I would have seen it.

There was a tiny jerk of recognition, and he changed his direction slightly, to match that of his quarry. His seemingly aimless air didn't change at all, and he didn't look in the least as if he was in pursuit. There was no doubt in my mind, however, that Chris was hunting this guy.

And he was surprisingly good at it. I wondered where he'd picked it up.

Saturday morning cartoons, probably. It's amazing how sophisticated some of the stuff kids watch has become.

The guy we were following was dark-haired, fairly tall, and about forty pounds past his prime, despite the well cut navy suit. He was still good-looking, if you liked that chubby, slightly pouty look.

A good bone structure saved him, but there was something about his face I instinctively disliked. It was the way he held his mouth, I think, and something too smooth in his appearance.

Whoever he was, I was quite prepared to class him as one of the bad guys.

Nick and I followed the Chris and his quarry back to the market at the Quay, a two-story building housing an upscale farmers market surrounded by trendy boutiques on two floors.

We nearly lost Chris and his target a couple of times in the crowd. The market's always busy, a favorite place for people on the way home to stop for a drink, to pick up something for dinner, or to buy a little something as a reward for having made it through another workday.

As our odd little procession wound its way among the stalls, I breathed in the rich scents of olive oil and herbs, cheeses, and ripe fruit from the produce stalls, the roasting chickens and grilling burgers from the food stalls.

Vancouver's various markets are some of my favorite places to spend time, and I appreciate even fleeting contact with them. My eyes feasted on the rich tapestry of form and my fingers itched for a paintbrush.

Nick touched my arm, gestured. I looked to see what he was seeing, and caught a glimpse of Dark Hair, who'd paused to buy a bunch of fresh basil. Chris was hanging back, waiting for his quarry.

Within moments, both disappeared through a side door. We quickened our steps and followed.

Outside was a maze of people flowing in every direction. I spotted Dark Hair, and pointed him out to Nick. As we followed, Nick looked at Chris, then back at me, one eyebrow raised. The roar of homebound traffic along Marine made conversation a challenge, so I just shook my head in response.

As we walked, I studied Chris's back, and the occasional side glimpse of his face. He was intent on his pursuit, oblivious to anything else.

I couldn't tell if he knew where they were going, or if this was new to him, too. Presumably, Chris thought the guy he was following was somehow involved in his father's murder.

I wondered who he was, and how Chris had caught up with him.

I spotted Dark Hair turning into the small Greek restaurant just before Nick did, and put a hand against his arm to slow him down. Chris hung back while Dark Hair went inside, then came to a stop just outside the restaurant, a disconsolate expression on his face.

I turned to Nick.

"Time to talk to Chris."

CHAPTER THIRTEEN

efore Nick had a chance to react, I was in motion. I walked up behind Chris as quietly as I could. Not that he was likely to hear me against the traffic rushing by.

"Hi, Chris."

He jumped, and spun around.

"Miss O… I mean Barbara." He looked stunned and a little sheepish, then very relieved. "I was just going to call you. How did you get here? And how did you find me?"

"Nick followed you," I said, indicating Nick, who was strolling over to join us.

Chris just looked at him, and his face went pale. "Mr. Markham."

I looked from Nick to Chris and back. "Well?"

I could hear the challenge in my tone. Nick didn't miss it, either. Good. Gorgeous smile or no, Nicholas Markham had some explaining to do.

His first words were reassurance for Chris. I had to give him points for that.

"Hello again, Chris." Nick held out his hand for Chris to shake. "It's okay, I'm on your side."

Chris didn't look as if he believed him. A little color came back into his cheeks, but he kept that wary look. Nick turned to me.

"I was retained by the insurer that issued Forrester's life insurance policy," he said. "Crestlife don't want to be accused of taking the easy way out of paying a legitimate claim. I recognized Chris the second time I saw him outside your office."

"You're an investigator, too?"

He nodded.

"There's no sign on your office door, and you're not listed in the yellow pages." I'd done that much checking, and at this point I didn't mind letting him know it.

"I specialize in financial cases, particularly insurance fraud, and my work is mostly through referrals. It's easier to get my job done if I'm anonymous."

I nodded. There was a note of truth in his voice, and his explanation was at least plausible. Which didn't mean I trusted him. We'd finish out today's little exercise, then I was going to do some digging into his past and current interests.

Chris had been looking from one to the other of us. I'd love to know what was going on in his mind, but his expression wasn't giving anything away.

"Who are you following?" I asked him. "And does he know you by sight?"

"His name is Cliff Walters."

Forrester's former partner. Now that I'd seen the man, I could believe a scenario in which he'd been bribed to look the other way.

"I've never actually met him," Chris was saying. "My dad pointed him out to me on a job site a couple of times, but it was at a distance. They didn't spend time together outside work. As far as I know, he has no idea who I am."

"He knows you exist though?"

"Yeah. Dad trusted him."

Obviously Chris didn't. "Why are you following him? And why did you call me?"

"I think Walters is up to something. I never liked what Dad used to tell me about him, and he acted like scum when Dad died." His voice almost broke on the last words. I made a mental note to find out exactly how the scum had behaved.

" I've been following Mr. Walters for two weeks," he said.

Interesting. I wondered why he'd started following him. Wasn't that my job?

Except I'd told him I was too busy to help him until I'd solved Andrea's case. I felt guiltier than ever.

Was that why Chris was doing this? Didn't he realize how dangerous it could be? Or did he not care? That idea scared me.

"He's pretty much got a routine, and he lunches with guys from the office," Chris was saying. "But today he met a guy right after lunch that I'd never seen before. The guy gave him an envelope of some kind."

"What did this guy look like?"

"Older, mid-twenties. Tall, kinda thin, long brown hair. Messed up face."

"Messed up? How?"

"Acne," Chris said. "Anyway, I figured Walters was up to something, and I came looking for you. I figured you'd know what to do."

"But I wasn't there so you followed him yourself."

Chris nodded. We both looked at Nick.

"I saw you outside Barbara's door and heard the message you left," he told Chris. "So I followed you to North Van and arranged for Barbara to meet me here. When you picked up Walters, we followed you both."

Chris nodded, seemingly accepting the explanation.

Me, I was waiting for the opportunity to have a quiet chat with Chris, find out what he really thought. I wanted a quiet chat with Mr. Markham, too. But that could wait.

"Have you ever met Walters?" I asked Nick.

"No."

"Then let's go in." Even if Walters had seen Chris, it was unlikely he'd connect him with the family group we appeared to be. Actually, that's one of the things I try not to think about, the fact that I could quite plausibly be the mother of a twelve-year old.

Inside, it was the typical North American version of a Greek restaurant—red checked cloths, dark beams against textured white walls, large posters of various Greek Islands, the wonderful smell of garlic and roasting meats. Walters was seated two tables away from us, deep in conversation with another dark-haired man, similarly clad in business attire.

If I concentrated, I could just about make out their conversation. Not that it helped much. They were deep in discussion of the stock market, in particular a small company that had just listed on the CNDX. Walters seemed very positive about the value of the stock, his companion wasn't so sure. They went from stocks to rating trendy restaurants, which lasted all through dinner.

Nick and I had just reached the stage of mock-arguing over the bill, when Walters and his buddy called for their check. They threw down cash, then I heard the question we'd been waiting for.

"You've got it?"

Walters glanced around, then opened his briefcase. He passed a white 9" x 12" envelope to the other man.

I looked at Chris, who gave a slight nod. It was the envelope from lunch.

The two men stood and left. Chris made "bored twelve-year old" noises and followed them. That kid really didn't miss a beat. If he were a few years older, I could use an apprentice like him.

Picking up Chris's cue, Nick had followed him, expostulating. Between the two of them, they almost had me convinced we were a family. When I got outside, Nick was nowhere in sight. Chris grabbed my arm and began propelling me back towards the Quay.

"Mr. Markham's tailing the other one," he explained. I wondered where he'd learned that an undertone is less carrying than a whisper. "We're to follow Walters. We'll rendezvous at the Bistro at seven."

The melodrama of his words was the first sign I'd seen that Chris truly was twelve years old. It was reassuring. I'd begun to wonder if he was actually a short, very young looking twenty-something.

We followed Walters as he made a beeline straight back to the office tower he'd emerged from earlier. As he used a key to let himself into the building, Chris and I looked at each other. He voiced both our thoughts.

"Now what?" He sighed dramatically, his expression frustrated. "That's his office. He works late. He'll probably be there for hours."

I almost laughed at how long that 'hours' sounded. "Which office is his, do you know?"

"It's on the 14th floor. Around the side. C'mon, I'll show you."

We made our way around the side of the building, and he pointed out the window, the fourth from one end. There wasn't much to see because all the lights were still on, so there was nothing to distinguish that window from any other.

"I think we're done here," I said.

He nodded, resigned. It was nearly seven, so we adjourned to the Bistro to wait for Nick.

Who was already there, looking very pleased with himself and the dark beer he was halfway through. Chris grinned when he saw him. "How'd you get here so fast?"

"Ah, I have my ways." Nick signaled for a waitress, then, after some discussion, ordered nachos for the table, a beer for me and a root beer for Chris.

Chris was sitting on the edge of his seat, practically squirming with impatience. I suspected Nick was well aware of the kid's anxiety to know what had happened, and was drawing out the ordering process on purpose. The twinkle in his eye told me I was right.

I hid a grin behind the menu, and watched the relief in Chris's face when the waitress finally left.

"So what did you find out?" he burst out.

"I've got an address, and a name. Knight. Byron Knight."

Chris looked puzzled. "That's not a name I know. But I don't get it. How did you find all that out so fast?" Then his face cleared. "Oh, I get it. You traced his license plate."

"Got it in one. How did you guys do?"

I let Chris tell him. I was still trying to figure out how Nick had traced that license plate so fast. He had connections somewhere, and I needed to know where.

"Not nearly so well." Chris was leaning forward, eyes sparkling. "Walters just went back to his office. How do we find out what was in the envelope?"

"Barbara and I will take it from here," Nick said. "If your Dad didn't commit suicide, this could be dangerous. You've done a great job so far, but now it's time to leave it to the professionals."

It was a great speech. I was tempted to applaud.

Nick had the grace to look slightly sheepish. 'Barbara and I' indeed. Last time I checked, it was still my case.

There wasn't a lot left to say. Chris told us what little he'd learned by shadowing Walters, though I had the feeling he was leaving out a few key details. My reluctant client and I were overdue for a long talk.

Meanwhile, we polished off the last of the nachos, Nick and I finished our beers, and Chris inhaled his third root beer.

We detoured by Walters' office. His light was still on, but there was no point following him further that night. I drove Nick back to our office building, dropping Chris at his home on the way. When we got to my floor, I said good night quickly and disappeared into my office.

Until I knew a little more about Mr. Nick Markham and his connection with my case, I planned on avoiding him.

———

I'D JUST CLOSED my office door behind me and flipped on the lights when the phone rang. It was Andrea. She'd finished the summary of what she knew about Jake, and could I come over and go through it with her?

Mentally shelving my plans for an early night, I told her I'd be right over.

First, though, I e-mailed Doug to let him know that it was Crestlife Insurance that held the policy on Forrester's life. Knowing Doug would keep digging into the case while I was focused on Andrea's problems made me feel better about Chris.

Though Chris deciding to trail Walters on his own still bothered me. I'd have to have a talk with him, and soon.

When I got to Andrea's, I went around to the kitchen door in back and tapped on the glass. Andrea's kitchen is a little too country for my taste, and the appeal of cow-embellished dish towels and tea cozies completely escapes me, but it was bright and warm, and smelled of freshly brewed coffee. She offered me beer or wine, but strong coffee was what I needed if I was going to concentrate.

She poured two cups, and we sat down at the round oak table that looks out over the back yard. With a flourish, she produced a thick sheaf of typescript and set it in front of me. I looked from the stack of paper to her.

"All this?"

"Well, you said you wanted everything I knew about him."

Right. I should have known better. "Why don't you summarize it for me. I'll read it in detail later."

"Okay. Jake sold insurance and mutual funds, and he mostly worked from home. There's a couple of pamphlets in there. I think it was some kind of weird pyramid scheme, because he kept talking about downstream opportunities and telling me how much money I could make if I changed businesses."

"Was he successful, then?"

She shrugged. "He always paid the rent on time. And that Harley of his is new, he bought it a few months ago. Even I know those things don't run cheap."

She was right, they didn't. "Has he always ridden motorbikes?"

"Pretty much. I think that's the third one I've seen him with."

"Was he home a lot?"

"It varied. I don't think he saw clients here, and he'd sometimes head off on his bike and I wouldn't see him for a few days. He didn't exactly have a predictable schedule."

"Anything else?"

"Most of the rest of it is details."

I flipped through a few pages, shuddered. Andrea had detailed the arguments she'd had with him and the incidents of violence she'd already told me about. She'd even included the times she'd run into him at the corner store, and what he'd been buying (mostly bread, milk and cigarettes). She'd done exactly the kind of precise, thorough notes I'd expected from her.

I took a swallow of coffee and looked over to see her watching me expectantly. Well, her look seemed to say. Can you prove me innocent now?

I took another quick swallow of coffee. This was going to be hard.

"This is good work, Andrea. It'll give me a start on figuring out who Jake was, who might have wanted him dead. But finding his killer—well, it's going to take some time. You know that, don't you?"

She nodded wordlessly.

I took another mouthful of coffee, then reached over and gripped her hand. "We'll get through, this, Andy. Just like the time we got caught jumping off the cliffs at Capilano. It was pretty stupid, but we managed not to kill ourselves on the way down, which was pretty amazing all by itself. And we managed to talk our way out of being grounded for life. Given your parents and mine, that's pretty amazing too."

She grinned. "It wasn't your finest moment, Babs."

"I had a feeling you'd remember that. Well, it wasn't exactly my fault they doubled the punishment after they heard my explanation. Besides, that's why you hired Claire. She's the one who's supposed to talk you out of things. I'm just supposed to…"

"To find the real killer," she finished. "I know it's a tall order, Barbara. I'm sorry. It's an unfair pressure to put on anyone. But I don't seem to have any other choice at the moment."

I hated seeing my bubbly, competent friend shook up like this.

Of course, given the events of the last few days, she was probably still in shock. I gripped her hand a little tighter. "It's okay, Andy. You'd do it for me."

She nodded.

"Besides, you know how I love to figure things out when other people are sure they already know the answer, and they're wrong. This is right up my alley."

Andrea smiled a little at that. She knows me too well, though. Both she and I could hear the ring of false heartiness in my voice. I decided I'd better stop while I was ahead.

"I'll do my best, Andrea," I said. "I don't know how it'll come out, but I'll do my best. I promise you that."

"I know you will." She paused for a long moment, tracing aimless little patterns on the cow-bedecked tablecloth, then looked up and met my eyes. "And I do know I may be asking the impossible. But I have to ask it."

"Yeah." There was no comfort or reassurance I could give her. I knew too well how hopeless the task ahead of me might prove to be.

I didn't stay long after that. There was nothing more to say.

When I got home, I sat down with a highlighter and started to go through Andrea's report on Jake. That came to an abrupt halt when twenty-some pounds of fur planted itself in the middle of the page I was reading.

"Get off, Cat!"

"Rrrowrr?"

"Yes, you. Get off now. Or I'll tell Andrea you're the reason I couldn't find Jake's killer."

He purred.

"If you don't get off, you don't get any dinner."

Cat licked his front paw, ran it slowly over his whiskers, then stood up and strolled to the edge of the table. He jumped down, landing with a thud that had to be audible to my downstairs neighbor, and sauntered to the kitchen. When I didn't follow, he looked back at me.

"Rrrrowwr."

Shaking my head, I got up and poured him a saucer of milk. It was clearly the only way I was going to get anything done.

I made myself a tuna sandwich while I was up, and ended up sharing half of it with him. The wine I refused to share, and he was too smart to argue with me.

Several hours later, exhausted from reading and re-reading Andrea's notes but no further ahead, I turned in. And lay staring at the ceiling for far too long, until I felt a familiar bulk settle itself against my legs.

I fell asleep to the sound of Cat purring.

CHAPTER FOURTEEN

I wasn't quite sure why I was in the office on a sunny Saturday. We'd have few enough of those before the rains set in next month. I doodled a series of question marks on a sheet of paper and stared at them for a moment, then loaded Jake's spreadsheets and went through them.

Still nothing.

But there was one question that I'd forgotten to ask Andrea the previous evening. I called her office.

"Hey, it's me. What are you doing working on a Saturday, anyway?"

"Same thing you are. What's up, Barbara?"

"Have you heard anything else that sounds like the noise you heard in the alley the night of the murder?" I wasn't hoping for much, but you never know.

"I've been listening to sounds for the last day or so, and I think it must have been a motorcycle."

"Any idea how big a motorcycle?" It was a stupid question. Of course she wouldn't know that. But I was forgetting who I was dealing with.

"I knew it was important, so I did some research. And the

sound was kind of odd. I ended up going to the Harley dealership, out on Boundary. And I think it was a Harley, one of the big ones."

"What made you think of Harleys?"

"Jake's bike. He rode one."

That made sense.

"I'm not sure what model I might have heard, but the guy I talked to was really helpful," Andrea was saying. "I got his card in case you wanted more specifics."

I could just imagine how helpful that poor Harley dealer had been. Andrea is an efficient businesswoman, but men mostly notice her fragile blond femininity, which they seem to misinterpret as helplessness.

I can't count the number of times I've watched her get something done while men fall over themselves to help her.

She often doesn't need the help, but she accepts it with a grace that I sometimes envy. I tend towards the "I can do it myself" school of thought. But Andrea is thorough, and regardless of the difference in our methods, I was grateful for this particular result.

As I pictured her talking to the Harley guy, my mind made one of those sudden connections.

"Andrea, is Jake's bike still out back at your place?"

There was a pause on the other end. "I think so. Why?"

"It might be useful to know what model he rode."

I could almost hear the wheels turning as Andrea tried to figure out why I'd want the information. Since I was operating on a hunch, and not entirely sure of my own reasoning, I was relieved when she uncharacteristically restrained her curiosity.

"I can check it when I get home, if you like," was all she said.

She must really be worried about how I was going to find Jake's killer, to be so diplomatic. I tried to keep that realization out of my voice.

"That'd be great. Leave a message on my cell when you have it. I'll get back to you."

"Will do. And Barbara, if I didn't say it last night, thanks."

"Don't mention it. Talk to you later." And I disconnected before she could thank me again.

As I replaced the receiver, the phone rang.

"O'Grady Investigations."

"What are you doing working on a Saturday? And have you talked to Mom yet?"

"I've been a little busy, Susanna."

"I know, I know. But I'm worried, Barbara."

"Has something happened?"

"No, it's still just a feeling. But I just talked to her, and she isn't herself."

Well, that was helpful. "What did you talk about?"

"Dinner tomorrow. The kids. The usual stuff. Are you going to be at dinner tomorrow?"

"Don't think I can make it. So how do you know something is wrong?"

"If I knew that, I wouldn't be calling you. Just call her, will you?"

"I said I would."

"And call me back."

"Look Susanna, I'll get to it as soon as I can. But Andrea's been charged with homicide, and I'm working on the case."

"You are? I didn't know that. But I really am worried about Mom."

I could hear it in her voice. "I'll call."

"Thanks, Barbara."

I'd just disconnected when the phone rang again. I glared at it. Why hadn't I signed up for call display yesterday? Or better yet, last month?

Shaking my head, I turned back to the notes I'd made during my call with Andrea, and one word leapt out at me.

Motorcycles. Was that the common thread? Jake had a passion for motorcycles. His killer had probably left the scene on a motorbike he'd stashed in the alley.

What about Jake's client list? Had any of them owned bikes? Did his any of his friends own bikes?

I suddenly remembered the gas receipt I'd spotted the night of the murder, and opened the scanned copy. I'd assumed that Jake had dropped it, as it was near his bike. But what if it had been dropped by the murderer?

Enlarged five times, the receipt still didn't tell me much other than where and when the gas had been pumped, but that was a start. It might be worth a visit, especially if I could track down the attendant who'd been on duty that night. And gas stations are always open, even on weekends.

———

TWENTY MINUTES later I was driving slowly through Stanley Park, trying not to rear end any of the end-of-season tourists who kept slowing down to gawk at the views. When I got to the bridge, luck was with me—the signals had changed and two lanes of the three lane bridge were open for north-bound traffic.

It's always a challenge driving the Lion's Gate when the traffic flow is being switched from two lanes southbound to two lanes northbound, or vice versa. The traffic patterns are all controlled by overhead lights, and there always seems to be some yahoo who stays in the middle lane long after the amber warning lights go on.

Why there aren't more accidents, I'll never know. Every few years City Hall tries to figure out a way to rectify the situation, everything from twinning the bridge to adding a second layer of bridge underneath the first, but no-one's yet come up with a solution everyone can agree on. And since the bridge is now a National Heritage Site, I doubt that will change much.

Probably just as well, though—the bridge is a Vancouver landmark. I'd hate to see them ruin it.

On the far side of the bridge, I followed the long curve beneath the bridge and continued west. Judging by the address, the gas station I was looking for was located just past Dundarave, West Van's trendy boutique and restaurant stroll. It was easy to find.

Which was where my luck ended.

It was a typical gas station, maybe neater than most. I'd been hoping for a connection—maybe a specialization in motorcycle repair. No such luck. The attendant, whose embroidered name tag identified him as Bill, was an older man with faded brown eyes. He watched me as if he expected me to steal something.

"Hi. My name is Barbara O'Grady and I'm a private investigator."

"Yeah?"

"I'd like to ask you a few questions."

He peered up at me. "Why should I tell you anything? Hah?"

"Because it will only take a moment of your time. All I need to know is the name of the attendant on duty on last Thursday night."

"What's it to ya?"

"My client needs to prove she was on her way to Whistler that night, and not in Toronto. It's important."

"Mmmph. Well, I guess young Tad was on that night," Bill said, his head held at an awkward angle.

"Thanks. Can you tell me Tad's last name?"

"Nope. Can't do that."

"How about where I can reach him?"

"Nope, can't do that neither."

"When is Tad scheduled to work next?"

"Not sure I should be telling you."

"Look, my client is desperate. Her husband wants a divorce, and he's trying to blackmail her." I had no idea where that one came from.

Bill thought for a moment. "Guess it won't hurt. Tad'll be working tomorrow night."

"When does he start?"

"Six."

"Thanks for your help," I said, groaning at the delay. Maybe Tad would remember one customer out of many. Maybe.

As I sat in traffic inching its way back across the bridge, I turned the question of Jake and motorcycles around in my mind. What exactly was I following here? I had nothing concrete, but a little surge of energy told me I was onto something important. I stuck the bluetooth gizmo in my ear, dialed Andrea's number.

"Hi, it's me," I said when she answered. "What was the name of the guy you talked to at the Harley dealership?"

"Just a sec while I find it. It's been an absolute zoo here this morning."

I could hear the tension in her voice. There was a clunk, and the sound of paper shuffling, then Andrea's voice again.

"Got it. His name's Dave, Dave Jennings. Why?"

"And does Mr. Jennings work on a Saturday?"

"I think so. You going to talk to him?"

"Yup. I have a few questions that he might be able to answer."

"I'll meet you there."

"I thought you were swamped."

"I am. But this is more important."

True. "Okay. It's the one on Boundary just off First?"

"Yes. It's on the west side of Boundary."

"Got it. I should be there in," I checked my watch, eyed the traffic, "about three-quarters of an hour."

"See you there." I could just hear a female voice, calling Andrea's name. "Gotta run."

———

ANDREA WAS STANDING by the double glass doors at the Harley dealership, watching for me. Dave Jennings was with a customer, so we looked around the showroom. It was a large room, well laid out, with long rows of shiny new motorbikes running from one side to the other.

"These ones," she said, pointing to a row of mid-sized monsters. "It sounded something like these ones."

"How did you check?"

"Oh, Dave started some of them for me," she said with a grin. "When I explained why I needed to know, he couldn't have been more helpful."

I'll just bet he was. I grinned at the image of Andrea surrounded by roaring motorbikes.

We hadn't been there very long when Dave came over to us, hand extended. He was about my height, dark-haired, with a weight lifter's muscles and a broad smile.

"Dave Jennings," he said as we shook. "And you must be Andrea's friend Barbara. The investigator?"

"That's me."

"How can I help you?"

"Andrea says you helped her identify the sound she heard as a Harley bike, probably one of these larger ones?"

"Yeah. Harley's all have a distinctive sound. Here, let me show you."

He led the way to the front parking lot. "This is the newest model. Listen."

He started the bike with a roar, then throttled back to a steady ta-tock-a, ta-tock-a sound. I could see why Andrea had recognize it.

"And the smaller bikes."

"Ah. Listen to this one."

Another roar, another ta-tock-a, ta-tock-a. Same, but different.

Okay, then. "What model's the first one?"

"It's called the Street Glide."

"That's the bike Jake had," Andrea said.

Interesting. I turned back to Dave. "How many of this model would you sell in a year?"

"A lot," he said with a grin. "The tourers are all pretty good sellers. The bigger the better, and money no object." And he laughed a little at his own humor.

"The guy who was murdered. Andrea told you about him?" At his nod, I continued, "He had a fairly new Harley that was his pride and joy. Any chance he bought it here?"

"I can check. I can't give out information on our customers, but if the guy's dead… What was his name?"

"Jake Scott."

"Jake is dead? Murdered?" The lines on his forehead stood out sharply.

"You didn't know?" I looked at Andrea, who shook her head. Dave's sudden pallor suggested he'd known Jake personally. "He was a customer of yours?"

He nodded wordlessly. All three of us were silent for a few moments.

"It's a shocker," he finally said. "I sold him his last bike. Just like that one," and with a jerk of his chin he indicated one of the bikes we'd been discussing, "only black."

Now, I don't know much more about motorcycles than Andrea does, but in my business you develop a fairly keen eye for detail. And even in the dim light of early morning, the bike I'd seen parked behind Jake's suite the night of his murder had looked a little different. Maybe it was a trick of the light.

"You're sure it was that model you sold him?"

"Yup. He'd come by every week or so, show it off. Oh, he'd get some minor adjustments made, but nothing he couldn't have done himself. Of course, he did try to sell me some insurance too, but it was really the bikes he was interested in." Dave grinned. "He was pretty good with bikes."

"What does a bike like that go for?" I asked him.

"This one? Base model is around twenty-three. Fully loaded, twenty-six, twenty-seven."

Thousand? "And did Jake get the base model?"

"Jake? Not hardly. He put everything he could on that baby. She was a beaut."

Add taxes and that easily took care of Jake's thirty thousand dollar windfall." When did you see Jake last?"

"A couple of days ago."

"Wednesday?"

"Must have been. Wednesday or Thursday."

"What time?"

He looked startled. "Five-ish, I guess."

"Jake was killed late Wednesday night. You may have been one of the last people to see him alive."

At this news Dave looked sick again.

"How did Jake seem to you? Any different than usual?"

Dave seemed to be having difficulty finding his voice. "I need a smoke. D'you mind?"

Without waiting for an answer, he led the way outside and lit up, inhaling deeply.

"Last time I saw Jake, he seemed okay," he said through a cloud of smoke, then inhaled again. "Joking around, the way he did. He had a temper, y'know" looking at us to see if we did know. "But that day he seemed relaxed. Got a little annoyed when a part wasn't in yet, but it didn't last. I can't believe he died that day."

"Did he say where he was going when he left here?"

"I don't remember. I think he was headed home."

"Hmmm." I made a few notes and took one of Dave's cards, giving him one of mine in return.

"If you think of anything else, anything that might be relevant, even if it seems a long shot, please give me a call. Anything you can do to help Andrea will be appreciated."

Dave gave Andrea a soulful smile, and took the card.

As we walked out, I glanced over at the bikes we'd been looking at, then back at my friend. "Andrea, are you free for the next hour or so?"

"I can be. Why?"

"Meet me back at your place in about twenty minutes and I'll tell you then. I have a hunch I want to check out."

She raised an eyebrow at me. "This better be good."

She had no idea.

———

HALF AN HOUR LATER, we were standing in Andrea's shady backyard looking at Jake's gleaming monster of a motorcycle. Sure enough, it was the same model as the bike we'd seen at the dealership, except for the color. I walked around it, looking at it from different angles.

Andrea watched me with her head cocked to one side.

I circled the bike again, slowly. My hunch had been right. I pulled out the eight by ten glossies I'd just had printed off and handed them to Andrea. "Notice anything?"

She looked from the photo I'd taken the night of the murder to the bike in front of her and back. Both had the same shape, the same gleaming chrome, both were black.

To my eye they weren't quite the same shade of black, though it was hard to be sure in the night photo. And small details were different.

"It's really hard to see this one clearly, Barbara," she said, waving the photo taken the night of the murder. "But something's not quite the same as this bike. I can't put my finger on the differences, though."

"Look at the detailing."

"You're right. This one," and she waved the day-after photo at me, "is Jake's bike. The other one... isn't. Not quite."

"I think so too."

"But how could that be?"

"I've been thinking about that. Come with me."

I stuffed the photos back and headed inside. A minute later, we were standing at the top of her bedroom stairway, looking down into the kitchen. "How far down were you when you saw something moving in the yard?"

"Umm—about here," she said moving down two-thirds of the staircase.

That was about what I'd expected, giving the slant of the stair-well. Until you got pretty close to the bottom, you couldn't even see the window, much less see out of it.

"Why don't you go back up, and we'll try recreating that night. When you hear a bang, get up the way you did that night. Just remember you were asleep, so allow a bit of time for the sound to register. And don't forget to get your robe from wherever it was that night and put it on. I'll be out in the yard. I want to know exactly where I am when you first see me. Okay?"

Andrea just nodded. I went down to Jake's suite, and into the kitchen. When I figured Andrea had time to get into position, I banged two pots together to simulate a gun shot, then paused for a moment as if looking at the body. Then I raced for the back door, banged it behind me and headed for Jake's motorbike.

Kicking up the stand, I wheeled the heavy bike through the backyard towards the alley at a pace as close to full speed as I could manage.

The killer could have wheeled the bike out of the yard using the same route I'd used to get in that night, probably without leaving any tracks or broken bushes. But could he have done so fast enough to have been where Andrea said she saw movement?

I got the bike to the alley with no problem, and only slightly out of breath. I stopped there and waited for Andrea to cross the yard to where I stood.

"I did exactly as you asked," she said. "I even tried to allow for the fact I'm slow when I'm just waking up. But I don't get it. Why did you wheel the bike into the alley? And how did you get the bike across the yard so fast?"

"Did you hear the gunshot?"

She nodded.

"And the door bang?"

Again a nod.

"Where were you when you heard the door bang?"

Her expression amused me. Andrea's no dummy, and she likes puzzles, but she hadn't put this one together yet. And it was driving her nuts.

"Just starting down the stairs," she said. "Why?"

"Bear with me. I'll explain it all in a minute. Or at least I think I will."

Andrea smiled at that, but assumed her patient expression. Knowing her, that meant I didn't have long until she started asking questions again.

"Where was I when you first saw me?"

"Near the back of the yard, about to go into the bushes. It's so dark there I could barely make out the bike."

"And where were you standing when you saw me?"

"At the foot of the stairs. Oh." I could see her putting the pieces together. "You mean, because of the angle of the stairs, I couldn't see most of the yard until I got further down. So I wouldn't have seen the killer until I got to the foot of the stairs. And then it was too dark to see much."

"Congratulations, Sherlock."

Her face went white. "I nearly ran into the killer. You said I had, but I didn't really believe you. But you were right. I did. I nearly…"

She stopped, took a deep breath. Then another.

"I'm… I'm okay now. But I still don't get it. What did the bike have to do with it?"

Andrea may look fragile, but she's tough where it counts.

"I'm guessing that the killer took Jake's bike that night, and left their own bike here. That's why I needed to re-enact it, to make sure it was possible. Jake may have been killed for something that was on that bike. Or in it. It's very possible that bike holds the key. I just wish I knew to what."

"You'll figure it out," Andrea said. "You always do."

CHAPTER FIFTEEN

When I got to Rick's Place, there was no sign of Jerry. The restaurant was still mostly empty, so I got a table in the back corner and glanced around. Battered wood chairs and tables, red and white checked tablecloths, candles in amber pebbled glass holders. I inhaled the combined aroma of rich tomato sauce, basil and garlic bread.

When Jerry had phoned and asked me to meet him for dinner, he'd sounded deeply worried. I immediately suggested Rick's. Located in the old Italian section of town, Rick's serve the world's best pasta, and probably the largest portions.

Unlike the newer places, which tend to specialize in unusual combinations of ingredients from different cuisines—sometimes I picture the chef standing in front of an open refrigerator, wondering what to combine this time—Rick's has about four basic pasta sauces, all delicious. Comfort dining at its finest. I love this place.

I ordered a carafe of the house red. There are advantages to having been friends for years. I know Jerry's as fond of red wine with pasta as I am, and that, like me, he likes the rough red that serves as Rick's house wine. While I waited, I reviewed my notes on Andrea's case.

It was nearly an hour later when I looked up to see the place nearly full, and still no Jerry. It wasn't like him to be this late, especially when he'd wanted to see me so urgently.

I tried his office, then his home, getting voice mail in both places. I'd give him another half hour, in case he'd been delayed somewhere. I ordered some antipasto to go with the wine—I was hungry.

Jerry arrived half an hour later, out of breath and apologetic. "Sorry, Barbara. I got called in on another case."

"Oh?"

He shook his head. "I can't tell you about it. Except that I had no choice but to deal with it immediately."

I nodded. It was a given in our business. When a case is breaking, you're working. End of story. It doesn't matter what you'd planned, or who you'd made promises to. The job had to come first.

Sometimes I think it's a shame that Jerry and I never became a couple—we understand each other's pressures and temperaments so well. Maybe too well. That kind of familiarity tends to kill romance.

Which is just as well if he and Andrea are a couple. Though given Andrea's behavior lately, I was starting to have my doubts about that one.

"We should order, before they get any busier."

He nodded, and I caught the server's eye. Once we'd ordered, I looked across at him. "So, what's up?"

"Andrea."

Uh oh. I really didn't want to get in the middle of whatever situation he was about to tell me about. "And?"

"I'm worried about her."

"Go on."

"Look, if she killed the guy, she killed the guy. There's no point you trying to come up with some mythical killer so she can plead not guilty. She'll just end up making herself look worse. All she needs to do is plead self-defense, and come up with some explanation for what she was doing in that guy's apartment at one in the morning."

What was this? I looked at Jerry a little more closely.

His expression would have fooled most people, but not me. I considered the face I've known so long, with its square shape, given character by level brows just a shade darker than the hair.

There were faint lines bracketing his mouth and between his brows, and one eyebrow seemed to have gotten stuck in a half-raised position. For Jerry, this was distraught.

"What happened? Last time we talked, I said I thought she was innocent, and you seemed willing to consider the possibility. Now you're convinced she's guilty. Who have you been talking to?"

He looked taken aback. Jerry's always had a tendency to be bull-headed about things, and once he's made up his mind, he tends to forget that other opinions exist. I was suddenly glad he'd removed himself from the case.

"Talking to? What makes you say that, O'Grady?"

So I was right. "Never mind that, just tell me who's been convincing you that Andrea is guilty."

"Well, you must admit the evidence is pretty overwhelming."

"I'm not convinced. Why don't you go through it for me," I said, drawing out my notebook. He's always been good at thirty-second summaries. Maybe hearing his version would help clarify his thinking. And mine too.

"Okay. First," he said, bending down the forefinger on his right hand. "Andrea was found holding the murder weapon, and standing over the victim. Second, her fingerprints, and only her fingerprints, were everywhere. Third, she had the master keys to the suite with her. Fourth, her pen was under the body. Fifth, she was afraid of him, and had tried to get the police to intervene. Sixth, he'd sworn out a complaint that she was harassing him. Seventh she'd hired you to deal with the situation. Eighth," and here the change in Jerry's voice would have alerted me even if his words hadn't, "she'd been spending time with him socially, despite five, six and seven. Ninth..."

"Wait a minute. Spending time with him socially? What do you mean?"

He gulped down some wine. "The Friday before Jake's murder, Andrea and Jake had drinks together at Fiasco's. And they were there the previous Wednesday, as well."

"Andrea and Jake?" I could hear the pitch of my voice rising, and stopped for a moment. "Who on earth told you that?"

"George."

That stopped me for a moment. Of all Jerry's friends, George is my least favorite, but it's not because he's a liar. Quite the opposite. George is one of the most boring, least imaginative people it's ever been my misfortune to meet.

If George says they were at Fiasco's, the local restaurant and bar a block and a half from Andrea's place, then they were at Fiasco's. I'd trust George for data, but I wouldn't trust his interpretation of that data.

"OK, if George saw them, he saw them. But how does that prove her guilty?"

"George says they had their heads together all evening, that they looked quite cosy. And she refused to see me that Friday night. Said she had other plans, in that mysterious voice she uses when she's up to something."

So there we had it. Jerry was jealous. I knew exactly what tone he meant, and with Andrea it often meant that she'd met someone new. But not always.

I'd learned the hard way that it sometimes meant that she was about to do something that scared her.

She'd been holding out on me. In her circumstances, she had no business keeping anything back. And especially not this.

I watched Jerry down his wine. The fact Andrea hadn't told him she was meeting Jake was a bad sign—not for her innocence, but for their budding relationship. She'd shut him out, and generally in Andrea's relationships, that's the beginning of the end.

Now was not the time to break that news to Jerry, though. I'd nursed him through a few broken romances in my time, but this one was with my best friend.

Who just happened to be under suspicion of murder.

Or maybe just manslaughter.

"I don't know what Andrea was up to. I do know that she was afraid of Jake, but I also believe her when she says she didn't kill him. Come on, Jerry, you know Andrea better than that."

I could see from his expression that he wasn't convinced, and nothing I said would change his opinion. "I'll talk to Andrea."

"You'll let me know?"

"Sure." I'd tell him as much as I could, depending what I found out. "And can you find out something for me?"

He looked warier than he had any right to. "What?"

"One of my cases involves a guy who says he's an insurance investigator, but he isn't acting like one. Can you check if he's legit or not?" I had other ways of getting the information, but Jerry could do it quicker and delve deeper.

"Yeah, I'll have a look. What's the guy's name?"

"Markham. Nicholas Markham."

He nodded, made a note.

Our food showed up then, so we concentrated on eating. It was a pretty silent meal. Neither of us wanted coffee. We finished our pasta and left. Jerry picked up the check, despite my arguments.

I didn't feel I'd helped much, but the words he really wanted to hear, the reassurance that Andrea wasn't avoiding a relationship with him, I couldn't say with any truth.

———

IT WAS STILL EARLY, so I went back to my office with the intention of putting all the facts I'd been collecting in some kind of order. As I inserted the key in the door, the phone began to ring.

I did my usual mad dash and caught it just before it went to voice mail. I have no idea why I do this to myself—that's why I have voice mail. Sometimes I feel like a trained seal, automatically responding to a familiar sound.

"Hello?"

"Hi, Barbara," said Nick. "You're working late."

"Yeah, well. That's the joy of self-employment."

He laughed. "True enough. I've got an update for you on Gordon Knight. Seems he works for Rawlins Construction."

"Pretty big firm. And judging by Mr. Knight's attire, I'm guessing he doesn't work on-site?"

"Nope. Exec. Assistant to Rawlins himself."

I scrawled the name down. "Wonder what was in that envelope. And why all the secrecy? Think it's to do with Forrester?"

"The kid seemed to think so."

Yes, he had. I ran through the description he'd given of the guy who'd given the envelope to Walters and added it to the note I'd just made. "So now what?"

"I'm going to do some more digging. If I come up with a connection, I'll let you know. In the meantime, it's late. And it's Saturday night. Care to join me for a drink? We can toast to the freedom of self-employment."

This was a bad idea. I'd just asked Jerry to check him out.

But after my depressing dinner with Jerry, I could use a drink. And I liked Nick's dry sense of humor. A lot. Maybe I could pump him for information, find out what his involvement with Crestlife really was.

Who was I kidding? I was attracted to him, I still hadn't heard from Alessandro and an element of risk can add spice. "I'll meet you at Fiasco's? They make a great martini."

By the time I got to the restaurant, Nick had snagged a table near the back. I glanced around. Very different from Rick's Place—Fiasco's had a more urban vibe. The tables were set just far enough apart to allow conversation, the overall buzz was loud enough that conversations stayed confidential and the lighting wasn't too intimate. Perfect.

"Good to see you, Barbara," he said, standing as I reached the table.

"You too, Nick."

He didn't sit down till after I did. That kind of courtesy is rare these days. The more I see of Nick, the more intrigued I am. Maybe that martini wasn't such a good idea after all. I ordered one anyway. Nick ordered a beer.

"I'm glad you could join me, Barbara. I'd like to know you better," Nick said once the waiter had left, and smiled at me.

This guy was either one of the best things to have come my way, or he was up to something. And my usually reliable instincts were refusing to tell me which. I smiled back, hoping it didn't look as strained as it felt.

Our drinks arrived. Nick lifted his glass and as I raised mine to clink against it. I hoped he wasn't going to be the type that invented pseudo-significant toasts for every occasion. He wasn't.

"*Salud,*" he said, and took a long swallow of his beer. "Heard from Chris today?"

I sipped my martini, which was excellent. "Nope. Hopefully that means he's keeping out of trouble."

"He's a real pistol."

"He is that." And he'd just handed me the perfect lead-in. "I'm curious—did you recognize him when you saw him hanging around my office? I mean earlier, when he first showed up?"

"Not then. I only saw him from the back, and he wore a baseball cap pulled down. Yesterday was the first time I'd seen him without it."

Okay, that made sense. "Guess he figured he'd be too noticeable when he was after Walters. He'd make a good detective someday."

"Yeah, I had the same thought. You making any progress on that case?"

"Some. It's a challenge fitting it in around other cases right now."

He nodded, drank some beer. "Want some nachos or anything?"

"No thanks."

"So how is Andrea doing?"

The question surprised me so much I nearly swallowed a mouthful of martini the wrong way. "How do you know Andrea?"

"When I need a receptionist for appearances sake, I hire a temp. Andrea's agency is the most reliable one I've found."

"Yes, it's why she's so successful," I said automatically. It was such a reasonable explanation, it should have quelled my doubts. It didn't.

"I've seen the two of you leaving our office building together a few times," he added. "I assumed you were friends."

"Oh. Yes, we are. She's fine." He'd caught me off balance. All my suspicions of the man blazed back, simply because he knew one of my friends. Logically it made no sense, but my emotions didn't care.

"How's she coping with her tenant's death?"

How did he know about Jake's death?

Nick took my silence for the question it was. "Andrea told me. I was in her office a couple days ago, and she was a little upset. Anyhow she told me." He paused. "Is that why you're looking so strained?"

"Thanks a lot," I said with a grin. It was a reflexive response.

I really needed to talk to Andrea. It wasn't like her to talk about her business, and especially not now. First she doesn't tell me about meeting with Jake, now this.

She'd never so much as mentioned Nick, yet she was comfortable enough with him to share this? What was going on? And why did Nick suddenly seem to be turning up everywhere I looked?

Something was wrong somewhere, but whatever it was would come to me in its own good time. It always did.

Meanwhile, it was Saturday night and I was off duty. I'd begun to suspect I'd heard the last of Alessandro. And here I was, out with a man I found very attractive, who seemed to be interested in me. Why not enjoy myself?

I put my doubts and questions on a back burner, and gave Nick the first genuine smile I'd given him all evening. He blinked, then smiled back.

"So how did you end up as a P. I.?"

"Would you believe I started out as an artist?"

"Whoa. That's quite a detour. What happened?"

I gave him the short version. "There's no money in art, unless you're very good. And it turns out I'm not that good."

"No? I'm surprised."

"Why, thank you. But economic reality suggested I either spend my life supporting my art by temping, or find a real job."

"So why investigating?"

"I was temping at a security firm, and I found the work interesting. Guy named Sid Fluxgold said I had potential and offered to mentor me if I passed my exams."

"How long ago was that?"

"Nearly five years now."

"Fluxgold retired last year, didn't he?"

How did he know that? "Yes, that's right."

"Is that when you set up your own firm?"

He was quick. "No, I'd gone into business the previous year. It seemed like it was time to be my own boss. I misjudged the economy, though. And I just didn't count on the frequency of the bills."

"I can relate."

"So what's your story?"

He raised an eyebrow. "What makes you think there's a story?"

"There's always a story."

"True enough. Not too different from yours, actually. I kind of floated from career to career until I fell into insurance, and it seemed to fit. So here I am."

I grinned at him. "Why do I have the feeling you've left a few things out?"

He laughed. "No man likes to recount his failures."

"Aw, come on."

"Well, there's the time I decided that the world needed a new ski racing champion."

"Downhill?"

"Is there anything else?"

"What happened?"

"Knee gave out."

"Ouch. How far did you get?"

"Tryouts for the Olympic team."

"You were good."

He shrugged. "Didn't do me much good, though."

"Hey, at least you got that far. You can't hold yourself responsible for your knee. So what came next?"

"I tried to sell used cars."

Used cars? I couldn't picture it. "And?"

"I stunk."

"Oh. Still, is it really something you'd want to make a success of?"

"Well, when you put it like that…"

"See, it wasn't a failure. Just a self-defense mechanism."

He chuckled. "I like the way you think, Barbara. Where were you back then, when I needed to hear those words?"

"Probably getting turned down for gallery shows. Getting torn to pieces by the few critics who deigned to notice my work. You know."

"Yeah. And you probably didn't hear the words you needed then, either."

I grinned. "I heard all kinds of words. Just not the right ones. And I can't believe I just told you that."

"I'm glad you did." He lifted his glass. "Here's to us, Barbara. We didn't let them stop us."

I raised my glass, touched his. "They were fools to try."

"They were indeed. Another martini?"

"Sure."

We ended up closing Fiasco's, talking and laughing until they literally threw us out. I liked this man. I might have gone further than kissing him good night, except that I still couldn't trust him.

And there was still a question mark about Alessandro. Were we done? Did I want us to be?

So after my toes uncurled, I said good night, and walked home. Alone.

CHAPTER SIXTEEN

Sunday morning I started the day with a pounding headache. I'd tossed and turned all night, and the little sleep I did steal was fractured by dreams of painting endless canvases in grays, blacks and chrome yellow. No wonder I had a headache.

It took two Extra Strength Excedrin and three cups of coffee to even come up with a coherent list of the questions I needed to answer. And my thoughts kept switching to the night before and to Nick.

Which reminded me. I picked up the phone and called Alessandro. It would be nearly six in Venice. No answer, not even voice mail. Figures.

I was just finishing my fourth cup when Cat parked himself in the middle of the table.

"I wondered where you'd got to."

He blinked at me.

"Who do you belong to, anyway?"

Cat yawned, showing sharp incisors and pink gums speckled with black.

"Don't give me that. Someone must be feeding you your kitty kibble. You can't survive on the milk and tuna you cadge from me."

He blinked at me.

"Why am I asking you? Now I know I'm losing it."

Cat purred.

"Oh, now you're agreeing with me? I'd like to see you solve this case. Who do you think killed Jake?"

Cat began to wash his face.

"That's what I thought. Okay, if you won't help, I'm going for a run. Maybe that'll clear my thoughts. Something has to," I added under my breath.

I changed into running gear and headed out along shaded residential streets. On a sunny Sunday, the Seawall is just too crowded to be enjoyable—it becomes the place to see and be seen.

An hour later I was in the office, feeling revived. I checked voice mail, but there'd been no calls. Picking up the phone, I called Andrea. It went to voice mail. That was odd.

Andrea isn't exactly a morning person, especially on a weekend. And I was pretty sure she hadn't been over at Jerry's.

I left a message saying I needed to talk to her and to call me. I also invited her to dinner at my place at six if she could make it. We needed to talk.

I called Nick at the number he'd given me last night. Voicemail again. I left a message for him, too, but without the dinner invite.

I tried Alessandro again. Still nothing.

I glared at the phone, then called my mother. She answered on the first ring. I've never figured out how she does that.

"Hello?"

"Hi. It's Barbara."

"Barbara? Is something wrong?"

"No, nothing's wrong, Mom. Andrea and I won't be able to make it for dinner tonight, though."

"I understand. I heard about Andrea."

"Yeah. It's keeping me pretty busy. But how are you?"

"Oh, I'm fine. Just fine."

Not a normal Mom-type response. "So what's new? How's the Hundred Mile diet going?"

"Nothing much is new. And I gave up on the diet—it was just too much trouble."

I began to see what Susanna meant. This didn't sound like my normally caught-up-in-the-latest-project mother. "Since I can't make dinner, would you like to go out for tea and a chat next week instead? There's a new teashop on Broadway that specializes in different tea blends."

There was a short silence. "Tea?"

My mother hates coffee, but she knows I don't drink tea. "I thought you might enjoy this place. It's supposed to be good. And they have coffee, too."

"Oh. Barbara, is everything all right?"

"Everything's fine, Mom. I just thought it might be nice to get together and catch up."

"You never do that."

She was right. The guilt I'd been trying to ignore since Susanna's first call suddenly hit me full force. "Well, I'm doing it now. Would you like to go out for tea next week?"

"Well, I don't know if I'll be able to. But thank-you for the thought."

Now I was getting worried too. "What about next Tuesday morning? I could pick you up."

"Are you sure there's nothing wrong?"

That's what I was supposed to be asking her. How long had it been, anyway, since I suggested to my mother that we do something together? I suspected I didn't want to know the answer. "Yes, I'm sure. I'll call you that morning to confirm a time, okay?"

"Well, I suppose so. If you're sure?"

"I'm sure. I'll talk to you then."

I disconnected, my emotions confused. Why had I done that? I didn't have the time, and my mother and I had little that was positive to say to each other. But somehow, it felt right. Shaking my head, I called Susanna.

"Hello?"

"Hi, it's Barbara."

There was a pause. "Are you at work?"

"Yeah, why?"

"Barbara, it's Sunday. You're not supposed to be working."

Susanna's Laws for Happy Living. "Uh huh. Just wanted you to know that I can't make dinner tonight, but I talked to Mom."

"You did? How did she seem?"

"She says she's fine."

"She always says that. How does she seem to you?"

"It's pretty hard to tell over the phone. I'm meeting her for tea on Tuesday—I'll let you know what I think."

"Tea? You and Mom are going for tea? Who suggested that?"

"I did."

"You did. Barbara, are you all right?"

"Very funny. That's what Mom said, too."

"You have to admit it's out of character for you."

No I didn't. "I'll let you know how it goes."

"I absolutely can't wait to hear."

"And stop laughing."

"You have to admit, the idea of you in a tea shop…"

"Funny, Susanna. Look, I'll talk to you later—I've got a case to solve." And disconnected to the sound of her laughter.

I spent some more time on my notes, but Andrea still hadn't called, so I called the Harley dealership. Dave Jennings wasn't working again until Monday. I tried Alessandro again. Still nothing.

I went back to my notes, feeling unsettled. There were no answers there, either. I was still feeling worried about Chris and guilty about not doing more for him, so I called Doug. No answer. Doesn't anyone work on Sunday any more?

I was getting hungry, anyway. So I called Sid.

It took about four rings, but he answered, somewhat blearily. I'd got him out of bed. He said he'd meet me as long as we went to his favorite greasy spoon for a very late breakfast.

I knew I'd have to watch him demolish a mountain of bacon, eggs, pan-fries and toast, which he considers the only possible reason for getting out of bed on a weekend, but I agreed anyway. I'd just call it brunch.

———

WATCHING Sid digging into his feast of fat and cholesterol, I felt very virtuous about my own poached eggs, despite the pan fries I'd also ordered. Sid sure looked contented, digging into his Lumberjack's Breakfast, which he'd covered with ketchup from a red plastic squirt bottle.

"You'll go to an early grave, eating like that," I told him, keeping a straight face with difficulty.

He ignored me, so I took mouthful of coffee—fresh, but lacking a little body—and took out my notepad. Sid gave me a sideways glance, but took another bite of a particularly crisp looking strip of bacon. Obviously his curiosity only emerges after breakfast, unless it retired when he did. Which I doubt.

I briefly filled him in on the Forrester case, and how I'd met the whisperer. "Turns out he's Forrester's kid."

Sid kept chewing, though he quirked an eyebrow at me.

"The thing that worries me, there's another guy involved, says he's an investigator, but I've never heard of him. Name's Nick Markham. Ring any bells?"

Sid shook his head. He sliced off some toast and bacon, swirled it in the egg yolk, and popped it in his mouth. I watched in fascination while a blissful look spread across his face.

"Would you prefer I not talk till you're finished?"

He motioned me to go ahead. Terrific, a mute audience. Some days that would be perfect. Not today.

"Okay, here's where I'm at. Forrester had life insurance, quite a bit of it, it seems. This guy, Markham, says he's working for the insurance company, but I haven't figured out how he ties in. The son would stand to benefit if Forrester's death were proven not to be suicide."

Sid spoke around a mouthful of bacon. "Let me guess, you're on contingency. Right?"

I ignored that. Sometimes I wonder if he reaches the conclusions he does through years of experience or ESP.

"I haven't had time to look much further into the case, though Chris, my client, has been following some guy named Walters, who's Forrester's old partner. Who met up with another guy named Knight, who works for a guy named Rawlins."

Sid looked up at that. "Kenneth Rawlins?"

"Yeah. You know him?"

Sid shrugged. "Pretty big cheese," he said, forking up another slice of bacon.

"Yeah, I guess. Trouble is, nothing seems to be leading anywhere. And my primary focus is Andrea's case, so I don't see that changing fast."

"So what are you planning on doing next?"

"Proving Andrea innocent."

"Besides that."

"Besides finding a killer the police are convinced doesn't exist? Well, I guess in my spare time I'll just, oh, I don't know, prove Forrester didn't commit suicide."

"Have some more coffee, Barbara. You're sounding a little stressed."

I glared at him. Mostly for show, though. Just talking the Forrester case made it clearer in my mind.

He grinned. "What did you expect at this hour? Seriously, though, despite the fact that your client is a kid, it sounds like you've got something worth looking into, and the pieces are starting to connect. How are you doing on Andrea's case?"

I shrugged. "I'm convinced she didn't kill Jake. And I think the killer switched motorcycles with Jake's bike on the night of the murder, then switched them back later. Beyond that, I've got a few leads, but so far nothing's coming together. Have you heard anything?"

"Wish I had. I'll keep my ears open, though, for what it's worth."

"You old fraud. You're still connected in this town and you know it."

"Yup," he said, then picked up his fork and went calmly back to his food. It seemed like a good idea, so I followed suit. For the rest of the meal, our conversation was desultory.

I spent a few more hours in the office, then headed for the market at Granville Island. Being surrounded by good food, wonderful food smells and bustling people always cheers me up. In addition to my weekly rations, I picked up fresh prawns, garlic, cilantro and pasta, in case Andrea could make it for dinner. The way my day had gone so far, though, I wasn't counting on it.

CHAPTER SEVENTEEN

Things were looking up. As I pulled into the driveway, I saw Andrea sitting on the front steps of the building. I waved her over, unlocked the car door for her.

She looked pretty cheery, given her situation. Maybe she had the same feeling I did, that we were one step closer to finding Jake's killer.

"Hi."

"Hi, back atcha." As I pulled into the underground and parked, I concentrated on avoiding the concrete pillars that some idiot had placed just a little too close together.

Andrea, having been through this before, kept silent. Once I'd parked, the questions started. "So what's so urgent?"

"A couple of things," I said. "Before I forget, are you free to go with me to the Harley dealership tomorrow morning? I think they open at nine."

She pulled out her smartphone, clicked a few keys. "Yes, I can meet do that."

"Great. I'll pick you up at eight-thirty. Which brings me to the little matter of the secrets you've been keeping."

"Secrets?"

"Secrets. You know, the little things you don't tell your best friend, who's supposed to be trying to clear your name?"

Andrea grimaced. "Any secrets in particular?"

As if she didn't know. "Try Friday night at Fiasco's. And the previous Wednesday. When you were there with Jake."

"Oh. That secret."

When I looked over at her, Andrea looked drawn and so tired that I felt guilty. I reached over and touched her hand.

"It can wait till we get upstairs. We'll talk about it over a glass of wine. C'mon, give me a hand with this food."

We rode the elevator to the fourth floor in silence. I gestured for Andrea to put her bags on the kitchen counter. Setting down my own load with a sigh of relief, I got out the Pinot Gris and poured us both a glass.

"Barbara, who is this?"

I turned to see what had caused that cautious note in Andrea's voice. She was pointing to the orange and white lump on the carpet. "Oh, that's Cat."

"Cat?"

"Haven't you met before?" Hadn't Cat been around any of the other times Andrea had been over?

"Barbara, you have a cat? And you never told me? Now who's talking about secrets?"

"No, I don't have a cat. You know I don't like cats."

"I thought you didn't like cats. But that is definitely a cat."

"He's not a cat, he's just Cat."

"Are you listening to yourself?"

"Anyway, he's not mine."

"Then what is he doing in the middle of your carpet?"

She was enjoying this way too much. "He gets in. Somehow."

She gave me a skeptical look. "And who does he belong to?"

"Good question."

"You call yourself a P. I., and you haven't been able to find out who a stray cat belongs to? And why is there a dish on the floor for him?"

Andrea has always been too observant. "Never mind."

I handed her a glass of wine. "Are you hungry?"

She shook her head.

"Then let's take our drinks out on the balcony."

Cat didn't follow us out, for a change. It was a beautiful, clear evening. The sun was just beginning to sink, and my view of sky, a few trees, lawns, other apartment buildings and the Shopper's a block over on Granville was bathed in that golden light that I'm still struggling to capture on canvas without looking clichéd. I keep saying I've given up painting, but I'd have a hard time explaining those half finished canvases in the spare room if anyone ever saw them.

I took a sip of wine, and tried to hold that feeling of peace. It slipped away, as always. I turned to face Andrea.

"So tell me about your meeting with Jake."

"There isn't much to tell."

"That why you never mentioned it?"

Andrea wouldn't meet my eyes. "No. I just felt so stupid, I was trying to forget it ever happened. Who told you?"

"Jerry."

Her brows drew together. "Not good."

"George saw you."

"Oh, lord."

"Yup, you might as well leave town now. You're branded for life as a scarlet woman."

"The truly sad thing is, that's probably exactly how George views things."

"True. Ever wonder how he got that way?"

"Deprived childhood is my guess."

I laughed. "You might be right. So, why did you meet Jake? And what do you feel stupid about?"

Andrea drained her wine, then very deliberately placed the glass in the exact center of the side table. "I decided to take charge of the situation. I wasn't going to let Jake scare me anymore. I thought maybe we could talk it out like two rational human beings."

"Rational? Jake?"

"I know, I know. I said I felt stupid. But I had to do something. And I thought maybe if we could talk on neutral ground…" her voice trailed off.

That explained Fiasco's.

"So how did he react?" I had a feeling I didn't want to hear this.

"You won't believe it." She looked at me, her face solemn. "He thought I was coming on to him."

I would not laugh. She was my friend, and she was hurting. I couldn't laugh at her.

"And he rejected me."

That did it. There was no way I could restrain the bubble of laughter that lodged behind my lungs and expanded outward.

Andrea grinned at me. "I thought that would lighten things up a little."

"You're pulling my leg," I managed to gasp. "He didn't."

She nodded. "Yup. And he didn't even try to break it to me gently."

I lost it again. When I'd finally calmed down enough to speak, I said, "So why didn't you tell me about it?"

"I really did feel stupid. I knew that once I'd brought you in, I should avoid doing anything that might make it worse. But I can usually charm my way out of most situations. I thought it was worth a try."

"You do realize it could have been extremely dangerous?"

She nodded. "And the worst of it is, I didn't accomplish a thing. I didn't even learn anything."

"Don't be so sure. Maybe you learned something that you didn't recognize at the time. Anything I can learn about Jake's contacts, his social life, might help. Who suggested Fiasco's?"

"I did."

No help there. "Did he meet anyone he knew?"

"No. He didn't even scan the room, the way you usually do when you go somewhere. Wait, though. Come to think of it, he didn't have to order his beer, the waiter already knew what he'd want."

"Did you catch the waiter's name?"

"Zeke. The one with dark hair. Young, but cute."

I knew the guy she meant. Andrea and I have spent our share of time at Fiasco's. I made a mental note to go and talk to Zeke later.

Draining my wine, I picked up Andrea's empty glass and stood up. "Your efforts just might pay off after all. Depends what Zeke can tell me. Now I'm going to start dinner, and you can come and talk to me while I create. I don't know about you, but I'm hungry."

"Me too." Andrea got up and followed me through to the kitchen.

We chatted idly as I cooked. I didn't want to lose my concentration, as I have a bad habit of slicing my fingers with the cleaver if I'm not paying attention. Andrea sipped her second glass of wine and filled me in on all the gossip she picks up from her temps. It's amazing how much she knows about what's going on in the city's businesses.

As soon as I'd served, Cat reappeared. "Rrrowwr?"

"I think he's hungry, Barbara," Andrea said with a snicker.

"Too bad. He's already eaten," I said to her. I'd taken enough ribbing for one day.

"Go away," I told him. "You wouldn't like prawns anyway."

Cat blinked.

"Especially not prawns with garlic."

Cat purred.

"Fine, then, see for yourself." I held out a morsel of prawns. And nearly lost a finger, it was devoured so fast. "Cats are not supposed to like garlic," I told him.

Cat purred, then looked at me.

"All right, prove me wrong." I gave him another prawn.

He practically inhaled it, then purred louder.

At her end of the table, Andrea was laughing so hard there were tears running down her face. "Barbara, that is the funniest thing I've ever seen."

"What? A cat eating prawns with garlic?"

"No, you being bossed around by a cat."

"He is not bossing me around."

"You should hear yourself."

"He's good company."

"Some cat hater you are."

"I never said I hated cats."

"No, just that you didn't like them much."

"Well, I'd never gotten to know one. And besides, he's not a typical cat."

"How would you know?"

Time for a change of subject. "What do you know about Nick Markham?" I asked.

"He's totally hot," she said. "But what is this? Don't tell me that you're interested in another man? First Alessandro, now Nick. This has to be a record for you. But then it's been four years, hasn't it, since Jayson did such a number on you?"

"Oh, shut up." I should know by now that the only way to deal with Andrea's teasing is to ignore it.

"Nick is working on a case that affects one of my clients, that's all. But he mentioned you, said you'd told him about Jake. I wondered how you met. And what you know about him."

Andrea gave me a knowing look. "When he needs a receptionist for a short period, he hires them from me. He became a client—oh, five or six months ago, I guess. He seems a decent guy, he pays his bills on time. He's easy to talk to."

She looked thoughtful. "I think he's in insurance. And I still think he's hot. I'm glad you haven't lost your judgment, after all this time. Your mother will be pleased."

I grinned. "Until I have a husband and kids like my perfect baby sister, nothing I do will please my mother."

"You could become a high-powered corporate executive."

I snorted. Andrea knows my mom pretty well. "Like that'd ever happen."

"But your Mom would approve of Nick."

I gave her a look. She laughed.

"Come on, Andrea. Be serious. How did Nick find out about your agency?"

"Yellow pages, I think he said."

"Any way he could have known Jake?"

She looked at me in silence for a moment. "You think Nick might be involved in Jake's death?"

"No. I just don't like it when someone I meet in one context turns up somewhere else."

"Come on, Barbara. Now you're sounding paranoid. Vancouver can be a pretty small city, that's all. Are you sure it's not just that you're attracted to him, and it's making you nervous? Not all men are like Jayson, you know."

She could have a point, but until I knew a little more about the man, I wasn't taking any chances.

I still didn't like the unexpected connections, even his concern for Chris. It could be genuine, or he could be using that situation for his own ends, whatever those might be.

"So why did you tell him about Jake's death?"

Andrea shrugged. "As I said, he's easy to talk to. The day he came in, I was pretty upset. I just found myself telling him."

She must have been extremely upset. "And what did he say?"

"I can't remember anything specific. I guess he mostly made appropriately soothing noises, because by the time he left I was feeling much better."

I gave her a skeptical look.

"You're sure you're not attracted to him yourself?" Soothing noises indeed.

Andrea grinned. "Nope. I think he's a nice guy, but that's it. He's all yours. So when are you seeing him next? And what happened to Alessandro, anyway?"

"I've no plans with Nick. And nothing has happened to Alessandro. He should be here next month." Or not.

"So you're still seeing him?"

"Why wouldn't I be?" It was the question I planned to ask the currently missing-in-action Alessandro, just as soon as I caught up with him. No way I was telling Andrea that. "But enough about me. What's the story with you and Jerry?"

She looked uncomfortable. "Story?"

"He tells me you're dating. But when I saw him the other day, he seemed uncertain about where he stood. What gives?"

She sighed. "Never date a friend. Especially when he's also friends with your best friend. Every time I break one of my rules, I end up regretting it."

I could relate to that.

"Look, I'm not sure how it started. We've always been good friends, you know that. Maybe there's always a question mark on that kind of friendship. You know, could it be more? Maybe that kind of chemistry is what makes a friendship interesting.

Anyway, I realized pretty quickly that when he gets into a relationship, Jerry gets possessive. And protective. He was driving me nuts, and I didn't want to lose the friendship. The problem is, I'm not sure Jerry feels the same."

I knew he didn't, but telling Andrea that wasn't likely to improve the situation. I just hoped Jerry would recover quickly, for all our sakes. Andrea had enough problems, without worrying about Jerry too.

I offered her another glass of wine, and we ended the evening watching Casablanca.

CHAPTER EIGHTEEN

The day was warming nicely as Andrea and I drove to the dealership. Andrea had brought travel mugs of coffee, and the rich scent hung on the air. Neither of us said much—we weren't awake enough for scintillating conversation.

When we arrived, Dave looked surprised to see us. He didn't look particularly pleased, either, which seemed odd given how helpful he'd been the last time. Maybe he thought we were wasting his time. Not that the place was very busy on a Monday morning.

He walked quickly over to where we were standing just inside the doors. "What's up?"

Andrea started to say something but I nudged her and she fell silent. Some instinct told me not to give him any more information.

I pulled out the eight by ten from the night of Jake's death and handed it to him. "Can you tell us which bike this is? Jake seemed interested in this one, so I hoped it might provide a clue."

"Not a great shot, is it?"

"It was the best one he had," Andrea said. She'd run with my lead, bless her.

"Well, it's another Street Glide, but this is a CVO, the custom model. You can just make out some of the details." He pointed to a couple of things I'd noted. "That's a lot of bike."

Andrea and I exchanged glances. "Do you sell a lot of them?"

"At these prices? Not hardly. There's maybe only a couple dozen of these babies in the Metro Vancouver."

"Did Jake ever talk to you about this bike?"

"Yeah. He talked about trading up all the time. Really interested in the new models, too."

I wondered where the money was coming from. "Any of your other customers own one of these? It'd help a lot to talk to someone who owns one."

"No, I haven't been lucky enough to sell one yet." His eyes flickered away, then back.

He was lying. Why? "Do you have one of these in the showroom?"

Seems he was okay with that request, because he didn't hesitate. "Sure, follow me."

The bike was a beauty, all black and chrome. One look at the thirty-six thousand dollar price tag and I could see why there were so few of them around. Which just added to the weirdness of that midnight switch.

"It can be customized from here," Dave said. "Puts the price up a bit, though."

We had what we'd come for and Dave wasn't likely to give us any more information. There was no point in hanging around. I thanked him, and we left.

———

I DROPPED Andrea at her office and headed for mine. Neither of us said much on the way. Once I was back in my office, I considered the leads I had on this aggravating case.

Jake's new bike was nagging at me. Where had those extra funds come from? Could it have been some kind of company bonus? I checked my watch.

Breyers Financial would be open now. A meeting with Jake's former boss was definitely called for.

An hour later I was sitting in the office of one Mr. William Brighton, discussing the operations of the Breyers Financial Agency.

"Call me Bill," he said, with a hearty handshake and a heartier smile, both of which I distrusted on sight.

"Thanks, Bill. As you know, I'm looking into the death of Jake Scott—"

"So you told me, Barbara, and may I say I'm very pleased to hear you are working on it. He's a great loss to us, a great loss."

"I'm sure he is. Bill, when I called to ask about Jake, it was recommended I speak with you. Can you tell me what your relationship with Jake was?"

"I was his primary contact. In fact, I recruited Jake into the organization, so he was in my direct line."

"In your direct line?"

"Yes, indeed. You see, Breyers has a unique, and may I say, very successful model in place. Each agent is responsible for recruiting and training other agents. Our individual success is based on how well those agents do."

"How does that work?"

"It works very well indeed."

"No, I mean, if you are spending time recruiting and training other agents, that's time you could be cultivating sales, isn't it? How can you afford to do that?"

"Very true, very true. That's the beauty of it, you see. Each agent is recompensed for this work through a "reward" based on the sales of the agents in their line."

"The agents they've recruited and trained?"

"Now you've got it! Yes! And the beauty of the system is, you see, that the better the agents in your line do, the better you do. So there is a built-in incentive to help others."

It sounded like a pyramid scheme to me. "If you train your recruits well, isn't there a danger they'll cut into your own sales?"

"Not at all. We're rewarded based on a fixed percentage of what our line makes. The better they do, the better we do. In fact, if an agent knows the business, if he's really good, he can retire from selling. The money will still flow in," Bill said with a big grin.

"From where?"

"It's a percentage from the sales of the agents he's already recruited. I'm telling you, this is a great business."

As long as those other agents kept bringing in the customers. So where did Jake fit into all of this? "Was Jake really good?"

Bill's smile faltered a little. "Well, Jake. He really only recruited a couple of agents. Decided that side of the business wasn't for him. Too bad, he could have made a killing. He made good money from his clients, though."

"How good?"

Bill didn't even blink at the question. Maybe he was used to would-be recruits asking similar things. "His combined income, from sales and commission, you know, was steady. Nothing like the money I'm bringing in, but hey, Jake seemed happy. And the opportunity was always open to him."

"So his income was steady? No big accounts occasionally? No bonuses?"

"Well, no. Not they way Jake worked. Forgive my blunt speaking, but Jake seemed to work just hard enough to keep his income steady. So hard, and no harder."

Personally, the whole thing made me nervous. "And you recruited Jake?"

"Yes."

"So you would have preferred him to have brought in more agents. His commissions would have been higher, and so would yours."

"Well, that's true, but hey, it all works out. Not all of us have to be stars, you know. Slow and steady paid his bills, and was a nice little addition for me."

Uh huh. I asked a few more questions, but the only thing that was clear was that Jake received his checks at the end of each month, and in predictable amounts. There would not have been a check mid-month.

Wherever the thirty thousand had come from, it hadn't been from Breyers Financial. I thanked Bill for his time.

———

BACK IN MY OWN OFFICE, which suddenly seemed a haven of sanity after talking to Bill Brighton, I was just adding to my notes on Jake when the phone rang. I grabbed it.

"I've tracked down the money behind the building deal," Doug said.

"And?"

"It ties back to one Kenneth Rawlins, who, among other things, owns Rawlins Construction. And Crestlife Insurance."

"Crestlife holds the policy on Forrester's company. And his life insurance." And Nick was working for them.

"Yup. And guess what else Rawlins has a majority interest in?"

Oh no. "Crendall and Barton?"

"Got it in one. I always said you were a smart one."

Cliff Walters worked for Crendall and Barton, aka Rawlins. Gordon Knight, the guy Walters had passed the envelope to, worked for Rawlins Construction. My mind went off on a tangent, suddenly seeing connections everywhere.

"Doug, by any chance does Rawlins have an interest in Breyers Insurance?"

"Hang on a sec," he said, and I could hear the clicking of a keyboard over the phone lines. There was a pause, then his voice came back. "Well, what d'you know. He has a controlling interest in it, through a couple of other firms. Why, is that significant?"

"It may not be, it's just that Jake Scott, the guy Andrea's accused of killing? He worked for Breyers."

I could hear the clicking of keys. "You find a connection?"

"Maybe. I can't say more now, but let's just say I find it interesting." Even more interesting was the role Nick played in all of this.

"Huh. What d'you have on Scott?"

I could hear that bulldog tone in his voice. When I'd worked with Doug before, I discovered that once he gets onto a story, nothing short of an earthquake is going to get him off it. The more convoluted a story gets, the better he likes it. And he's a hell of a researcher.

"He's looks pretty clean, except for an unexplained infusion of cash."

"What about the kid?" Doug asked. "You got anything more on him?"

"Haven't heard a peep from him since Friday."

"Huh. Let me look into the Breyers connection."

"Thanks, Doug. And I'll keep you…," I began, but he'd already disconnected.

I considered our conversation, and what I'd learned about Breyers. I couldn't seem to get a clear read on who Jake Scott had been. Or what Nick was up to.

I had the feeling that somewhere in the information I already knew there was a connection or a bit of information I was overlooking. I've learned to trust that feeling when it comes. Unfortunately, I've also learned that the only way to pin down that missing piece is to make lists of everything I can think of and hope the critical bit pops out.

It's a slow, exasperating process, but it works too often for me to give it up. And right about now I needed the focus.

I started with Jake and everything I'd learned about him. Where he lived, what he did, who his friends were. I looked at screen after screen, so many little bits and pieces of information. The remnants of a life.

A life someone had ended. Why? Somewhere in all of this detail was the connection, the reason someone had killed Jake.

I had the feeling that if I knew why, I'd know who. I went through the information again, slowly. Nothing.

Time to look at the client forms Jake had "filed" in his fish tank. Given the neat computer records he'd kept, that they had been left there was surprising in itself. Going through them, they seemed pretty straightforward. For the most part, Jake had convinced his clients to switch the form of life insurance they carried. As far as I could tell from the calculations he'd attached, that transaction had benefited both parties.

Looking through the forms, I could see no pattern in client type. All ages and occupations seemed to be represented, and they came from all over the Metro area.

I wondered idly how Jake had found his clients. I paged through the forms again, looking for any similarities, any discrepancies. Nothing. Going through the forms a third time still yielded nothing.

I got up and put on a pot of coffee. As I watched it drip through, breathing deeply of that incomparable aroma, it hit me. Jake was a salesman. His clients were probably all people he'd cultivated over time, built up a relationship with.

He'd have met with them at their convenience, on their schedule. If a client, or better yet a potential client, had wanted to discuss business at one-thirty in the morning, my guess was Jake would have accommodated him. Or her.

Insurance is a service industry after all, and dissatisfied clients don't come back. But the bills do, every month.

It's a reality I know only too well. Thinking about the inevitability of the monthly billing cycle, I suddenly recognized something I'd been overlooking.

To survive in the insurance industry, you had to make regular sales. To make regular sales, you had to be a 'people person'. A good insurance salesman has to convince virtual strangers to open up about their finances, and money is not a subject people are comfortable talking about. Especially when coupled with that other disquieting topic, death.

Somehow I'd been picturing Jake as an introvert, despite what Andrea's report had told me. Because he'd been violent, because she'd been so scared, I'd seen him as anti-social.

But to have made any kind of living in the insurance field, and particularly the kind of steady income Jake had made, the reverse had to be true.

My mental picture shifted, and I had an a-ha! moment. What if the outbursts of violence had been the aberration in Jake's life?

He'd built up a steady clientele, and, except for the fish tank, his business records had been in good order. The only problem in his life that I knew of—except for the fact that he was dead, of course—had been his outbursts with Andrea.

Yet if he was losing control in his private life, eventually it would begin to affect his business life. Or had that already begun?

There was no way to tell, not from the little information I had. It was clear I needed to dig deeper into Jake's life.

I'd start with Fiasco's. He may not have been a regular, but he'd been known there, maybe had friends there. It was worth a shot.

———

MY LUCK WAS IN. Except for a few patrons enjoying tapas and sun on the flower-bedecked patio, Fiasco's was deserted. And Zeke had just started a shift.

In the cool, dim interior I ordered a glass of Merlot and asked Zeke if he had time to answer a few questions. He knows me, or at least he's seen me there with Andrea often enough. He was more than happy to talk to me, especially when he discovered I wanted to talk about Jake.

People are funny about death. I usually run into one of two reactions when someone has died, and especially if it was a violent death. Either they look a little sick and refuse to discuss it, or they're eager to talk about the death and everything to do with it. Zeke was the latter type.

"Yeah, Jake used to come in now and again. He lived around here, you know. He'd come in and order a beer. Always drank beer, and usually domestic. He liked the micro-breweries—Granville Island or Okanagan Springs. Usually the Pale Ales. And he always ordered either pizza or the chicken wings. The extra hot ones."

I wondered if people who'd been in the restaurant business for a while started typing people by what they ordered. Probably. Maybe it even told you as much about someone as any other kind of personality test.

I wondered what they made of me. I like food too much to be predictable.

Zeke was still talking. "Jake would sometimes bring clients in. He sold mutual funds, you know. Always telling me that if I started putting money away now, I could retire a millionaire. He really believed it, too. Had some kind of book he always quoted, about how you could save a percentage of your income, put it in mutual funds, and end up rich."

He tapped a finger against the menus he was still holding. "Jake was a cool guy. Course, he had a temper on him. I only saw him lose it once, and I never wanted to see anything like that again. It was like he became somebody else. Like Dr. Jekyll and Mr. Hyde, you know?"

Bingo. This was what I'd come looking for—I just hadn't expected it to be this easy. I tried to keep my tone casual. "D'you remember what happened?"

"Naw, I was serving another table. Only thing I know is, he was having dinner with some guy I hadn't seen here before, and all of a sudden, Jake lets out this roar and stands up, and he looked like he was going to reach across the table and strangle this other guy. He was screaming at him, you know. I mean really yelling."

He shook his head. "He really lost it, man."

"So what happened then?"

"Well, we were going to throw him out, but nobody wanted to go near him. Then some lady talked him down. Weirdest thing I ever saw."

He gave me a direct look. "I looked at him twice the next time he came in, let me tell you. But he was fine, just like nothing had happened. Never saw him like that again. Weird."

"Did you recognize the woman who talked him down? Or the guy he was with? It could be important."

"You mean it had to do with his murder?" Zeke looked excited for a moment, like a small kid who's stepped into the limelight. Then his expression clouded. "Nah. I'd never seen the guy before. The lady—yeah, she comes in here a lot. I don't know who she is, but I could ask around, if it would help?"

"Thanks, it would help a lot." I handed him my card, then consulted my notebook. "You mentioned Jake used to bring clients here. Were any of them regulars?"

"No, mostly they'd only be there the once. The only guy I saw him with all the time was Earl."

"Earl?"

"You don't know Earl?"

I shook my head.

"He's here all the time. Great guy, and he's got a really cool bike. In fact, I'll bet that's why he and Jake got along so well. Jake used to talk about bikes all the time too."

"What's Earl's last name, do you know?"

Zeke thought a moment, then shook his head. "Sorry, Earl is all I know. I can ask around about that too?"

"That would be great. And it's pretty urgent, so please call me as soon as you find out something."

He said he'd do what he could, and left to wait on a couple who had just come in. I slowly drank my wine, and thought about what I'd learned.

Not nearly enough. But Jake had clearly had problems, and from what Andrea and now Zeke had said, he'd been starting to lose control. I wondered what other trouble his uncertain temper had got him into.

Had it gotten him murdered?

Had Jake grown violent the night he died, and been killed in self-defense?

Sometimes a solution can be so obvious, everyone overlooks it. The police were certainly convinced that Jake had grown violent and been killed in self-defense. I just didn't like their choice of killer.

What if I assumed the scenario was right, but they had the wrong player in Andrea?

There was only one problem with this theory. If it was self-defense, then why the exchange of motorcycles? Simple panic didn't fit. The risk that the substitute bike would be identified and traced to its owner would have been too great. Or would it?

I dropped a hefty tip on the table, leaving my wine half-finished. It was still warm and sunny out, but it was nearly five-thirty. I was in no mood to go back to my office.

And Tad, the gas station attendant I needed to talk to, was supposed to be starting work at six. It was worth fighting home-bound traffic over the Lion's Gate to cross that item off my list.

It was well after six by the time I reached my destination, and my frustration level was pretty high. Rush hour over the Lion's Gate is no picnic.

My luck was in, though. Tad was there. He turned out to be a tall, lanky teenager with bad skin and an even worse attitude. Given the expensive neighborhood, I'd expected a budding CEO-type. Wrong again.

"Hi, Tad. Mind if I take a moment of your time?"

"Guess not."

"I'm a P. I., Barbara O'Grady. I'm looking into the theft of a bike near here last Wednesday night. Were you working that night?"

"Dunno."

Okay, this was going well. "One of your co-workers said you were. I could verify it with your manager, though?"

"Nah."

"So you were working."

"Guess so."

"Do you recall if any of your clients that night were riding motorbikes?"

"Nope."

"No, you don't recall or no, there were no motorbikes that night."

"Don't recall."

I brought out the photo I'd shown Dave that morning. Tad's eyes lit with the first sign of animation he'd shown.

"Cool," he said.

"Do you recognize the bike?"

He looked closer. "Yeah, maybe."

"You've seen it before?"

"Maybe."

It was a start. I brought out the sales receipt again and waved it under his nose. "Any chance that bike was this customer?"

He looked at the receipt, scrutinized the photo again, then looked warily at me. "Maybe."

"So this bike gassed up here on the 11th?"

"Could'a."

For Tad, that was a positive response, but I needed more. I hate to let a teenager, especially one with an attitude like this, get the better of me. " What's it worth to you?"

Tad reached for the photo. He looked at it carefully, then at me. "Hundred."

What can I say, it's a consumer society. "Not likely. Twenty."

"Sixty."

"Forty, and that's as high as I'll go."

"Yeah, this bike was here. He came in late on the Friday, wanted a fill up. I like bikes, so I noticed."

"So who was riding it?"

He looked at me and shook his head. "For forty? Nah."

"Fifty, then."

"I didn't notice the guy. Just the bike."

I didn't believe him. "You must have noticed something."

"Just that he was an old guy, nearly thirty, I guess." I winced at that one.

"Dark hair? Light? Tall? Short?"

He shook his head. "Nope. Didn't notice."

"Did you notice anything else at all?"

"Nope."

I still didn't believe him, but for some reason he'd changed his mind about talking. And I didn't think it was about money. I couldn't tell if it was fear or just attitude, but he'd said all he was about to.

I shrugged and gave him his forty and my card. "If you remember something, give me a call. It's important."

He grunted, stuffed the card in a greasy pocket and went to deal with a car that had just pulled in.

I didn't expect to hear from him, but I had a feeling I wasn't done with his customer, whoever he was.

CHAPTER NINETEEN

The following morning I overslept. I'd gone to Guido's the previous evening for some good jazz and a little distraction, and stayed longer than I should have.

I sat at the kitchen table with my coffee and toast, feeling logy and uninspired. Not that it mattered. Wrapping both hands around my favorite mug, I took a bracing swallow, then headed for the shower.

In the office I put on a pot of extra-dark French Roast, then called Claire to see if she had a date for Andrea's hearing yet.

She did—Monday morning. Which gave me exactly six days to find some proof that there had been someone else in Jake's apartment that night. What I needed was new information, not more time spent rearranging the information I already had.

I considered having another conversation with Dave at the motorcycle dealership, but remembering our last meeting, abandoned the idea for the time being. Instead I called Jerry. Who answered on the first ring.

I guess my luck had to be in sometimes.

"Jerry, it's me. Look, can you find out if there was a motorcycle stolen that night?"

"Morning, O'Grady. What night?"

"The night Jake was murdered, of course. You remember, when they arrested Andrea?"

"Cute, O'Grady. A motorcycle, you say." There was a pause, and I could just picture him pursing his lips in disbelief. "Okay, I can check into it. You're running up your tab though. It's going to take more than ice cream this time."

"Yeah, yeah. Just find the information, will you?"

"Speaking of information—you know that investigator you asked me to look into?"

"Nick?"

"Uh huh. Well, he's not a private investigator, but other than that I can't tell you anything about him."

"You mean you still haven't found anything on him?"

"No. Listen to the words, Barbara. I can't tell you anything about him."

This time I listened, not to the words, but to the way he said them. The emphasis told me what he couldn't. It probably meant Nick was a cop of some sort, undercover.

So what role did Nick play in this whole mess? Why was he working with Crestlife? And what was he doing renting an office in my building and trying to date me?

Unless I was a suspect? Or he thought I was somehow involved?

It would explain why I kept running into him.

I pushed the unwelcome thought away. "Okay, I've got it. Thanks, Jerry."

"What are you mixed up in now?"

"When I figure it out, I'll let you know."

I knew my flippancy would only make things worse, but sometimes I just can't help myself, especially when I'm dealing with Jerry at his most bureaucratic. It's a good thing we've been friends as long as we have. Otherwise he'd probably stop taking my calls.

As it was, I could practically hear him frowning over the phone line.

"Look, O'Grady, if you've got yourself into more trouble..."

More trouble? "Calm down, Jerry. I'm not the one who's in trouble here, remember? I can handle this." Whatever it is, I muttered under my breath.

"What was that?"

"Nothing. Look, just find out if there were any bikes stolen. I'm going to need all the help I can get to get Andrea off." It was a low blow, but I didn't have time for this nonsense.

"You wanted to know about any motorcycles stolen on the eleventh? I'll get back to you shortly." His tone was crisp, professional.

"Thanks, Jerry. And you can collect your ice cream as soon as Andrea's in the clear."

"Funny, O'Grady. Very funny," he said, and disconnected on me.

I drank some coffee and thought about what he'd told me. So Nick was one of the good guys. And I wasn't denying the spark between us—there was no faking that. But I still didn't trust him.

Andrea would have a field day with that one.

But it wasn't cynicism talking, or at least not totally. Sure, I could hear her say. It was true, though. I still didn't know what his involvement was in my case, and I didn't trust his motives. I don't like being used, for any reason.

While I waited for Jerry to get back to me, I went back through Andrea's case file. I was scrolling through my notes for the fourth time when I happened to glance at my watch, and sighed. Time to meet my mother for tea.

I called first—maybe she'd forgotten and made other plans. No such luck.

"I've been thinking," she said instead. "And the place you suggested sounds lovely, but I'd heard about another place I thought would be fun to try."

Oh no. It sounded like I was in for the full treatment. Uber-healthy food, here we come. "Oh?"

"Have you heard of Ellie's?"

What was this? Ellie's is famous for their full English tea, complete with thin watercress sandwiches and fragrant scones with thick Devon cream and homemade cherry preserves. Not to mention french pastries to die for. The kind of eating that usually makes my mother cringe.

And she was suggesting it? Voluntarily?

Maybe my sister was right. Something was certainly going on.

"Mom, are you sure you want to go there? We can go anywhere you like."

"No, no. I'd like to try it. And I think you'll like it. Shall we say ten-thirty?"

She was doing this for me? No, if it was for me, it would have been a coffee shop. Or maybe the neighborhood bar. At best, this was a compromise. At worst? I wasn't going there.

"Perfect," I said with as much enthusiasm as I could muster. "I'll pick you up."

"Nonsense. I'll meet you there. See you in half an hour."

Huh. Well, at least the food would be good.

As I put the phone down, inspiration struck. Maybe it was my reward for calling Mom. I made a note.

The phone rang again.

———

AT TEN-THIRTY I was sitting across a cozy table from my mother. She ordered Ceylon tea, I stuck with English Breakfast. It wasn't coffee, but I had to admit it was pretty good.

My mother looked around her, taking in sunny windows with bright window boxes, white wicker and chintz, fine china and gleaming silver, and gave a little sigh. Sinking back against the thick padding of her chair, she said, "This is such a nice change. Thank you for suggesting tea, Barbara. We haven't done something like this together in a long time."

Maybe ever. "Would you like another scone, Mom?"

"No, thank you. I'm enjoying my indulgence, but my body will only forgive me for one."

I nodded, reached for a second lemon-cranberry scone. As long as I keep up the running, my body will forgive me for just about anything. And these were good.

"You know, I've been wanting to have a long chat with you for a while. Just the two of us."

Uh oh. "Another sandwich, Mom? Pastry?"

She ignored me. "I worry about you, you know."

What was this? "You worry about me?"

She nodded, and took a sip of her tea. "You haven't chosen an easy path. Nor a safe one."

"I thought you hated my life."

"Sometimes I do. It wasn't what I'd hoped for, for you."

"What did you hope for?" I needed to hear it, for once, straight out and honest.

She lifted one shoulder. "The kind of security I never had, I suppose. Someone to love you, who'll be there for you. A home. A family."

"That's Susanna's choice. It isn't mine."

"I know. But if you are choosing a career over a family, I don't see why it shouldn't be a career with prospects."

"And a pension plan."

She smiled. "Yes, that too."

I took a breath. "It isn't me, Mom. Any of it. Why can't you accept that?"

Though I really knew the answer, knew it from all the times I'd seen her after Dad died, late at night after she'd worked all day and we were in bed, struggling over the bills, tears sliding down her cheeks as she downed another glass of cheap wine. When she looked at my life, it was her own fears she saw.

But she surprised me. Again.

"Maybe because you don't seem happy."

"I'm happy."

"Are you?"

"I'm happier than I'd be working for some bureaucratic corporation. Or with Susanna's life."

"That's because you don't like Godfrey."

Godfrey was only the beginning of my problems with Susanna's life, but I was surprised to hear her acknowledge it. "He seems to be good for Susanna."

"Yes. He is." She picked up her teacup, examining the fragile lilies painted on it. "He wouldn't have been my choice for her either, though I'll swear I never said that. But she does seem happy."

I couldn't believe what I was hearing. "Most of the time."

"Most of the time," my mother agreed.

For a change we seemed to be having a real conversation. Now it was my turn. "And what about you?"

"What about me?"

"Are you happy?"

My mother's face took on an odd expression, as if she'd tasted an unfamiliar flavor and couldn't decide whether she liked or hated it. "I don't really think about it."

"Maybe you should."

"I have you girls. I have my interests, and my crafts."

We weren't girls anymore. "Is it enough?"

"Oh. Well," she said, and took a sip of tea. "Most days it is. Like anyone, I guess. Can I pass you another scone?"

The look on her face made me ask. "If you could do absolutely anything, Mom, what would you do?"

There was a pause, then she smiled. "I've done most of it. And when you've lived as long as I have, you learn that you can't do everything."

"I'm not talking about everything. I'm talking about one thing. What if I asked you to name one thing you've always wished you could do."

Like painting.

I pushed the thought away. I didn't have enough time for two passions. I was lucky enough to love what I did for a living. That was enough.

She tipped a bit more tea into her cup, added milk, stirred slowly. "I always used to want to go parachuting," she said eventually.

Now that I wasn't ready for. But I was the one who'd started this. "Why didn't you?"

"I couldn't afford the lessons. Then as a single mom, I couldn't take the risk something might go wrong, and you two would be left alone. It was just a foolish girl's thought, anyway."

"Doing something important to you is never foolish." Too bad I didn't listen to myself.

She gave me that Mom look. "And what about you, Barbara? What have you always wanted to do?"

Damn. My mind flashed to the idea of having a show of my paintings, then dismissed it. "I'm doing it. And you're changing the subject."

"Are you? Doing what you've always wanted, I mean?"

"I'm good at what I do, Mom. And I like making things right."

"Yes, you were always that way, even as a small girl."

I was?

She drained her cup. "And now I think it's time for me to go home. I know you have your hands full with Andrea's situation. I won't take any more of your time. But thank you, Barbara. I enjoyed this."

"So did I." And much to my surprise, I meant it.

————

BACK IN MY OFFICE, I sank back in my vintage leather chair, put my perplexing conversation with my mother firmly out of my mind and started in on my calls. Somewhat to my surprise, Breyers Financial operated exactly as I'd been informed. And it was legal.

Though I got the feeling that the insurance regulators kept a rather close eye on the operation. That's one of the things I love about my job—I find out such interesting things.

The phone rang. I grabbed it.

"I've got a few reports of a bike stolen that day. Can you be more specific?" Jerry said with no preamble.

"A Harley. Street Glide or CVO Street Glide."

"Well, that's specific. Hang on." I could hear keys clicking. "Well whaddaya know?"

"What?"

"I've got a CVO Street Glide reported stolen earlier that evening," Jerry said. "Recovered the next day, abandoned in West Vancouver."

West Van again. "Thanks, Jerry. Any chance I could talk to the owner?"

"I can't give you their information," he said. No surprise there. "But I can ask them if they'll talk to you, give them your number."

"I'd appreciate it."

"I don't suppose you're going to fill me in on what you're up to, O'Grady?"

"I'll call you if I need anyone arrested." I knew he'd appreciate that one.

"Gee, thanks."

"Hey, I thought you'd be happy."

"Good-bye, O'Grady."

———

MIKE CHALMERS PROVED to be a fit, distinguished looking man in his late forties, with well-cut salt and pepper hair and a charming smile. I met him at a small coffee house in Dundarave, one that I've always liked for its unpretentious service, bright yellow walls and off-beat artwork.

You could say I collect coffee shops, especially ones with atmosphere, and this was a good one.

Once we were both seated, him with a latte and me with a cappuccino, I pulled out the photos I'd taken the night of the murder. He looked at the ones showing the bike, then looked at me thoughtfully.

"Yes, that's my bike," he said. "Or one identical to it. Too bad you didn't get the full license plate. Mind telling me what's going on?"

"It's a long story. Basically, I think whoever stole your bike killed a guy in Vancouver, then used the victim's bike as a getaway, leaving yours behind. Sometime the next day he went back and exchanged the two bikes."

"The night my bike was stolen—that would be the Jake Scott case."

"Yes, but how did you know?"

Mike smiled. "I'm a lawyer, and I do a fair bit of criminal law. You hear things."

I had a feeling that was an understatement. "So what do you hear about the case?"

"Just that Andrea Fisher has been charged, and Claire Chan is representing her. I'm guessing you're working for Claire."

"That's right." I saw no reason to keep my client's identity quiet this time.

"She's lucky to have you. I've heard good things about your work from Brian Stewart."

Was he flirting with me? "You know Brian?"

"He and Cassie are friends of mine."

Friends of his, not of him and his wife? A subtle way of saying he wasn't married? He was flirting with me. "They're good people."

"They say the same about you."

Enough already. I had a case to solve. Why did the interesting guys always show up when I didn't have time to even think about dating them? On the other hand, all this attention was kind of flattering… "Do you know when your bike was stolen?"

He gave me a sharp look, then smiled. "Sometime in the late evening last Wednesday. I'd parked it by the garage around ten, and when I went to put it away about eleven, it wasn't there."

"Is the driveway visible from the street?"

"Yes."

"From the house?"

"Yes, from the living room and from one of the guest bedrooms."

"Were you home?"

"Yes. And the lights were on in the living room," he added, taking a sip of his latte. He'd seen what I was thinking.

Wow. "This is one brazen thief."

He nodded. "Not only that—my bike was found abandoned down by the beach on Thursday morning."

"How far from your place to the beach?"

"About eight blocks, straight uphill."

"So he practically brought it back. The guy really likes West Van."

"Either that or he lives around here."

Now there was an interesting idea. "He's either very stupid or very arrogant. He even gassed up at the station down on Marine. Which is probably what, five blocks from your house?"

Mike nodded. "About that. So now what?"

I drained the last of my cappuccino. "So now I pay another visit to that gas station attendant."

"You've talked to him before?"

"Yeah, and I got a partial description before the guy clammed up. Maybe his memory will improve when I tell him the bike was stolen."

"I'll go with you."

Not a chance. "Thanks for the offer, but I work better alone."

"If the thief is local, maybe I can identify him from even a partial description. I gas up at that station all the time. I probably know the attendant, maybe he'll tell me more than he told you."

I wasn't sure about Mike's motives, but he did have a point.

And to catch the killer, I'd take any help I could get. I nodded. "I'll drive."

CHAPTER TWENTY

We were in luck. Tad had come on shift half an hour before, and the station was otherwise deserted. I took one look at that sullen face, and began reviewing my persuasive techniques.

Mike's reaction was different. He took one look, and barked out, "Tad."

"Mr. Chalmers?" I've never seen a kid's attitude change so fast. Tad practically swallowed the wad of gum he'd been champing on, and his suddenly straight back made him a good six inches taller.

Mike didn't look like the relaxed guy I'd been chatting with, either. How much time had he spent in the military, anyway?

"I have a few questions that need answering."

"I didn't do anything, I swear. I'm clean."

Mike looked him up and down and let the silence stretch for a long moment, then produced the pictures of the bike. "You see this bike?"

"Yeah. Yes, I do."

"It's my bike, and it was stolen last week. Somebody brought it in here Wednesday night and gassed up. You know anything about that?"

"Maybe," Tad said. Mike looked at him. "Okay, okay. Yes, I saw him."

"I thought perhaps you had. What did he look like?"

"It was too dark to see much, but he had dark hair, really long."

"How long?"

"To his shoulders. And messed up skin on his cheeks and forehead."

Tad's complexion was typically teenage male awful, so I wasn't surprised he'd noticed the latter. "Go on."

"He was pretty tall, and skinny."

"How tall?"

"Shorter than me, but not by much."

We both looked at Tad. He had to be six foot four.

So Bike Guy was six two or three. And his description was sounding a lot like the guy Chris had described handing an envelope to Walters. Or was I reaching? "Ever see this guy before?"

Tad's eyes darted to me and he licked his lips nervously before looking back at Mike. "I think I've seen him around, but I couldn't swear to it, like."

"Where?"

Tad shrugged.

"Know who this is?" Mike asked him.

Tad eyes skittered towards the car that was just pulling in. "Uh-uh. Look, I gotta go now. Can't afford to lose this job."

"You'll go when I say you can go. You're sure you don't know who he is."

"No, really, I don't."

Given the way his eyes wouldn't meet Mike's when he said it, I didn't believe him. He knew who this guy was all right.

But whoever he was, Tad was more scared of him than he was of Mike. And that was saying something.

"Well, if you see him again, or if you remember anything else, give me a call," Mike said, holding out his card.

"You can count on it, Mr. Chalmers."

Back in the crowded confines of my aging Civic, I turned to Mike. "Let me guess, Tad is one of your clients."

"Let's just say that his father is. And that Tad has no record."

"Dealing? Or possession?"

"No comment."

It figured. "His memory sure improved when you showed up."

Mike nodded. "I thought it might have. And it sounds like your killer is local."

I shook my head. "I still can't believe Bike Guy had the gall to steal your bike and gas it up six blocks from where he stole it."

Mike laughed. "Bike Guy?"

"I can't keep calling him 'the guy I think might be our killer.' And he seems to have a weakness for bikes."

"He does indeed. Okay, Bike Guy it is. The amazing thing is, he seems to have got away with it. And with murder, if your theory is correct."

"Tell that to the police. As far as they're concerned, they've found their killer."

I must have sounded as discouraged as I felt, because Mike suggested dinner. Now I have a lot of faith in food as a solution to most problems, and Mike had some hidden depths, but I had a case to solve.

And it wasn't just that his smile didn't make my knees go funny —I simply didn't need the distraction. I was finally beginning to make some progress on this case. I wasn't about to risk losing that momentum.

Mike said he understood. He graciously accepted both my promise that I'd take him up on the offer when the case was completed and my card. As he accepted the latter, he promised he'd call me if he thought of anything else that might have a bearing on the case.

And I forgot about him as soon as I drove back across the bridge.

Finally I had something to go on—a partial description of a possible murderer. I ignored the turnoff towards my office and headed back to Fiasco's.

I'd follow this one as far as it would take me.

———

ZEKE WASN'T ON SHIFT, and none of the other staff at Fiasco's had known Jake, at least not by name. When I asked about Earl, it was a different story. Not only did they know him, they pointed him out.

Earl was the big bald guy with massive, heavily inked arms and a nose that looked like it had been broken a few times, sitting in a strategic corner of the bar. Looking at that rocky face, my fingers itched for a piece of charcoal. And the hairs on the back of my neck prickled.

From where Earl sat, he had a good view of the bar, with its dark wood and clean modern lines, and beyond that the small groupings of square tables. He was making good use of his strategic position, eyes moving rapidly from one table to the next, head cocked slightly to one side as if trying to listen to the variety of conversations.

He caught my look and checked me out, then his gaze moved on. I'd obviously been evaluated and dismissed. I wondered what criteria he was using, then decided I probably didn't want to know.

I walked over and introduced myself. The look he gave me then held wariness, but some interest.

"Yeah, I knew Jake," Earl said, his voice gravelly. "He was a good guy, and a straight shooter. There's not many guys could get me to buy life insurance."

I could believe that.

"Jake was, well, Jake was real. Didn't mess with your head, just said it like he saw it. And he knew numbers." Earl looked around, then lowered his voice and said, "He's got me set up in a little scheme, I won't have to worry about money later. Know what I mean?"

I didn't, exactly. "What kind of scheme?" I asked cautiously, more than half-expecting to hear about drug deals or kidnappings.

"Mutual funds," said Earl, with a hint of triumph in his voice. "I put away the same amount every month, see, and in fifteen years or so I'll be a millionaire. Jake called it 'the miracle of compound interest'."

It wasn't compound interest I would have called the miracle in this little scenario. I'd heard the phrase before, Jake certainly hadn't originated it. But how had he sold Earl on the idea?

I was still trying to contend with the incongruity of discussing financial planning with a guy who looked and sounded like Earl. It seemed that Jake had got Earl, of all people, planning for his financial future. I was finding Jake more intriguing dead than I'd ever found him alive.

But intriguing or not, it was too late for Jake, and I was here to help Andrea. Before I could formulate my next question, Earl made a statement that drove other lines of inquiry out of my head.

"I'm not surprised somebody killed him, though."

"Oh?" Earl seemed to take that for encouragement, instead of the stunned surprise it really was.

"Jake had enemies, you know. Anybody that successful would have. But he'd been looking nervous lately, and I figure he knew they were getting closer."

"Who?"

Earl looked around again, and leaned towards me. "He wouldn't tell me. But I could tell when they were around, cause he'd get really tense, and when I asked about my funds, he'd tell me to wait for my monthly statement. Usually he'd just look it up for me, but when they were around, he wouldn't."

"Do you have any idea who 'they' are?" I probed, watching Earl's thick eyebrows drew together.

After a pause, he answered. "No, but I saw him with this guy a couple of days before he was killed, and they didn't look very happy."

"Where was this?"

"Here."

"Do you remember what the guy looked like?"

"Young guy, longish dark hair, kinda skinny. Bad complexion."

Bike Guy. I couldn't believe it. The pieces of the case were falling into place like dominoes, one after the other. It made me nervous, and suspicious.

Things never work out quite that neatly in real life.

Was Earl up to something, or was I just on the wrong track? "Had you seen this guy before?"

"Yeah. Couple of times."

"Here?"

Earl nodded. But that was the extent of his knowledge, it seemed. He hadn't seen the guy anywhere else, didn't know his name, his business or even when he'd seen him with Jake.

Or maybe he'd just clammed up and had a really good poker face.

I now had two people who had seen and described Bike Guy. Whoever he was. Tad had connected him with the stolen bike, now Earl had connected him with Jake.

It felt just a little too neat. But I couldn't see any holes in my thinking. Unless they weren't the same guy?

I thanked Earl and bought him another beer, then gave him my card and left.

———

BACK IN MY OFFICE AGAIN, I stared at the sun patterns on the wall while I waited for the coffee to brew, and thought about Bike Guy. How did I go about finding him with a description but no name?

Could he be one of Jake's clients?

I opened Jake's client spreadsheet and scrolled through it again. Jake had set up a record for each client, with names, addresses, likes, dislikes, appearance and financial details. Scanning a couple of records, and calling up the files they were linked to, I was amazed at the level of detail he'd gone into. If the murderer had been a client, I could find him.

I looked up Earl. Even without knowing his last name, I found him easily. Jake had everything on file, names, addresses, contact numbers, descriptions, likes and dislikes, recent purchases. He'd separated the names into first and last name fields, so I did a search on first name Earl, and came up with four matches.

My Earl was in the comment field—Jake had entered "Bald, broken nose, gravelly voice, Fiasco's".

I pulled up his client file. Earl's name was Earl Martin, he was 58, a retired fisherman on disability payments, and he liked beer, baseball, boxing, motorcycles and opera, of all things. He disliked his ex-wife, government in general, and any kind of culture except opera.

Earl lived in East Van, which made his affection for Fiasco's a bit odd. It was quite a distance to go for a beer, especially in traffic. I wondered how that had come about.

Earl had been investing with Jake for about four years. He was doing quite well, incidentally, owning stock in four funds that had been appreciating nicely. So far so good.

I went back to the spreadsheet and searched for male clients living in West Vancouver whose age was between twenty-one and forty. The search yielded twelve matches. Of those, seven had dark hair. When I pulled up the files and compared addresses to a map, three of them lived within walking distance of Mike Chalmer's home.

None of the three files mentioned motorcycles, though. And Bike Guy really knew his motorcycles. So, Bike Guy probably wasn't a client.

What next?

I considered what Earl had told me, the escalating argument in Fiasco's. What was Bike Guy doing there, anyway? If he lived in West Van, there were two bridges and a whole lot of traffic between him and Fiasco's.

Maybe he went there to meet Jake.

Maybe Jake had his clients meet him at Fiasco's. It was a little odd, but then so was his client list. But Bike Guy wasn't a client, so why would he have been meeting with Jake, and on Jake's turf?

What did they have in common?

A passion for bikes. What else? I stared at Jake's spreadsheet again. It was pretty thorough. Would Jake have had an equally thorough file for prospective clients?

I scanned the various files I'd copied from Jake's computer, until I located a spreadsheet that looked similar to the client one. I grinned when I realized he'd called it "Wish List" which , then lost the smile when I remembered the owner of that rather quirky sense of humor was dead.

A search on this file gave me five dark-haired male prospects living in West Van. Of these, two lived within walking distance of Chalmer's place, and both apparently liked motorcycles. I was back in business.

I saved the results of the search as well, then printed them. My current suspects were Richard Mayland, twenty-six and Anthony Rawlins, twenty-three. I looked at that last name again. It couldn't be.

I checked the phone book, and sure enough, the address listed for Kenneth Rawlins was the same address Jake had listed for Anthony Rawlins. And I just bet I knew what Anthony Rawlins looked like.

If I was looking for a connection, I had just found it.

Or had I?

As I considered the implications of that connection, the phone rang again. It was Nick.

"Have you heard from Chris?" he asked.

"Not a word." Which was odd. "You?"

"Nothing since I told him about Knight. I'm guessing he's up to something."

"Should we worry?"

He laughed.

Nice to know I'm amusing. And that we share a sense of humor, which right about now was the last thing I wanted to know. I was still pretty annoyed with Mr. Markham. Or Detective Markham, or whatever his title was.

"I just thought he might have called you."

"No, but I'm sure I'll hear soon." And since Nick had called me, he might as well be useful. "Nick, do you know who Forrester dealt with at Crestlife?"

"Let me check."

I wondered if he already know about a connection between Rawlins and Jake? It might explain why he was so interested in Andrea's case. And maybe his interest in me?

I heard the rustling of papers, then his voice came back on the line. "Forrester was a client of one Les Saunders."

"Was it Saunders who hired you?" Obviously it hadn't been, since he was a cop, but I was curious how he'd answer a direct question.

"No. But anything else is confidential," he said, cutting off further questions.

Which was probably true, as far as it went. At least he hadn't ducked the question entirely.

"Okay. Thanks." I made a note of Saunders' name.

If Nick wanted to keep pretending to be an insurance investigator, that was his choice. I know those rules pretty well—I play by them myself. But apparently Nick had another agenda.

"Look, there's a baseball game on Saturday afternoon. Want to go?" Then, before I could reply, he answered for me. "I know, I know. It depends on the case. How about you let me know by Friday?"

"Thanks, Nick. I'll do that."

"Good enough. I'll call you then."

I was left contemplating a silent phone, wondering why he'd really called.

CHAPTER TWENTY-ONE

The following morning was gray and damp. I added a vest over my hoodie and I was still cold. And the heater in my Civic was malfunctioning again, so by the time I got to the office I was truly frozen.

First thing I did was turn up the heat. Not that I really expected it to do any good, not in our building. A couple of cups of coffee later, I was ready for a little chat with Mr. Saunders.

Only it wasn't Mr. Saunders at all. It was Ms. Saunders. And she was a barracuda in panty hose. Every now and then I suffer from the delusion I'm tough, and then I run into someone like Ms. Saunders, who sets me straight.

"I'm sorry, Ms. O'Grady. Client accounts are confidential," she said.

"Even when your client is dead?"

"Our clients expect confidentiality. They get it. Regardless."

"I appreciate that, Ms. Saunders. However, my client is the beneficiary on this particular account. And he has engaged me to look into it for him."

"I see." I could hear the clicking of a keyboard. "The beneficiary's name?"

"Christopher Forrester."

"I see. I will need confirmation of that before I can release any information. In writing."

Of course she would. "Well, can you tell me why the policy has not been paid out?"

More clicking. "Our records show it was not a natural death."

"Not a natural death? Are you suggesting Mr. Forrester committed suicide?"

"That is what my records show."

"But Ms. Saunders, my client advises me that there is some question as to whether he did indeed commit suicide."

"Nonsense. The police reports said it was suicide. People don't just accidentally fall off bridges."

"I wasn't suggesting it was an accident."

Her frosty silence practically crackled down the phone lines. "Are you suggesting murder?" she asked, only moments before the lines started to develop permafrost. "That is absolute nonsense. He committed suicide, that was very clear. Unfortunate, but clear."

Well, Ms. Saunders was either a terrific actress, or she was not involved in whatever this was. I was betting on a conspiracy, but I was going to need more information to prove it. And I wasn't likely to get anything more out of Ms. Saunders.

Okay, I wasn't stymied yet. I put through a call to Bill Brighton.

"Bill here."

At least someone was having a good day.

"Hi, Bill. It's Barbara O'Grady again. I've a few more questions I'd like to ask about Jake Scott's business, if that's okay with you?"

If possible, Bill's voice got even cheerier. "I'd be more than happy to help."

"Was Jake was at all involved in the management of Breyers Insurance, Bill?"

"Well, depends on what you mean by management, exactly."

"So what was Jake's involvement?"

"Well, you see, all the salesmen are involved in goal-setting meetings. We get together and determine quarterly and annual goals. Jake was part of that."

"Was Jake at all involved in strategy for Breyers?"

"What do you mean by strategy?"

"Determining the direction of the company."

"Jake?" He laughed. "No, strategy was not Jake's forte. And only the top man in any of the consistently productive lines is involved at that level."

"Like yourself?"

"Well, yes, actually."

"So Jake wouldn't have known about Breyers' links with Crestlife, for instance." From Bill's hesitation, I didn't think he'd heard of it either.

"No, no reason for him to know that. It's not public information, after all. Is it?"

"No, no. Which is why I wondered if Jake had access to it," I said, then changed the subject before he could start wondering how I knew about it. "Jake had a prospective client named Tony Rawlins. He ever talk to you about him?"

"No. But Jake was quite protective of his clients and his prospective clients. You have to be, in this business. We work together, and we share information, but you have to protect potential clients. If you know what I mean."

I couldn't detect the slightest hesitation or change in his tone.

"I know exactly what you mean, Bill, and I appreciate you being so frank about it," I said. I doubted the man knew irony when he heard it.

After I'd rung off, I sat and contemplated the crack in the wall opposite my desk for a few minutes, trying to get the bad taste out of my mouth.

It was certainly possible that Jake had known nothing about Kenneth Rawlins or about Forrester. He and Anthony Rawlins had shared an interest in motorcycles—they could have met through that, or through mutual friends, or even at Fiasco's.

I had no proof at all that Anthony Rawlins was Bike Guy, after all, nor even that Bike Guy was the killer I was looking for. Just because both cases involved interconnected insurance companies owned by Kenneth Rawlins, didn't mean that Jake's death had anything to do with Forrester's.

Except that I had a feeling about this one, and it got stronger with every call I made. I just didn't think Kenneth Rawlins' connection to both cases, however peripheral, was a coincidence. Not when you added in a connection between his son and the late Jake Scott.

I put another call through to Jerry. One of these days, he's going to start refusing to take my calls. Or maybe he already had—I got his voice mail. I left a message, then called Doug. Again.

"Have you run across anything on Kenneth Rawlins' son, Anthony?"

"Hello to you, too. No, why? Is he important?"

"I don't know. He seems to have showed up in Andrea's case."

"You think there's a connection?"

"Could be. But other than Rawlins himself, I can't find it."

Sometimes I swear I can hear Doug thinking. I shut up and waited till he finished. It sounded like he was drinking coffee while he thought, or at least I hoped it was coffee.

"I wonder if Forrester knew the kid?"

"What makes you say that? Unless...did Forrester know Rawlins?"

"Yeah. They're both architects, same year."

"Rawlins is an architect?"

"Yup. Never practiced, though. When he graduated, he took over his old man's construction firm, and he hasn't looked back since."

"Interesting. Did Rawlins and Forrester keep in touch?"

"Now that I don't know, but there was a class reunion a couple of years ago, and they're both listed in the write-up."

" How'd you find that out?"

"I get the Alumni magazine."

"I didn't know you were an alum."

"Yup, creative writing. Not a very useful degree, even then."

I laughed. "Try a degree in fine arts, if you're talking about useless."

"Fine Arts? You're an artist?"

"Not any more. I gave up painting a few years back. Investigating is more rewarding." Or so I keep telling myself. "And it pays the bills."

There was a thoughtful silence. "Do you paint at all?"

I wondered what he'd heard in my voice, decided I didn't want to know. "Once in a while, when I have time. Just for my own enjoyment."

"I'd like to see them sometime. You know I used to handle the art beat, right?"

He did? "How did you end up there?"

A dry chuckle. "The editor hated me."

Okay, then. No way I was showing him my paintings. "About Forrester? You'll let me know if you hear anything more about Rawlins, junior or senior?"

"Yup. And when this is over, I still want to see your paintings."

"Yeah, yeah. Thanks, Doug." I disconnected.

Time for a little digging in the university archives.

You have to love technology. Instead of dashing off to the main UBC campus to dig through dusty archival boxes, I got to sit back in my comfy chair and troll the web. They've put a lot of the old publications on-line, and it makes my life easier. And greener, come to think of it.

I miss driving along Jericho Beach though—it's the alternate way to get to UBC, and it's unbelievable. Thick cedar and pines on your left, miles of flat sandy beach leading to the ocean, with the North Shore Mountains and the islands in the Salish Sea ghosting blue on the horizon.

On sunny days it looks like a postcard, on our much more frequent rainy days it's a palette of dark greens and grays softened by mist and clouds. In any weather, it makes my fingers itch for a paintbrush, and makes me wish I were a decent watercolorist. Acrylics are often too robust for the feeling I want to capture.

Maybe I'd go down to the beach with my paints once I'd cleared Andrea. Yeah, right.

Shaking my head at my lack of focus, I loaded the archives site. Before long, I was wondering what it would cost to add more computer memory. I had to guess at the year Forrester and Rawlins, Sr. might have graduated, which meant I had to open a lot of very large, very slow documents.

I'd just found a photo of the two of them playing rugby, of all things, in the student yearbook, *The Totem,* when the phone range.

"O'Grady Investigations, Barbara O'Grady speaking."

"Don't you get tired of saying all that?"

"Hey, Jerry. No, I don't. I'm fond of eating."

He laughed. "So, you called?"

"You ever heard of a kid named Anthony Rawlins, lives in West Van, about twenty-three or twenty-four?"

"Rawlins, huh? And this is related to Andrea's case?"

"Of course." I heard keys clicking in the background.

"Uh huh. Officially, no I haven't heard of him. Unofficially I might know quite a bit about him. Why?"

Which meant either they'd never been able to make charges stick on one Anthony Rawlins, or he had a juvenile record, which had officially ceased to exist once he became an adult. I grabbed a pen. "So, unofficially, what kinds of things might he be involved in?"

"Off the record, a young punk like him could be into drugs, maybe fraud. Or not. So why are you suddenly interested in him?"

"He apparently knew Jake."

"Huh. Young Tony runs with a pretty scary crowd."

"Gangs?"

"Unproven."

Which meant it was a possibility. I'd have to check into it. "What about his father?"

"Who, Kenneth? Good question. Nothing proven, but rumor has it he's bought the kid out of more than one sticky situation. Rawlins, Sr. has a stable of high powered lawyers, as you can imagine."

Maybe I'd learn more by investigating the son's recent past than by delving into the father's history. "They've always lived in West Van?"

More keys clicking, then Jerry said, "For the last fifteen years or so."

"And where did Anthony go to school? Or need I ask?"

"St. John's. "

Of course. "And did he cause trouble there?"

"If he did, we didn't hear about it. Either the school dealt with it, or Daddy did."

"I'm betting on Daddy."

"Mmmph."

I interpreted that to mean he agreed with me, but didn't feel free to say so. "Wonder if they'd like to tell me about it?"

"I'm sure they'd be happy to tell you all about it," he said. "I could warn you not to annoy them, but I get the feeling you're not in a mood to listen."

He had that right. It riles me that so often there's one set of rules for the privileged, those with legal advice on retainer, and another for the rest of us. When I get a chance to challenge that status quo, I tend to take it on, as Jerry knows only too well.

"Just don't bring me into it, that's all I ask," he said, correctly interpreting my silence.

I agreed, crossing my fingers as I did so. I wouldn't bring him into it unless I had no other choice, but that was the best he could hope for and Jerry probably knew it.

———

THE HEADMASTER'S study at St. John's, with its heavy Victorian décor and the centuries of male privilege it invoked, was deliberately intimidating, but I refused to let it bother me. I focused on Stuart March, headmaster at St. John's for nearly ten years now, or so he had pompously informed me, who looked like he'd been out in the sun several years too long. Everything about him was thin and dry, his voice, his manner, his appearance.

This was a man who wouldn't cooperate unless he thought either he or his reputation had something to gain.

"And what can I do for you, Ms. O'Grady?"

"I'm writing a story for the *Globe and Mail*, comparing the results of a private versus a public education on today's disaffected youth," I said. "St. John's has been mentioned as a sterling example more than once, and confidentially, your name has come up also."

As he took in my words, he seemed to expand, like a sponge. I watched in fascination as his facial muscles relaxed, giving him a more open, approachable air. Even his voice was different.

"Why certainly, Miss O'Grady. I'm always more than happy to cooperate with the press."

Which I knew to be untrue. I'd spent most of an hour in the newspaper archives before arriving at St. John's. March talked to the press as little as possible, and kept his school out of the press as much as possible.

I hadn't found anything on Anthony Rawlins or any of his schoolmates. Either St. John's pupils were unusually circumspect, or the school had grown adept at keeping a low profile. I was betting on the latter.

"Thank you, Mr. March. I just have a few questions?" I said, with a smile that I managed to keep just this side of phony.

"Of course, of course." He didn't exactly rub his hands together, but he came close.

I started off with a series of innocuous questions, the age of the school, the number of pupils, what geographical area the school draws from. He answered readily. Then I zeroed in. "I understand you have the sons of a number of prominent people at St. John's, Mr. March. Including the sons of several prominent politicians, for instance. Do you find it creates a sense of inequity among the pupils?"

"Not at all, Miss O'Grady. Quite the contrary, in fact. Since all our pupils are treated equally, and all wear the same uniform, the boys develop a sense of their own individuality. They are here on their own merits, as it were."

Their own merits and their parent's bank accounts. I was sorely tempted to ask why, in this supposed age of equality, St. John's was still a boy's school. The question wouldn't have helped my investigation, so I held my tongue.

I wished I really were writing an article for the *Globe,* though. I decided when this case was done and I had some time, I'd write a letter to the editor. It made me feel better about the things I couldn't say.

"What about when the boy comes from a wealthy family? Does that cause conflicts? I understand that the son of Kenneth Rawlins was at St. John's, and Rawlins is one of the wealthiest men in the province. Was the younger Rawlins a good student?"

"Young Tony? Nice lad, that." Did I detect a forced note in his voice? "Tony was no trouble, no trouble at all."

"But was he a good student?"

"Oh, you mean scholastically. Well, academics were never his strong suit. But we worked with him, until we uncovered his true gifts."

"And those were?"

"Well, Tony has a gift for mechanical things. And actually, quite a flair for finances."

"Finances?"

"Investments, you know. Increasing the value of money."

Translated, that probably meant he'd been dealing drugs, or swindling somebody. Or both. "So you developed these gifts at St. John's"

"Oh, yes. Once we recognized where his gifts lay, he came along quite nicely."

Which meant they'd let him do pretty much what he chose. "And did he go on to university?"

"No, no." That stopped March for a moment, but he recovered quickly. "He opened his own motorcycle repair business. Making use of both his gifts, and doing quite nicely, too."

Motorcycle repair? I wondered if Tony had ever done any work for Jake. "You must feel a sense of pride when you see former students making a success of their lives."

"Yes, indeed. One of the joys of my life." He sounded even phonier than I did.

"And young—Tony was it? He's still in business?"

"Yes indeed. In fact, he works out of his father's estate. Works by referral only—quite a sign of success," March concluded hurriedly.

I looked at him askance. I couldn't tell if he actually believed this nonsense, or if he hoped that if he gave me the facts quickly enough, I wouldn't question him. He certainly looked more strained than he had at the start of our conversation.

He shifted slightly in his chair, his gaze not quite meeting mine. No, this wasn't a stupid man, just a self-interested one. Interesting that he hadn't been able to do a better job of fending off my questions about young Rawlins. I didn't delude myself it was my skill as an interviewer. I'm good, but I'm not that good.

I could only speculate that whatever trouble Tony Rawlins had caused when he was a St. John's "boy" had been pretty bad, if this was the best March could do to whitewash it.

Now I really wanted to know what he'd done.

I was debating my next question when the intercom on March's desk sounded. He looked relieved as his secretary informed him that his presence was required in one of the classes. I wondered if he'd prearranged the signal with her, or whether she just buzzed after a certain length of time.

I'd pretty much got all I was likely to get out of him anyway, so when he apologized, I accepted the apology and left with handshakes all round.

Time to talk to Tony himself. If I could find him, that is, and if he was willing to talk to me.

Which was a big if.

CHAPTER TWENTY-TWO

The following day I got to my office late and put on a pot of dark French Roast, waiting impatiently for it to brew. I was tired. I'd spent too much time at Fiasco's, in the hope Tony would show.

He hadn't. He didn't seem to be a regular there, either. A couple of the servers recognized my description of him, but no-one except Zeke had seen him lately. It looked like he really had only gone there to meet with Jake. That fit the theory I was slowly assembling.

Unfortunately nothing else seemed to fit. I didn't find much online on Tony, and nothing that suggested another avenue. Too bad I didn't own a motorbike I could take to him for service.

Of course, I knew someone who did own a motorbike. Someone who might be talked into doing me a favor. I dialed Mike Chalmers office.

"Mike, it's Barbara O'Grady," I said, when to my surprise I was put straight through to him. "I've reached a sticking point in my investigation and I could use your help."

"Sounds intriguing. What can I do for you, Barbara?"

"Do you happen to know a mechanic named Tony Rawlins? He specializes in motorcycles."

"I don't know him personally, but I know of him. And of course I know his father."

Of course he did. "I need to meet Tony casually, ask a few questions. Would you be willing to take your bike to him for service, have me tag along?"

"I don't see why not. I'll set something up, let you know the where and when."

"I'd appreciate it, Mike. Thanks."

"Not a problem, I'm happy to help. I assume time is of the essence?"

"I'm afraid so."

There was a pause, and I could hear keys clicking. "Looks like there's a hole in my schedule later this afternoon. Are you free then?"

"I will be."

"Then I'll have someone set it up and let you know."

I gave him my cell number. "Just have them leave a message with date and time. I'll be there."

"Will do."

———

IT WAS NEARLY three-thirty by the time Mike Chalmers and I wheeled his Harley towards the large garage set behind the sprawling mansion belonging to Kenneth Rawlins.

A tall young man with long dark hair pulled back and a really bad complexion came out to meet us. He was wearing dirty jeans and a T-shirt and smoking a thin cigar. Bike Guy, as I live and breath.

"Tony Rawlins?" Mike said.

His eyes swept over me, then he dismissed me and turned to Mike.

"Yeah?"

I'd just become invisible. I didn't like it much. And I wasn't much impressed with him, either.

Tony Rawlins was in his early twenties. His features were hard and set, and his tone was an odd combination of curtness and arrogance. The concept of service obviously eluded him.

His posture and his gestures said he was the one who mattered here, and it was our role to earn his attention.

As he and Mike discussed a performance problem with the bike, I considered Tony. Was this Jake's killer? My latest theory put him on the top of my suspect list. But then, I'd been wrong before, with nearly fatal consequences.

Tony seemed intent on what Mike was saying, but his eyes were in constant motion, checking out the bike, checking out the yard around him, checking what I was doing. If he was Jake's killer, he had to recognize Mike's bike. I wondered how good his game face was.

Did he guess we knew something?

After watching him for a few more minutes, I decided he didn't have a game face—it simply hadn't occurred to him that we could suspect him. There was no fear in the way he was talking to Mike, and no respect, either. If anything, his attitude was one of superiority.

The eye movements were compulsive, a reflection of personality rather than a reaction to the situation. I tried to imagine what I'd do if I'd stolen a bike and killed someone, then been confronted with the owner of the bike. I wasn't sure what my reaction would be, but it certainly wouldn't be calm superiority.

Did this kid have ice water in his veins? Was he too stupid to imagine consequences to his actions? Or had Daddy's money bought him out of trouble so often that he thought he was above the law?

I'd bet on the latter, personally.

But then, there was something about Tony that set my teeth on edge. And Kenneth Rawlins' influence had kept him out of quite a bit of trouble over the years, judging by his former headmaster's reaction.

Of course, he could be innocent.

My gut told me otherwise. I'd be willing to bet on that this kid had been born to trouble, and had traded far too long on Daddy's influence. Still, murder was another story.

Or was it? Watching Tony, I could see him as a killer. He had that kind of disdain for others that was the mark of a sociopath, though they usually hid it with a lot more charm than Tony was displaying.

But Jerry hadn't mentioned violence in Tony's past. I think he would have told me that. And if Tony had killed Jake, and if this was his first killing, would he be so cool now?

Unless he thought no-one would ever make the connection? Or assumed Daddy's lawyers could get him out of a murder charge, just like they'd done with all the other messes Tony had undoubtedly got himself into.

But I still didn't get why Tony might have killed Jake in the first place.

Rage? Yeah, I could see it. In self defense? Not so much, but possible. I considered insurance agencies, and Kenneth Rawlins.

What if Tony had killed Jake to protect his father? What if he thought Daddy would be pleased to hear about Jake Scott's death?

I suspected Rawlins senior would have had other thoughts on the issue, but Tony didn't strike me as particularly perceptive. Not a deep thinker, this one.

Mike and Tony were still deep in their conversation about the bike. Mike pointed out something near the engine, then Tony started the bike, and revved it, listening intently. You could tell he loved bikes.

Yet it didn't change his expression or his attitude. Clearly, the only things that mattered were himself and the bike. Mike and I might as well not be there.

It didn't matter what I thought of Tony Rawlins. What mattered were the facts and whether I could prove them.

Starting with fact number one—a current picture of my suspect of choice. I pulled out my iPhone, pretended to make a call and got off a couple of quick shots of Tony with the bike.

That meant it was question time, though I was much less optimistic about the results than I'd been before I met him. "You have an impressive place here, Tony," I said. "Have you been fixing bikes long?"

He shot me an impatient look, then looked back at the bike. "Yeah."

"Do you have a lot of clients?"

"Enough."

"Are they mostly local?" I persisted.

He didn't even bother to answer that one. Clearly talking to him wouldn't get me anywhere. Tony Rawlins' social skills would fit into a thimble. A small thimble.

Either I identified myself as an investigator and asked about Jake directly, or I gave up for now. Neither option appealed. Before I could get myself into real trouble, Mike intervened.

"I'd been thinking of selling this, getting one of the new models that are supposed to be coming in. I may not get the CVO this time, though, just the Glide," he said to Tony. "Heard much about them?"

"Sure. Slightly stiffer ride than this baby, but good bikes. Bit of a downgrade, though."

Mike shrugged. "The economy, you know. And I've heard they're solid. Have you worked on them?"

"Yeah. Lot of my clients have them."

"Can you suggest anybody I could talk to?"

"I'll have to let you know. Check it out with them first."

"Sure thing. I'd appreciate it. Actually, one of my clients had one, but he was killed before we had a chance to talk bikes. I'm a lawyer, you see."

Tony looked a little wary. "One of your clients was killed? On the bike?"

"No, nothing like that. He was murdered, actually. Fellow named Jake Scott. Don't suppose you knew him."

"Jake Scott..." Tony drew out the name, as though searching his memory banks. "Nope, doesn't ring a bell."

Tony's eyes had stopped darting about, and were fixed on the bike in front of him. Maybe he wasn't as cool as he'd seemed. He wasn't looking at Mike, but I could almost feel the intensity with which he was focused on every word.

And he'd denied knowing Jake, in front of a lawyer and investigator. That would come back to haunt him. I was prepared to guarantee it.

"This Scott. What was he into? I mean, did he come to see you about whatever got him killed?"

"I don't know what got him killed," Mike said. "He came to see me about a will."

Nice one, Mike, I cheered silently. Puts you beyond suspicion, but you got a rise out of our friend Tony the imperturbable.

"Guess he should have come sooner, eh?" said Tony with a half-smirk. "Unless you got the will finished?"

"No, he was to come in the next day. He'd called me all excited, too, said he had something to show me."

I don't know what hunch Mike was following, but it was effective. I just hoped he'd keep it up.

"He tell you what, man?" Tony asked with a pretense of casualness.

Mike shook his head. "He said he couldn't trust the phones. But he said something odd."

"Yeah?"

"He said that he might not need the will, that he had it covered and nobody would be able to touch him."

"He said he had it covered?"

"Uh huh."

"You know what he meant?"

"No idea. But it was something he could bring to my office."

By this point I felt as if I was watching an uneven contest, as the conversation ricocheted back and forth. Tony had given up all pretense at disinterest, and Mike was playing him like a fish.

It looked like Tony had suddenly figured out that killing Jake might not have solved all his problems, whatever those had been. Tony wasn't about to let go, and he seemed to have no sense that he might be betraying himself

"And he really said that he might not need a will? Like it was protection?"

"That's what he said."

"Then he was killed. Didn't it make you wonder?"

"Well, I only had his word. Hearsay, you know."

That made sense to Tony. He nodded, and his face relaxed a little. He obviously had some familiarity with the laws of evidence. I had a pretty good idea where he'd gained it, too.

Tony wasn't finished. There was one more piece of reassurance he wanted. "So, you didn't go to the cops?"

"No. There didn't seem to be much point. They'd already arrested someone, charged her with killing Scott."

"Yeah," said Tony, nodding. "Guess there wasn't at that. I heard they'd arrested some chick, lived upstairs."

I bit my tongue to keep from reacting to his description of Andrea as "some chick", taking the rap for a killing she hadn't committed. He didn't care, but I'd make him pay.

The two guys seemed to feel their conversation was finished, and went back to discussing the bike.

I stood in that well lit, well-equipped garage and fumed. Then it occurred to me that Tony's uncertainty could create an interesting result. If he'd bought Mike's story of Jake having a document that 'covered' him, maybe Tony knew such a document might exist.

What if Tony now felt he had to have another look for that document, just in case? Given what I now knew about Tony, I'd say there was a strong possibility that he'd go back to Jake's suite. This time, he'd probably break in.

So what could I do with that?

———

HALF AN HOUR LATER, Mike and I were sitting sipping lattes on the geranium bright deck of a little café that overlooked the water. We both wore shades against the bright sunlight, but the air was crisp and there was a slight breeze, so we had the deck to ourselves.

Which was good, given that we needed to talk about a potential killer. Always better not to have those conversations overheard.

"What did you make of young Tony?" he asked.

"I didn't think much of him. Definitely an attitude."

He grinned. "I didn't expect such understatement from you. The kid's a punk. But did he do it?"

"My guess? Yes. What do you think?"

"I agree. He was far too interested in my late 'client'."

"Your strategy was brilliant. How did you know he'd react to the implication of protection?"

"Logic, mostly. If he killed Jake, he must have had a motive. And there's usually a paper trail somewhere, unless it's a crime of passion. Between you and me, I don't think Tony is capable of that kind of passion for anyone except himself."

"Dangle the bait, and if he's guilty, he'll go for it."

"Exactly. Now, what do you think he'll go after? What would Jake have had on him, anyway?"

"That's the problem. I'm not sure. Could be something to do with Jake's business."

"Which was?"

"Insurance."

"Interesting. Rawlins senior has ties to the insurance industry."

"I know. But how did you?"

"You don't practice in this town for as long as I have without figuring out who the players are. And where they're playing."

It made sense. "Know anything about Rawlins' insurance plays?"

Mike shook his head slowly. "Nothing that seems relevant now. What firm did Scott work for?"

"Breyers."

He raised his eyebrows. "Interesting outfit. Was he involved in anything else?"

"Not that I've been able to pin down, anyway." I was pretty sure by now he'd had no gang affiliations, though some of his clients might have been members.

"So where do you go from here?"

"I figure Tony will have to go back to the suite, check to see what he can find."

"Don't tell me you're planning on being there."

What business was it of his? "Okay, I won't tell you."

"You're dealing with a probable murderer here. I trust that hasn't escaped your attention?"

What is it with the men I deal with? I could accept that Mike had dealt with more than a few hardened criminals and it made him wary, but that was his job. This was mine.

"I know what I'm dealing with," I said. "And as long as the police are convinced that Andrea is guilty, the most they're going to pin on him is breaking and entering. If Tony is the killer, I need something more, something that will tie him to Jake's murder."

Mike looked at me with a speculative gleam in his eye. "What if I help you create that something?"

"Set him up?" I had no problem following Mike's train of thought. We must both have devious minds. "I like the way you think. What did you have in mind?"

He leaned forward a little, and the wind ruffled the ends of his silver streaked dark hair. "I have a some research to do before I tell you. How about I call for you about six? We can talk about the plan over dinner, then stake out Jake's. How early do you think Tony might show?"

I wasn't keen on having my planning on this case usurped, but I wasn't about to pass up a good idea. I'd have my own fallback plan, though.

"Give me a call when you've finished your research, and we'll sort out the details."

CHAPTER TWENTY-THREE

I got to Joe's at ten to six. The place is a local institution that has recently gone upscale, though for a change without diminishing the quality of their food. It's main advantage tonight is that it's in the opposite direction to Fiasco's, when the starting point is Andrea's place. Joe's is closer to the university, on the edge of upscale Point Grey, and we were highly unlikely to run into our buddy Tony there.

The restaurant wasn't busy yet, but already had the buzz good food and good conversation create. Mike was seated at a small square table near the back. He'd been watching for me, raising a hand in greeting as I came in.

I joined him with a smile, and we ordered dinner. I decided on the pasta special, fettuccine with spicy sausage in an organic tomato basil sauce. Mike chose the four-pepper steak with *pommes frites*. He suggested a particularly nice bottle of Cabernet, but I passed. Drinking on a stakeout is a really bad idea.

Once the waiter arrived with our Pellegrino and departed again, I looked over at Mike and raised my eyebrows. "So?"

Mike's grin reappeared in full force. "I left my bike parked outside my garage this evening, just in case."

"You're thinking Tony might steal it again?"

"Maybe. It's a little extra encouragement, in case he needs it. Why, you think he's not arrogant enough to try it?"

He was definitely arrogant enough. "Go on."

"Right. I checked the specs on the Glide, and there are a number of very small, hard to get at spots on that bike. You'd have to disassemble the whole thing to get at some of them."

"Presumably Tony didn't have time the night of the murder," I said dryly.

"Presumably not, or he wouldn't have been so interested in what I had to say this afternoon."

"Odd. If that were the case you'd think he would have kept looking. Unless…"

"Unless?"

"Unless he didn't really expect to find anything. Maybe he was looking for proof that something didn't exist. Maybe Jake had something, and was supposed to have destroyed it."

"Then why was Tony so interested in what I had to say?"

"Because he didn't trust Jake."

Mike nodded slowly. "He'd be concerned to hear that Jake had told me about a document that would protect him."

"Because it would mean that something still existed, something he hadn't found the night he killed Jake," I said. "And it could be a threat to him."

Mike looked at me. "Which brings us right back to where we started. So what do we do now?"

"Finish our dinners. We should be at Andrea's place by seven-thirty, just in case. And before we leave, I want to call Fiasco's. I've just thought of a loose end I need to tie up."

Mike looked at me inquiringly, but I shook my head at him. I'd tell him later, if my hunch proved right.

We finished dinner without talking about the case or Tony again. Mike proved to be as good a conversationalist at dinner as he'd been over coffee. We touched on a wide range of topics, and our ideas were dissimilar enough to make the conversation interesting.

I could feel the tension in both of us, though, the anticipation of what the rest of the evening might hold.

Just before we were ready to go, I put a call through to Fiasco's. I was in luck. Zeke was working, and free to come to the phone. I identified myself, and asked the one question I'd forgotten to ask the last time I talked to him.

"Zeke, you remember the guy with long dark hair, the one you'd seen with Jake a few times?"

"Yeah?"

"Do you remember what he drank?"

There was a pause on the other end. I could picture Zeke's face contorting in thought, and mentally crossed my fingers.

"Red wine," he said after a long wait. "He liked Shiraz wines, I think."

"You're sure?"

"Well, not positive it was Shiraz, but I know it was Australian, cause he'd always order a bottle to himself. Jake drank beer, you know."

"Yes, I know. Zeke, you're sure it was red wine, though? It's important."

"Oh, that. Yeah, I'm positive about it being red."

"And did he ever order anything else?"

"Nope. It was always red wine."

"Thanks, you've been a great help."

The only two pieces of physical evidence at the murder site had been the red wine, and the pen. Zeke had just linked Tony to red wine, which while not confirmation, at least didn't eliminate him.

When I got back to the table, I filled Mike in on what I'd just found out.

"Hmmm. Tony is looking more and more like our man."

I grinned at the "our". Mike was definitely taking on this case. He was in for a bit of a shock, though.

———

AFTER THREE HOURS of sitting in Andrea's darkened kitchen in total silence, the romance of investigating was clearly wearing very thin for Mike. I could sympathize. This wasn't my favorite part of my job either, but you get used to it.

At least we weren't outside. The nights were starting to get damp and chilly, full of the smell of dying leaves.

Andrea had gone to stay with another friend, so at least she wasn't having to sit through this. It would have been even harder for her—having your house broken into is a violation, waiting for someone to break in is unspeakable.

Just as I was beginning to wonder if I'd misjudged the situation, there was the muffled sound of a Harley engine in the alley. It cut out, and a minute or so later there was a hint of movement in the thick darkness where the yard bordered on the alley.

I nudged Mike and pointed. As we watched, a shadow detached itself from the surrounding darkness and began to move across the yard. A tall, thin shadow, one that moved with a suggestion of a slouch. Tony.

He made his way across the middle of the yard, not even bothering to hide his movements. He headed straight for the door to the suite, and vanished. Seconds later a light came on in the suite, spilling across the lawn. This guy really did think he was invisible.

After what seemed like hours but was really only ten minutes—I timed him—Tony reappeared empty handed, and loped across the lawn towards the alley. He was giving up?

Apparently not. Moments later the bushes shook, and Tony wheeled a bike into the yard. Another Street Guide? This one wasn't all black, though. It looked like it had a white or some lighter color upper, and striping.

"It isn't mine, but that's a CVO, too," Mike whispered. "Must be his bike."

I nodded, watching as Tony wheeled the bike across the yard to where Jake's bike had been stored and hauled off the tarpaulin.

Moving quickly, he covered his own bike and began wheeling Jake's towards the alley.

Mike nudged me. "He's really going to steal it again."

"Shhh." Sound carries at night.

Despite Tony's arrogance, he had to be on the alert for any hint of discovery, didn't he? Watching that shadow wheeling the bike across the lawn, I had to wonder. There was no furtiveness in his movements. He acted like he owned the place.

Mike was wrong—it wasn't fear that was motivating Tony. Greed, maybe, or pride, but not fear.

As the shadow of the man and the bike merged with the denser shadows of the bushes, I elbowed Mike, and gestured towards the front of the house. We sprinted through the house and out to my car, which I'd left strategically parked for a quick getaway earlier in the evening.

I started the engine but left the lights off. The alley only had one exit, which was further down the next block. Spotting Tony on the bike should be easy. And it was.

Mike saw him first, as he pulled out onto the street. There was almost no traffic at that time of night, so I waited for a second or two before pulling out. As long as I could see which way he turned, and he didn't turn again too suddenly, we wouldn't lose him.

We didn't. Tony turned right onto Broadway and just kept going till he reached Burrard. Then he made a left and headed over the bridge towards downtown. I followed, keeping a measured distance behind him. He made another left on Georgia.

"I don't believe this," I said. "He's headed straight back to West Van. He isn't even bothering to disguise his route."

"This is one cocksure kid. What do you want to do about him now?"

I smiled. Mike had finally accepted our respective roles in this scenario. "For now we just follow him. See where he ends up, and what he does then."

So follow him we did. And as I'd suspected, Tony ended up back at his shop. I parked the car some distance away from the Rawlins property, and Mike and I walked in, very cautiously.

There was no real need for caution, though. No-one was stirring in the house or on the grounds. Good thing they didn't have guard dogs. We skirted the shadowed lawn on the edge of the property and made our way to the back of the house.

The yard was dark and still. There was no breeze, and the air felt cold and heavy with dew. The only sign of life was a light showing in the alley. It had to be coming from the back windows of Tony's shop.

Mike and I looked at each other, and reached a silent agreement. We crept closer.

Finally we were beneath the window. It was a quiet night. This far up, we couldn't even hear the freeway. There was only the occasional metallic clunk coming from the shop.

Stretching up very carefully, I peered through a dimly lit window.

Tony was at the far end of the shop, under a small spotlight. He appeared to be taking Jake's motorcycle apart, piece by piece. I was about to motion to Mike to look too, but he was already beside me.

We both watched, motionless, for some time. Tony was very definitely, and very systematically, taking that bike apart. If he was looking for something specific, he didn't appear to be finding it.

After what felt like hours, one of my legs began to cramp, protesting the unnatural position I was in. I moved away from the window and Mike followed reluctantly.

We walked far enough away that our voices wouldn't carry.

"He's determined to find something on that bike," I said.

Mike nodded, the motion more felt than seen in the darkness. "I've never seen such thoroughness."

"Is he going to be able to put it back together?"

"Depends how good he is. Regardless, it's unlikely he'll get it back together tonight. So what's our next move?"

"I should probably call the police and let them take it from here."

I could sense Mike's grin in the darkness. "Probably. So what are you going to do?"

"Watch him for a while. What if there really was something there to find?"

"What makes you think there might be?"

I shrugged, a futile gesture in the dark. "I don't, really. But wouldn't it be ironic if there was? After all, when Jake lived in LA, his apartment was broken into and his girlfriend murdered. He wouldn't have had much faith in the security of his home after that. Given his fondness for bikes, that just might be where he'd choose to hide something he valued. And it's possible Tony knows that."

"But if he had, Tony would've found it the first time."

"Not if Tony thought Jake had destroyed whatever it is. Or lied about it in the first place. Maybe he looked for it, but not really thoroughly."

"Why kill Jake, then, if Tony didn't believe there was any proof of whatever he's so worried about now?"

"You'd have to ask Tony that. Maybe he didn't need a reason, maybe Jake provoked him." I stretched out my leg a little, then headed back towards the window.

We watched Tony disassemble the bike for what seemed like forever but was probably another hour. Just when it seemed there was nothing left to take apart, he stopped and reached into an odd shaped part.

He stood there for a moment or two, staring at something and turning it over in his hand. Whatever it was, it was small. I caught a glint of metal.

A key? Mike and I exchanged glances, then our attention returned to Tony, who had slipped whatever he'd found into the front pocket of his now very greasy jeans. In short order he had that bike back together and looking as if he'd never taken a wrench to it.

Mike was shaking his head in either disbelief or admiration. Maybe both. No wonder no-one had caught the switch of the bikes the night Jake was killed. Tony must have stolen Jake's bike, disassembled then reassembled it and returned it the same night, with no-one the wiser.

Or at least no-one would have been the wiser if I hadn't taken those pictures while he still had Jake's bike.

While Tony was finishing up, Mike and I hiked, very quietly, back to my car. When Tony rode the bike back out onto the quiet street, we were ready to follow him back to Jake's, where he left the bike. Retrieving it, he headed straight for West Van.

By then it was just past four a.m. Tony was probably set for the night, but I didn't intend to take any chances. Dropping Mike back at his car, I wished him good night without mentioning what I intended to do next. He'd been great, but he was a lawyer, not a P. I.

And I was used to working solo.

CHAPTER TWENTY-FOUR

A thick mist sat like a blanket on the nearby lawns, and gleamed gold as the sun rose. I blinked tired eyes and slammed the sun visor down, then yawned, stretched.

Good thing I hadn't been trying to sleep in the car, I had enough cricks in my neck and back just from sitting here all night. I just hoped Tony was an early riser.

It was a vain hope.

Tony finally reappeared at ten after ten. I'd already called Andrea and told her not to go home yet, and was half-dozing in the sun coming through the side window when he rode out the gate.

I had a hard time keeping up as he skillfully wove his bike in and out of the traffic flowing into the downtown core. Eventually he pulled up in front of the main branch of the Royal Bank on Georgia, squeezing the bike into a space between a gray Lexus and a blue and white SmartCar.

There was no space to fit my Civic. With my fingers crossed, I stashed my car in a lane and dashed back.

To find no sign of Tony. Pushing through the glass double doors, I did a fast scan, spotting the safety deposit area in a far corner. I caught a glimpse of Tony just being admitted.

So it had been a safety deposit box key. But how had Tony known which bank? And how had he got past their security? I had no answers, just more questions.

Now what? Before I could come up with anything creative, which always takes longer when I'm short on sleep, Tony re-emerged. I hid behind a pillar. As he strolled across the space between us, he had a look of satisfaction on his face that made me long to hit him.

Not very professional, I know, but my dislike for this arrogant punk was getting stronger by the minute.

I looked him up and down. He wasn't carrying anything. None of his pockets showed suspicious bulges. Either whatever had been in that box fit neatly and unobtrusively into a pocket, or he'd left it there.

Looking at that smug face and thinking about the arrogance he'd displayed so far, I was willing to bet that he'd left it where it was.

Just to be on the safe side, I followed him as he roared away from the bank. Keeping up was a challenge, but he rode straight home. That was enough for me. I needed a couple of hours of sleep, then I had some planning to do.

And some calls to make.

A scant four hours later, I was sitting at my kitchen table, half-heartedly drinking a cup of the strongest coffee I could make. The sleep had helped—I now felt mostly coherent. No closer to clearing Andrea, though.

I still had nothing Claire could use in court, and I figured my odds of getting Jerry and company to have a look in that safety deposit box were pretty bad.

I reached over and patted Cat in an absent way. He'd re-appeared this morning as if he'd never been gone, and he'd vanished the saucer of milk I'd poured him as if he was starving. Which he clearly wasn't.

I wondered how many gullible neighbors he'd convinced to feed him.

"So, what would you do, Cat?"

Cat blinked at me, then purred.

"Well, I'm glad someone thinks it'll work out. I'm not sure I do."

I poured another cup of coffee, stared at the streetscape four floors down without seeing anything much.

Maybe I had enough to convince Jerry they needed to take a closer look at Tony, but maybe wasn't good enough. Not given the mess Andrea was in. And I just wasn't ready to hand the case over just yet.

Not till I could prove that arrogant young thug had killed Jake. It had become personal. I didn't want to see Tony get away with murder, the way he'd seemingly got away with everything else in his life.

The question was, what next? Whatever was in that safety deposit box probably held a big part of the information I needed, but I had no way to get at it. Still, as long as Tony thought he was the only one who knew that information existed, he'd probably leave it there.

And I fully intended to get my hands on it before I was done.

Tony was the key. He'd led me to the safety deposit box. Where else could he lead me? To his father, perhaps?

The senior Rawlins remained the unknown factor. Were the two cases connected, or was it just coincidence and wishful thinking on my part?

I hadn't talked to Doug to see what he'd found out, and I'd never had that little chat with Nick, either. The latter seemed the more urgent. I picked up the phone.

"Markham here."

"Nick? It's Barbara."

"Barbara. How are you?"

"I'm great, thanks. Look, there are a couple of things I'd like to talk to you about. Are you free for coffee?"

"With you? Anytime. What about Beans?"

Normally I would have agreed, but I wanted this meeting on my turf, so I stretched the truth a little. "Actually, I'm waiting for an urgent call. Could we meet in my office?"

"That works for me. See you in twenty?"

"Make it half an hour."

Half an hour gave me just enough time to get to the office and put the coffee on. It was also long enough to get nervous about what I was going to say. As I sat down opposite Nick, I noticed the way his dark hair ruffled onto his brow.

Not now. I needed to focus on the matter at hand. Namely the real reason he was involved in the Forrester case.

Looking at that strong face, I considered my strategy, then decided honesty was the only thing that was likely to work.

"Look, Nick. I need your help, and I think maybe you need mine."

There was that wonderful grin again. I ignored it. "I'm beginning to think the murder of Jake Scott and the Forrester case are connected."

That got to him. Nick straightened in his chair, and something changed in his face.

"Problem is, I've done a little checking, and nobody's ever heard of an insurance investigator named Nick Markham. Special investigations, maybe, but not a P. I.."

I paused for a moment, then went for the line drive. "If we're going to share information, it has to be honest. So how about it?"

He eyed me in silence for a moment, then grinned. "I knew you were good. And I'm not even going to ask who your source was. I can't tell you who I'm working for, or what I'm working on, but where our information overlaps, I'll be as up front as I can."

I nodded, appreciating his candor. I already knew from what Jerry so carefully hadn't said that Nick was one of the good guys.

My standards aren't high. As long as he wasn't lying to me, I could work with him. And sharing information would probably benefit both of us.

"You've got a deal." I extended my hand.

He took it in a firm grasp, and we shook on it. I resolutely ignored the effect that simple action had on my libido. I wasn't ready to trust him as more than a work partner. Not yet, anyway.

"I won't ask what you're working on. But I'll guess it has to do with Forrester's death and that disaster at the mall. And that Kenneth Rawlins is tied in somewhere."

Nick started to say something but I held up a hand. I wasn't finished. "In addition to Crestlife Insurance, Rawlins owns the real estate development firm that Forrester's former partner now works for, as well as the insurance firm that Jake Scott used to work for. And I'm all but certain that Rawlins' son Tony, who runs a motorcycle repair business out of the family garage, is the one who killed Jake Scott."

Nick let out a low whistle.

"You're right that we're very interested in Kenneth Rawlins. But we're not paying much attention to his kid."

"Just his businesses."

He nodded. "Someone pointed us to the Forrester case, and it was looking good. But Rawlins is a past master at covering his tracks."

"Sounds to me like you need to find a weak link."

He looked at me and slowly raised an eyebrow. "Young Tony?"

"Yup. I think Jake was blackmailing Tony, and Tony killed him for it. But I still can't prove it was Tony rather than Andrea who killed Jake."

"So how are you connecting in Forrester?"

"I think Scott uncovered a connection between Rawlins senior, Forrester and the mall disaster. But you have to understand I'm running on gut instinct, here."

To his credit, Nick didn't even flinch at that one. "So in your scenario Tony killed Jake Scott to protect his father?"

"Something like that. It sounds far-fetched, especially given that I haven't been able to find the actual connection. But it's either that or a huge series of coincidences."

"I don't believe in coincidence."

"Neither do I."

"Okay, partner. What's next?"

"Next? I'm glad you asked. That's where you come in."

"You mean you had an ulterior motive in talking to me?" There was mock-horror in his tone.

I grinned at him. "Always."

"I'll keep that in mind."

"You do that. But in the meantime, here's what I have in mind."

And I filled him in on what I was planning to do, and what I wanted him to do. And somewhat to my surprise, he agreed.

———

IT WAS MOSTLY dark and the streetlights were making pools of light on my office floor by the time Nick rapped on my door. Judging by the number of bags he carried, he'd bought out the neighborhood deli. As he unpacked the food, the smell of spicy barbecued chicken made me realize I was starving.

I helped myself to potato salad and a couple of chicken wings, waving a wing in Nick's direction. "You start."

He grinned, probably at the enthusiasm with which I was attacking dinner. "I had a look at Tony Rawlins' record. This is confidential—we never had this conversation."

I nodded.

"From the time he was about twelve, Tony had a habit of taking things that belonged to other people. He started with electronic equipment, which seems to have fascinated him for a while. Then he moved up to motorcycles. He seemed to have a real knack for breaking and entering—he could get through just about any kind of lock."

That explained how he'd got into Jake's suite so quickly the previous night.

"In most cases, either Rawlins' lawyers got him off or the victim wouldn't prosecute, probably after some monetary persuasion. He was convicted once at seventeen but the sentence was suspended, since it was his first offense. First on record, anyway. Then he got smart."

"You're not telling me he went clean?"

"Nope. He just changed his act. We've got a pretty good idea what he's up to but there's been no proof. And he's small potatoes, not worth a lot of effort."

"You mean he was small potatoes."

"Good point. Murder is something new for our friend Tony."

"So what was he into?"

"Deals."

"Deals?"

"Tony put people together. The B and E artist with the guy who'd pay big for a particular item. The drug dealer with the money man."

"That punk?"

"Hey, that punk has good connections. And in his business it's the connections that count."

"True for most anything. Is he running with a gang?"

"Not that we've been able to determine. More like he's got contacts in all of the gangs, at least the big ones. He knows who to call."

"So what was Tony doing with Jake?"

"Tony dealt with the biker community a lot, and he seemed to have made a specialty of financial deals."

"Insurance?"

"Insurance indeed. Though Jake seems to have been legitimate, which is more than can be said for most of Tony's connections."

"And Jake had a lot of biker clients. Does that mean he had gang connections too?" It didn't matter to Andrea now that Jake was dead, but the thought gave me chills.

"Not that we've been able to find. Jake didn't show up on anyone's radar."

"Hang on a moment," I said, putting down my half-eaten roll as inspiration struck. I flipped on the computer and loaded Jake's spreadsheets. A search on motorcycles, sorted by location and last name, resulted in a four-page listing.

I printed it and passed it to Nick, who had watched me with interest while chewing on a chicken wing.

"Jake had quite a few biker clients, from all over the Lower Mainland," I said. "I haven't found anything they had in common, though. Aside from the motorcycles, that is."

"What are the columns off to the right?"

"Mostly they seem to relate to the type of coverage. MF is mutual fund, IS is insurance."

"And RF?"

"I haven't been able to decipher that one yet. I probably need to talk to someone who knows more about the insurance business than I do."

Looking over his shoulder, I ran my eye down the RF column. There were two letter designations against each name. "Hang on, there's a lot of repetition here. It wasn't obvious in the whole list of clients. AR keeps repeating, so do JS and DJ."

Nick had no problem following my thought process. "Initials. If AR is Anthony Rawlins, JS would be Jake Scott."

"And DJ would be Dave Jennings, who sells Harleys. Which means RF could mean referral."

"So Jake and Tony were doing business together. Can you see when these people became clients?"

I nodded.

"And sort it in date order, so we can tell how long Jake and Tony had been associated?"

"Sure," I said, and did so.

"It looks like about a year and a half," Nick said. "And Forrester was killed nearly a year ago."

"I'd like to know what Tony was getting out of this deal. He doesn't strike me as the type to do favors without getting something back. And if Jake was legit, then why was he worth Tony's time?"

"Good question. Were there payments made to Tony?"

"I already checked that. Nothing. Unless—what name does Tony's company operate under? "

"Try NorthWest Cycles," he said, after rustling through the papers he'd brought with him.

I loaded the appropriate spreadsheet, and searched the "Paid To" column.

"How did you know he had a company?" Nick asked.

"It seems like his style. If you're incorporated, it lessens your personal liability."

"Good point. Find anything?"

"Just a sec. Yeah, here we go. Well, how about that," I said, then deliberately didn't say anything else, just to get a reaction. I got one.

"What? What?" Nick asked, getting up and coming around behind me so he could see the screen.

"There." I pointed to the relevant columns. "He started paying a thousand a month to NorthWest Cycle Repair just after the date of the first referral, and it continued till six months ago. Then nothing."

"But the referrals continued."

"That's not all. Have a look at this." I brought up the file showing Jake's income statement.

"His income was fairly steady all along, except for this thirty thousand dollar payment. Which occurs the same month the payments to NorthWest Cycle stop."

"How did he afford the payments in the first place? Do you have his previous year's statement?"

"Sure," I said, loading it. "And what do you know? His income goes up substantially when he starts getting referrals from AR."

"No wonder he was happy to pay out a thousand a month."

"He may not have been all that happy about it. I'd guess he took the first opportunity he found to get out from under that payment. And to do a little squeezing of his own. Because look here. Now Northwest Cycle seems to be paying him a couple of thousand a month."

"Blackmail? Was that in character?" Nick asked.

"For Jake? Oh, I'd say so."

"It may not help us much, though. If you're right, it gives Tony a nice clear motive of his own, without dragging Rawlins senior into it at all."

"Depends what Jake found to blackmail Tony with. The timing's awfully close to the Forrester murder," I said, reaching for another roll. "But there's another factor we need to consider. Jake had been getting more and more unpredictable. He and Tony had at least one violent, and very public argument. They were at Fiasco's at the time, and another customer had to break them up."

"Mmmm." Nick thought about that while he chewed on another wing. Between us, we were doing a good job of demolishing the food he'd brought. "So there was something personal between them?"

"It sounds as though it had become personal, anyway. Not that Tony strikes me as a particularly cool customer, but I somehow don't see him as a public brawler. Too arrogant."

"And Jake?"

"In the last six months or so, Jake had taken to brawling with everyone. Andrea was afraid of him, and lodged a complaint. So he lodged a complaint against her, which is one of the reasons she's been charged with killing him."

"Aside from the fact that she was found standing over the body holding the murder weapon," Nick said.

"Well, aside from that, of course. It wasn't just Andrea, though. Everyone Jake dealt with socially seems to have noticed the change in his personality."

"Huh. Jake's personality changes, and he starts blackmailing Tony instead of paying him." He ate an olive. "These are good."

I tried one. They were.

"Wonder if Jake's judgement was off. Blackmailing Tony wasn't the smartest thing he could have done."

"Not given what you've told me about Tony's connections. Did you dig up anything at all on Jake?"

"Nope. As I said, he seemed to be completely legit. As far as our records go, anyway."

"Mmmm. I checked with the insurance regulators too. No complaints that they were aware of, either. What about the companies? Breyers Insurance, Crestlife Insurance, Tony's shop?"

"Nothing on any of them."

"And I can't ask why you're so interested in Kenneth Rawlins, huh?"

"Nope."

"Damn. I was afraid of that," I said with a grin. "Can you give me the real scoop on Forrester's life insurance, then?"

"That I can do. He'd taken out a three million dollar policy a couple of months before he died, and his kid's the beneficiary. The insurance company's refusing to pay out on a suicide."

"So far, that matches what Chris told me. What about the mother?"

"Forrester's widow? No provision. But the house and some stocks and stuff were all in her name, so those weren't affected by his death. Still, I gather she's had a pretty tough time of it, and the insurance money is needed to pay for Chris's education."

"That's interesting."

"What?"

"That's the part that doesn't match Chris's story. He claimed that his mother and father never married, that he'd only got to know Forrester recently. Now why would he do that?"

Nick shrugged. "With a kid like Chris, who can say? Sounds like a coping mechanism of some kind. Has to be tough, having your father die like that and everyone saying it was suicide."

"Yeah, but I get the feeling there's more to it than that. He's up to something."

"Could have been a sympathy ploy, to make sure you took the case."

Personally, I doubted it. I had a feeling Chris was more complicated than that. "Anything else on Forrester? Debts? Gambling? Drugs? Women?"

"Nope. Aside from that building collapse, he seemed to have led an absolutely straight and narrow life."

"What about his partner? Walters. Any idea why he didn't have a financial liability in the mall collapse? "

"Cliff Walters has a history of gambling, and a tendency to run up some pretty impressive debts, but that's all we've got on him. As to the partnership, I don't know why it was structured that way. You'd have to ask a lawyer."

I made a mental note to talk to Mike about it, then grinned at Nick. "Well, I guess it's up to me then, as you don't seem to have come up with much."

Nick nearly choked on his chicken wing.

I kept my face bland. "I checked on a few connections. Walters has a history of working for companies that Rawlins has a controlling interest in. Except for once, when he took a job with Forrester."

"Huh. Wonder why Forrester took him on."

I shrugged. "Who knows? Anyway, building projects that Rawlins' company develops apparently have a reputation for coming in on time and under budget. They also tend to be insured through Crestlife insurance."

He nodded. "They do indeed."

"Given the mall collapse and young Tony's rather extreme reaction to Jake's blackmail efforts, I started wondering what Rawlins Senior had to hide. It certainly suggests some interesting possibilities, don't you think?"

"Like questionable building practices and a whole network of contractors and inspectors willing to look the other way. At all levels." He seemed to have lost interest in the half-eaten chicken wing he was holding.

Bingo. "That's what I figured. It would also be worth an awful lot of money, which would be at risk if someone was about to blow the whistle on it."

"Forrester." It was a statement.

"Again, it seems to fit the facts. But we've still got nothing concrete. We don't even know if Forrester was murdered. But does this all it fit with whatever angle you're pursuing?"

He nodded thoughtfully. "Quite nicely. And it may open up a couple of possibilities."

"What are you thinking?"

"Jake Scott."

"He seems to be the link. But quite frankly, I've come to a dead end there. Literally."

Nick groaned.

"Sorry, I couldn't resist. What did you have in mind?"

"Searching his records," Nick said.

"I've got most of them here. Other than our friend Tony, there doesn't seem to be mention of anyone else connected to this thing, not Forrester or Kenneth Rawlins or Crestlife Insurance."

"What about looking at any clients he might have dealt with around the time he quit paying Tony?"

That was an angle I hadn't thought of. "It's worth a try."

I ran the relevant printouts. We spent the hour going through them, in laborious detail. Finally Nick found the key we'd been looking for.

"Well, hello Angela Walters."

"As in Cliff Walters' wife?"

"I'm guessing so. Jeremy and Jessica Walters are the beneficiaries."

"Sounds like the kids. What's the address?" I asked, reaching for the phone book. He read it to me, and when I found the listing for Cliff Walters, I was elated to see that they were the same.

"Bingo."

"Finally. I think we should pay Mrs. Walters a visit."

"Good plan." I glanced at my watch. "But not tonight. Do you realize it's past midnight?"

"Time flies when you're having fun," Nick said, standing up and stretching his long frame.

I tried not to stare at the sight of all that muscle moving under the skin.

"But I guess we'd better call it a night. How about we pay an impromptu visit in the morning, say about nine?"

"Nick, it's Saturday."

"Ah. Nine-thirty then?"

"Make it ten and you've got a deal." I planned on sleeping in.

"Great. I'll pick you up. Here?"

I nodded. We cleared up the mess and left. When I got home, I did a hasty wash and brush and fell into bed.

I couldn't sleep. Despite the hour and my exhaustion from the previous night, I tossed and turned. Finally I got up, poured myself a glass of Merlot and watched the traffic go by.

I couldn't get Tony Rawlins out of my mind. I had the nagging sense that I was overlooking something important. I just didn't know what.

Thinking about it didn't help, but I couldn't seem to turn my mind off. I paced for a bit, then sat down and made lists: everything I knew about Tony, everything I knew about his father—everything I knew about Jake's business. Just as I was deciding I knew too little, Cat plopped himself down on my foot.

"And just where did you come from?"

Cat purred.

"One of these days I'm going to figure out how you get in."

Cat rubbed his head against my leg and purred loudly.

"You're right. I'm too tired to think straight."

I went back to bed, Cat a warm, noisy lump on my feet. I had no trouble falling asleep, but my dreams were of painting endless copies of Klimt's "The Kiss".

CHAPTER TWENTY-FIVE

On Saturday, the buzz of the alarm woke me far too early. I rolled over, trying to ignore it, but the noise was insistent. Getting up I felt like I was wandering around in a fog.

I needed to run. I didn't want to run, but I needed to. So I went, muscles protesting with every step.

By ten I was feeling ready for just about anything, despite my lack of sleep. Judging by Nick's expression, so was he.

At his insistence, he drove to the address we had for Angela Walters, an old, stone home on a tree lined street, located on the west side of town. It wasn't quite Shaughnessy, but it was close.

The woman who answered the door was in her mid-thirties, blond and pretty, with a helpless air about her. She was wearing fluttery pastels, which should have looked ridiculous, but somehow didn't. By unspoken agreement, Nick took the lead, smiling that charming smile at her.

"Mrs. Walters?" She nodded. "Good morning, ma'am. We're from the Breyers Insurance Company, and we'd like to talk to you about your policy."

"Oh," she said. "But I deal with Jake Scott at Breyers."

We exchanged glances. Didn't this woman read the paper?

"I'm very sorry to have to tell you this," Nick said with what sounded like real concern in his voice. "Jake Scott is dead. He was murdered just over a week ago. That's why we're here, you see."

Angela Walters turned even paler. I wouldn't have thought it possible.

"May we come in, Mrs. Walters?" Nick said. "You look like you should be sitting down."

"Oh, I'm sorry. It was a shock. Yes, please, come in." She stood back to allow us entrance, then preceded us into an over-decorated living room in shades of cream and gray. "Would you like some coffee?"

"No, thank you. Please, just sit down for a moment," Nick said before I could, which was unfortunate. I could have used a coffee.

Still, he had a point. Angela Walters didn't look like she had the strength to hold a coffee cup, much less make and serve the coffee.

"Pardon me, ma'am, but did you know Mr. Scott well?"

The question seemed to draw her out of a fog. "Oh. Oh, I'm sorry. No, not well. I met him at my health club, Hercules, in Yaletown? He was so sincere, and so interested in finances, and in such good shape."

Nick and I exchanged glances. That particular health club was the local hangout of the Beautiful People, more concerned about muscle definition and the perfect tan than about fitness. Looking at Angela, I could easily picture her there, but Jake?

Granted, the few times I'd seen him he'd been wearing grungy, oversized sweatshirts and jeans, though he had filled out the latter nicely. From Angela's tone, she was talking about more than the state of his muscles. There was a definite heat there.

Nick was thinking along the same lines. "Did you see Mr. Scott often?"

"Well, he was at the club two or three mornings a week, and occasionally we'd go for coffee. When he was talking to me about money, we went to his place where we could have the conversation in private..."

Her voice trailed off.

I was mentally picturing Jake's place as I'd last seen it. If he'd brought this woman there, it hadn't been for business purposes. One look at the mess he lived in, not to mention the files in the fish tank, would have sent a prospective business client running.

But I couldn't imagine a romantic liaison in that atmosphere, either. Had she been too enthralled by Jake to care?

"About your investments, Mrs. Walters," I said before she could start getting cautious about what she was saying. "Will you be wanting to increase them in the coming year?"

"Oh, I don't think so," she said breathlessly. "Cliff just had that one lump sum, you know. We aren't expecting any more."

I very carefully didn't look at Nick. "And you invested that money with Mr. Scott?"

"Oh, yes. Jake was very good about it—he made sure the money was invested safely. It's our nest egg, you know, it's important it be safe."

"I understand." Nick's voice was smooth. "Your investments will be secure. Now, Mrs. Walters, Head Office is very concerned when one of our people is murdered. Did Mr. Scott ever say anything about someone threatening him, or about being afraid?"

"Oh, not Jake," she said with some pride in her tone. "Jake could take care of himself. He was very strong, you know."

"Mr. Scott was shot, ma'am," Nick said.

That went right over her head. "Jake did talk about someone he was angry with. He was going to get even with him, or something. I'm afraid I didn't really listen," she said with a tiny laugh.

"Do you remember a name, ma'am?" I asked. "Anything at all?"

Anyone else would have wondered about supposed insurance agents asking such questions, but not Angela Walters. "I'm really not good with names. Jake talked about so many people, I couldn't keep it all straight. I'm sorry."

"Well, thank you for your time, ma'am," Nick said, before I could say something rash. "And we're sorry we had to bring such bad news. We'll be in touch about your investments."

She thanked him, and ushered us both to the door, fluttering with every step. I waited till we were back in the car before giving breath to my feelings.

"That is either the dimmest woman I've ever met, or she's a terrific actress."

Nick chuckled. We drove in silence for several blocks.

"We can check some of it," he said suddenly. "We know when she began investing, but we didn't check the amounts, and the frequency. And if she was making a habit of spending time at his apartment, someone would have noticed them coming and going."

"If she really is that ingenuous," I said, choosing the kindest word I could think of, "I think we've got a pretty good idea how Jake got interested in the Forrester situation."

"It's hard to imagine her husband telling her much about his business."

"Unless he couldn't resist talking about the deal he'd pulled off? And he figured she wasn't swift enough to do any damage."

"Then why let her invest the money?"

"I'd be amazed if Cliff Walters didn't meet with Jake at least once to set up that investment, and just put it in her name."

"Makes sense. And we can probably assume that Angela told Jake enough to put him onto the Forrester situation. Look at how much she told us, and we just showed up at her door."

"There is that. I'd still love to know why she told him, but it's probably irrelevant. Look, why don't we check out the neighbors, see if anybody remembers seeing Angela. We can always go through Jake's records again later, see what we can find out about the Walters' investments with him."

Nick agreed, and it proved to be a very profitable afternoon. I already knew from Andrea's scathing comments on more than one occasion that Jake's elderly neighbor across the street, a Mrs. Jacobs, was a bit of a busybody. And I thought I remembered Andrea mentioning her, too. It seemed like a good place to start.

And it was.

Mrs. Jacobs ushered us into her sunny yellow kitchen, insisted on making us each a cup of very strong tea. She was more than pleased to cooperate, and she proved to be a mine of information. She hadn't seen anything the night of the murder.

"I'm in bed long before that," she said. She had definitely noticed Angela with Jake though.

"Every Tuesday and Thursday afternoon," she informed us with pride and a hint of envy. "Regular, they were."

Nick and I exchanged glances. Maybe the mess in Jake's suite wasn't typical—had Tony searched the place before he'd stolen the bike the first time? And Mrs. Jacobs wasn't finished.

"They weren't the only ones. There was a whole group of them, all women, came every Wednesday. I asked him once. He said it was an investment seminar." She paused, and grinned slyly. "Seminar, hah. I wasn't born yesterday."

Nick solemnly agreed with her that indeed she hadn't been born yesterday, and thanked her for the information. We beat a hasty retreat. Good thing, because I couldn't have kept a straight face much longer.

Back in the car, I glanced sideways at Nick. "Well, I guess that confirms it. Angela Walters really did know Jake."

He cracked up. It was infectious. I started to chuckle.

"I don't know about you, but now I really want to have another look at those investment records."

———

BACK AT MY office I turned on the computer, then the coffee pot. While we waited for the two machines to do their thing, Nick imitated Mrs. Jacobs' probable reaction to us.

"Working together, huh," he sniffed, catching her intonations exactly. "Call it what you will, I wasn't born yesterday."

When I stopped laughing, I went and loaded the spreadsheet. Nick got the coffee. I sipped absently, then realized he'd got mine exactly right without even asking. The man noticed things. It was unsettling.

Angela Walters had placed two hundred and fifty thousand

dollars with Jake, followed by another two hundred and fifty thousand two months later. Beyond that, there was only the regular investments of fifty dollars every week.

"There's a note against these that isn't against the larger amount," I pointed out to Nick. "See this WS? Wonder if that's the Wednesday seminar he explained to Mrs. Jacobs?"

As I spoke, I did a search on the records, requesting a subset of only those records with the WS notation. There were about ten of them, all women. In each case, there seemed to be weekly deposits of fifty or a hundred dollars over a period of six to eight months.

"Let's see where these are going."

I pulled up another spreadsheet, checking the investors against the investments. Both the initial and the final two hundred and fifty thousand dollar amounts from the Walters had been divided amongst three mutual funds.

"Those three have been around for a while," Nick said. "They have fairly high management fees, but they're stable and have a reputation for good money management. Looks like Jake invested conscientiously for the Walters."

On Angela Walter's subsequent investments, and those of the other ladies with the WS notation, there was a long list of funds, some repeating, some not. I printed the list and passed it to Nick. He studied it in silence for several moments.

"This is a pretty speculative group. There's small caps, international funds, a little of everything. It looks like it was an investment group, speculating in different segments of the mutual fund market, of all things."

At my inquiring look, he explained, "Mutual funds are designed to spread the risk of individual investments. They're usually the investment vehicle of choice of those who are risk averse, because while they don't have the volatility of individual stocks, they tend to have a poorer return, certainly over the short term. Investment clubs would normally invest in stocks, because it's a way of diversifying into several stocks, of spreading the risk. Mutual funds are supposed to have already done that."

"So what was Jake up to?"

Nick looked at the list again and shook his head.

"Who knows? Could be a social group. Maybe that's how he found clients or set up affairs. Then again, maybe he was just dense about how the market works."

I wondered about Nick's background. He seemed to be very attuned to the market himself.

"Maybe Jake was really sold on the concept of mutual funds." I was thinking of my conversation with Earl. "I met one of Jake's clients, a very unlikely investor, who rhapsodized about the magic of mutual funds. Either Jake was a complete con-man, or he believed it himself."

Nick looked at the list again, shaking his head. "This is just strange. And it doesn't seem to be getting us closer to Rawlins. Either of them."

"Okay," I said, waving my half-full mug at Nick. "Suppose Jake was the ultimate con man. Smooth enough to convince all kinds of people to invest in mutual funds, smooth enough to make a stable living in a very unstable field. Suppose he finds out about Forrester. He already knows Tony Rawlins, in fact is in business with him. What's a man like that going to do with the information?"

Nick took a thoughtful sip of his coffee. Over his shoulder the lights of the city glowed warm through a thickening mist. "A real con man is going to take it as far as he can. Blackmail, maybe. And he'll use whatever or whoever he sees as the weakest link."

"So if we assume Jake was a con man, and saw Tony as the weakest link, a couple of the pieces fall into place."

"The payments that Jake suddenly wasn't making. The influx of cash. Tony stealing Jake's bike even makes sense, if Jake had tangible evidence that Forrester's death was not an accident."

"Or if he said he had."

Nick acknowledged my point with a lifted eyebrow.

"What I really want to know," I said. "Is why Jake's personality seemed to change so suddenly. He had his neighbors afraid of him, and Andrea terrified. Was it the stress of blackmailing Tony that caused the personality change, or did his personality change cause him to lose control of that situation? "

"Could be either. But if his business relied on his ability to manipulate people, and if the rages you've told me about were real, they must have played havoc with his ability to make deals."

"So maybe the deal with Tony got out of control?"

"If you call winding up dead out of control."

"I'd be tempted to call it that," I said, straight faced. "But, Nick, we've got a lot of speculation and no proof."

"True. But we do have connections now between Jake and all the major players."

"Except Chris," I added in an attempt at humor.

Nick looked thoughtful.

"Except Chris. Look, Barbara, I've been discounting Chris and what he might know. But when you think about it, why is he so convinced Forrester was murdered?"

"Well, if the alternative is believing your Dad committed suicide, I think I'd be convinced too."

"Yeah, but Chris doesn't strike me as the self-delusional type. Too smart, too self-aware."

"So what d'you suppose he knows?"

Nick just shook his head. Personally, I was inclined to think he was grasping at straws, but who knows.

"Wait a minute," I said, grabbing Nick's arm. "Nick, that's it. Who knows?"

I have to give the man credit for not shaking me off. I must have sounded demented. "Who knows what?" he asked calmly.

"Who knows—whatever it is that got Jake killed. Look, if this thing is about Forrester's death, then we have a lot of people suspecting something was wrong. But who actually knew anything concrete? Even if it isn't about Forrester, the question is the same."

Nick was looking thoughtful again. "If Jake learned something dangerous, who else had that knowledge?"

"That's it. But it's more than that. Who knew that he had the knowledge, and knew that it was dangerous to them?"

"So... Angela Walters might have suspected Jake had learned something, but not what it meant."

"And I have to wonder how much Tony actually knew. I mean, if you were Kenneth Rawlins, how much would you tell a kid like Tony?"

"Which makes me wonder about Chris. What he actually knows, and what he's just guessing."

"And what Jake actually found out. And how?" I added.

"We probably know what started him off. Angela and her half million dollar deposits."

"And her talk of it being one-time, a nest egg."

"Say Jake was intrigued, where would he go from there?"

"Start looking into Walters' background, maybe."

"And the trail led straight to Forrester," he said.

"And to Kenneth Rawlins, if he checked ownership on some of the companies involved."

"Which leaves us exactly where?"

"Well, it leaves me wondering if Kenneth Rawlins knew about Jake's little discovery, or if Tony kept it quiet."

"He kept it quiet all right. Permanently."

"You don't think Rawlins himself knew?"

"I think it would have been handled rather differently if he had. Which makes me wonder exactly how much Tony actually knows, and how much he's guessing."

I shrugged. "I think we're back to the facts on the Forrester death."

"There aren't enough facts to tell any kind of story. And I dug pretty deeply."

Looking at the frustration on his face, I believed him. But then how had Jake found out? Or had he?

"What if Jake didn't have the facts? If he was a con man, and especially if Tony didn't have the whole story, maybe Jake was blackmailing Tony with non-existent evidence."

"Do you really think Jake was that stupid?"

"Well, we already know something was wrong with his judgment on a personal level. Why not in this too? After all, it seems to have worked, for a while."

"You've got a point," he said. "Okay, suppose you're right. What's in that safety deposit box?"

I shook my head in disgust. "That's where my theories fall apart. I don't know. All I can suggest is that it's time we had another chat with Chris. Maybe whatever made him suspicious will help us. Besides, it's past time that young man came clean with me."

CHAPTER TWENTY-SIX

Chris lived with his mother, in a fifties era white stuccoed house on the East side. Mrs. Forrester was a nice woman. She was horrified to find out Chris had hired me.

Dark and thin, she had a harassed air, as if the details of life were too much for her. Or maybe it was her son that was too much for her. Still, the rich textures and warm reds and browns in her living room suggested there was fire there, somewhere. I was glad, for Chris' sake.

"That boy," she was saying, shaking her head. "His dad's death was so hard on him. He's been in denial ever since."

She attempted a smile. "I took him to a couple of therapists, and they said they could help him, but that he needed months, if not years of treatment. It would have been tough on just one salary," she made a half gesture with hands that were rough and too thin, "but if it would help him, I'd have found a way. Except he refused. Said he didn't need it. Said they were fools."

She met my eyes. "But I'm very sorry he's been wasting your time."

She paused and cleared her throat. "He's a good kid, really. I sometimes think maybe he's too imaginative for his own good. He's dreamed up this idea that Jim, that his dad didn't kill himself. And he just won't let it go."

"We think Chris may be right, Mrs. Forrester," I said. "It's possible your husband was murdered."

Beside me, Nick made a half-movement, as though to interfere, but stopped himself.

"Murdered?" It was a horrified gasp.

"It's still just a possibility at this point, Mrs. Forrester. But yes, it is possible. And that's why we need to speak to Chris. Unless you have some idea why he thinks his father might have been murdered?"

She shook her head. "No, he just came up with the statement one day. I assumed it was his way of trying to accept the unacceptable. It never occurred to me he might be right. And then, Mr. Rawlins was so understanding."

She stopped short.

"Mr. Rawlins?" I prompted. "Mr. Kenneth Rawlins?"

"I wasn't supposed to mention that. I suppose he doesn't like his charitable acts known. But he was so kind to us, to me, after—after the funeral. And the money—he didn't have to do that."

"How much money are we talking about, Mrs. Forrester?"

It was the wrong question.

"I don't see that it's any of your business, Ms. O'Grady," she began frostily, then hesitated. "Unless—what kind of money did Chris promise you?"

"Don't worry about that, Mrs. Forrester."

But I could see she was the type of woman who would worry. "He promised me a percentage of the insurance money, if I proved your husband was murdered. He was supposed to have got your signature on the contract."

She nodded, the fine lines in her brow and around her eyes suddenly in evidence. "He's been copying my signature since he was eight years old."

She gave a strained half-laugh. "He signs my name better than I do. And the money from the policy would go to him. But they'll never pay out. You do know that?" Worried still.

"I'm aware of the conditions of the policy, Mrs. Forrester. And I wasn't worried about the money. I just couldn't turn your son down."

She smiled, then. "He does have that effect on people. Which makes it even harder. But I'm being so rude. I haven't even offered you coffee. Would you like some?"

"It's urgent we speak to Chris," Nick said.

"Oh, of course. I'm sorry. He's—well, he should be at the park. That's where he said he was going, and he did take his basketball."

"The park?" I asked.

She waved her hand in a generally southward direction. "Over on 33rd. You can't miss it. Three blocks over, then two up. He should be on the courts."

I looked at Nick, who nodded. Thanking Mrs. Forrester, we left more quickly than was strictly polite.

I felt very sorry for her, for the situation she'd found herself in, and for the difficulties of dealing with a kid as bright and independent as Chris. But there was nothing I could say that wouldn't have sounded condescending.

Once we were back in the car, I looked at Nick. "Rawlins again."

He nodded. "That one I didn't expect. He must have given her cash, because it didn't show up on the records I looked at."

"Interesting."

"Yeah."

By then we'd reached the park. "What are the odds we'll find Chris here?" he asked.

"Not good would be my guess."

"Mine too."

We were both silent as he parked, then together we headed for the basketball courts on the far side. There were four or five kids playing there, all looking to be about Chris's age. Our approach didn't interest them in the slightest.

"There he is," I said, to my surprise spotting that familiar pale head. "In the red T-shirt."

"Got him." And without warning he bellowed, "Chris."

I hadn't heard that tone from him before. It was enough to stop the game dead, and to bring Chris to us at a run.

Impressed, I made a mental note to get him to show me how he achieved that volume and tone. Anything that effective was worth learning.

Chris didn't look surprised to see us, or that I'd been able to find him. His expression stayed open and friendly, and his eyes met mine evenly. He'd make a great poker player some day. It was hard to remember this kid was just twelve.

"Hi, Barbara. Hi, Mr. Markham." Even his voice was calm. "Whadda you guys want? I'm kinda in the middle of a game."

"I thought you wanted to prove your father was murdered."

He looked at me sharply, then nodded once. "Okay. I'll be back in a minute," he said and raced back to his group. He stood with them for a moment, seemingly explaining the situation, then ran back.

"Let's go."

I gestured towards a group of benches on the far side of the park, and we began to walk across the grass. When we got there, Nick and I sat on one of the benches. Chris dropped to the grass at our feet.

"Chris, we're close to proving your father was murdered, and we need you to level with us."

He gave us an innocent look. "I've told you what I know."

That was my cue. "Chris, you hired me to find your father's killer. But you've lied to me right down the line. Unless you come clean, I'm off this case. It's that simple."

Suddenly he looked like a twelve year-old. "But you can't. I hired you."

"I can. It's one of the basics of the business—if your client isn't straight with you, you ditch the case." Which wasn't strictly true, or I'd have no business at all, but he didn't need to know that.

Chris thought about that one for a minute. Whatever he knew, he really didn't want to share it. I waited impatiently for him to make his decision. Nick wisely stayed out of it.

"Okay," Chris said finally. "I'll tell you. It was that Rawlins character."

"Kenneth Rawlins?" I asked, barely managing to keep the surprise out of my tone.

"Yeah, that's him. The snake. After Dad died, he kept nosing around Mom. Offering help, money, whatever."

Chris looked down, seemingly intent on digging one sneakered toe into the grass. "She couldn't see through him, but I could. What a faker," he burst out.

"What was fake about him?"

"Everything. He pretended to like me, but I could tell he didn't, really. And everything he said about my Dad, well, there was a tone under it, you know?"

I did know. "So what made you think your Dad was murdered?"

"Suicide—well, it just wasn't like Dad. He'd never take the coward's way out, never leave Mom and me like that. I knew that. But I couldn't seem to think my way around it, cause nothing made any sense. Till he showed up." There was venom in his voice.

"Rawlins?"

Chris nodded. "He said he'd gone to school with Dad, university, you know? He said that's why he was helping Mom. But he didn't mean it. I could tell, even if Mom couldn't. And it wasn't like they'd worked together or anything. So I figured there had to be some-thing else."

"And?"

He shrugged, very offhand.

"And I went looking for it."

"And?"

"And that's why I hired you."

"I said come clean, Chris. And I meant it."

He was suddenly very interested in the patch of grass he'd been demolishing. Two could play that game. I waited.

"I knew Dad'd been working on something just before he died.

To prove his innocence. He told me so. I figured whatever it was, it would be at his office. So I snuck into my Dad's office," he finished quickly, then went back to his demolition.

"How—never mind that. What did you find?" I asked, focusing on the essentials. When he didn't respond, I let him hear just how pissed off I was getting at his games. "Chris."

"Nothing. Not there. His files had been pretty cleaned out."

Nick and I exchanged a look.

"When was this, Chris?"

"Day after the funeral. Somebody wasn't wasting any time."

I could only agree with him.

"But I figured my Dad was too smart to leave stuff where anybody could find it. So I went to his gym."

"His gym?"

Chris nodded. "He used to work out every day after work. Said it relaxed him. He even had a special arrangement, had a permanent locker and everything."

"Which gym?" I asked, half expecting the answer.

"Hercules Gym, in Yaletown. Why?"

I exchanged a glance with Nick. It was the same gym Jake had used. "It's not important. So, did you find anything in his locker?"

"I found a file—well, some notes, actually. About the mall." He darted a quick look at me.

I nodded.

Ducking his head, Chris said, "I was just looking, but I thought I heard someone coming. So I grabbed the notes and got out of there."

"Why didn't you tell me this before?"

"Because I don't have the notes any more," he said in a rush. "And I didn't think you'd believe me."

He lifted his head to face me fully, and now his emotions were clearly printed on his face.

"I'm just a twelve year old kid," he said, mimicking someone else's pedantic tone. "What do I know? I'm disturbed, not myself. You can't trust anything I say."

He broke off, and dug up some more of the park. "How could I tell you?" he asked, and I had to lean forward to hear him.

"Well, let's start with the assumption that I believe you," I said, not wanting him to hear the pity I was feeling. "What was in the notes, and why don't you have them any more?"

"The notes were a record of construction deficiencies, and the dates he'd reported them to the contractor. And some official forms stating that they'd been fixed. And I don't have them any more because Rawlins stole them."

———

THE WORLD SEEMED to narrow to the three of us. The sun on our backs hadn't taken the chill from the air, and the leaves on the chestnut trees were yellowing. Yells from the basketball court drifted across the grass, distant and unimportant. I watched Chris's face closely.

"Do you have any proof that Kenneth Rawlins stole your Dad's notes?" I asked him.

He shook his head, his expression resentful. "But who else could it have been? They were in my desk, in my room. No-one goes there. And right after they disappeared, he convinced my mom to take me to a shrink. The shock of my Dad's death, you know," he said with heavy sarcasm.

"Let me guess. The shrink is the one who decided you were disturbed, not yourself? And that you were making things up?"

He nodded.

"Assuming it was Rawlins who took the notes, how could he know you had them?"

"I think somebody saw me leaving Dad's office. Probably Walters," Chris said. His tone was peevish, as though he'd expected to slip in and out invisibly. I bit back a laugh and avoided looking in Nick's direction. The worst thing I could do right now was to belittle Chris's experience.

"Did it look like your Dad had sent this information to anyone else?" Nick asked him.

Chris looked thoughtful for a moment. "No," he said. "It seemed to be just notes to himself. Scribbled, you know. And his writing was always pretty hard to read. He used to get everything typed. We joked about it," he said in a rush, then swallowed hard.

I looked away quickly to hide my sympathy.

"I could read it, though. It was kind of a game, to see how much of his writing I could figure out. I got really good at it. So I could read the notes. Anybody else would probably have trouble with them."

"What about your Mom?" Nick again.

"She had trouble with Dad's writing. I doubt she could read these."

We talked a little longer, but there didn't seem to be anything more that Chris could tell us. As Chris ran back to join his friends, I leaned over towards Nick. "Time to check out that health club."

He nodded, but his expression was abstracted. "You go ahead. There's something I want to look into."

"Something Chris said?"

"No, something he reminded me of."

I pressed, but he didn't explain, just said he'd call me later and we'd compare notes. Fine, then. I headed for the Hercules Gym.

I pretended an interest in joining the gym, and they were only too happy to tell me all the details. Including that private lockers, located in a more secure area of the women's change room, were available for an additional fee. And my husband could rent similar lockers on the men's side.

It seemed odd to me that Forrester had left his papers in a gym locker. If he really had—I only had Chris's word for that. I casually brought up Forrester's name, but Brant, the assistant manager—a muscled kid with a great tan and a wide smile—hadn't known him. He'd known Jake, though.

"Great guy. Just great," he said. "Haven't seen him around for a while, though."

"Jake's dead."

I'd never seen anyone go so white under such a dark tan. He looked ghastly. "Was it the 'roids?" he croaked out, fear overruling caution.

Jake was on steroids? Now that was a factor I'd never considered. One that could definitely explain his increasing rages, his paranoia. I shrugged, watching Brant's face closely.

"I heard he was shot. But it sounded like he'd picked a fight with someone. And lost."

Brant looked relieved.

"Oh, if he was shot..." He tailed off, perhaps realizing how bad that sounded. "I mean, it's a real shame. Like I said, Jake was a great guy."

"Did he have any enemies here?"

"Jake?" Brant looked shocked again. If he was lying, he was a great actor. "No, like I said, he was a great guy. Everybody liked him."

"Had he been using steroids long?"

"Hey, I don't know for sure he was using. I mean, with his build, he probably was, but, like, I can't really say. He was an outgoing dude, you know? Like, he knew lots of people."

"Any idea who his source was?"

From the consternation on Brant's face, he himself had been Jake's source. But if that were true, there was no way he was going to admit it.

I listened to his verbal tap-dancing for a minute or two, then gave up.

"He was a great guy" seemed to be the depth of Brant's insight into what made other people tick. I mentally shook my head, hoping I'd never need to use him as a character witness. Thanking him, I made my escape.

It was getting late, so I headed back to my place and threw a frozen bacon and mushroom pizza in the microwave. As soon as I opened the fridge, Cat was weaving around my ankles and complaining about the day he'd had.

"You don't know the half of it, Cat," I told him as I put down a saucer of milk for him. "And with the week I've been having, there's not much to eat, either."

Cat didn't seem to care. His head went nearly into the dish and he was lapping the milk as fast as he could, that incongruously pink tongue flickering back and forth.

Watching him, waiting for my dinner to ding, my mind went to the case. I felt like I was one piece of information away from tying this whole thing together and clearing Andrea.

I just wished I knew what that piece was.

When the phone rang I nearly jumped out of my skin. I grabbed for it, hoping it would be Nick. It was. He was just around the corner from my place, he'd seen my lights, and could he come up?

"How do you know where I live?"

"I know many things," he replied in a deep, mysterious voice.

I could have done without the phony accent and told him so.

He laughed. A warm, deep laugh that sent quivers up my spine. I was in trouble.

"You can come up. But only if you promise to be good." And I emphasized each word, using everything I'd learned from watching the sirens in old movies from the 40's and 50's. He laughed again.

"I'm in trouble now," he said, and rang off.

"Damn," I said, staring at the dead receiver. "And I still don't know what he was checking on."

Five minutes later I did know. The coffee I'd put on hadn't even dripped through when Nick arrived at my door with a big grin and a bottle of Burrowing Owl Cabernet. I checked the year, and nearly dropped the bottle. Expensive, and hard to find. But worth the effort.

Accepting the wine from him, I found myself returning his grin without intending to. He was in big trouble.

Or maybe that was me. I headed for the kitchen.

"And who is this?"

I turned to see Nick regarding Cat, who now lay in the middle of the hall.

"That's Cat. I was just about to throw him out," I said, digging around in the middle drawer for the corkscrew.

"Cat?"

"He's not mine. He belongs to a neighbor," I said, jerking the cork out of the bottle of wine.

Nick looked from Cat's contented sprawl to the empty saucer. "I see," he said, bending to stroke Cat, who purred loudly.

I didn't think I wanted to know what he thought he saw. "So what's the scoop?"

"When Chris mentioned deficiencies, I started to wonder if a check had been done on the copies that are kept of all the inspection reports on a building, as well as the various plans, especially the final plans and the original plans. When there's a problem with a building, a comparison is supposed to be done to verify that all the versions match."

"Supposed to be?" I said, handing him a glass of wine.

"You are quick. Yeah, in this case it either never got done, or it got 'lost'. So I asked for another check, and I asked them to check the final drawings against the original architect's plans, if they could find them."

"And?"

"And we've got major inconsistencies. They don't show up when you compare various versions of the builder's plans—the differences there are minor. But when you compare Forrester's original architectural specs against the final building plans, there are huge differences."

"What happened?"

"As best we can tell, there must have been a second, redrawn set of architectural drawings that all subsequent engineer's plans were based on. And those plans cut too many corners. They weren't structurally sound. We're talking fraud, and a lot of people involved. Bribes and payoffs at all levels."

"How?"

"It looks as if Forrester's original drawings were presented to the money people..."

"Rawlins?"

"Yup. We've verified that Rawlins was the money behind the project. So those original architectural drawings were approved and then sent in for building permits. Then a second set of architectural drawings must have been done by someone else."

"Leaving Forrester as the scapegoat," I said slowly. "Why didn't they cover it up better?"

"Except for Forrester's original drawings, they did. My guess, based on what happened later, is that the second set of drawings were supposed to replace the first ones, with the approvals faked," he said.

He frowned. "Probably a substitution was supposed to be made. Forrester wouldn't have agreed to any of this, so maybe whoever did the second set of drawings—most likely his partner, Walters—couldn't get his hands on the original drawings. Or he wasn't quick enough at making the substitution."

"So this implicates who?"

"Pretty much everybody who ever touched the project. Except Forrester, ironically."

Ironic because Forrester was the one who'd been blamed for everything. And only his son had believed in his innocence. "Including Rawlins?"

"Probably, though it'll take a little more digging to prove. Given some of the things we already know about Rawlins, though, we'll find the links," he said. "That's what the wine is for."

I touched my glass to his in a mute toast, then said in tones of mock hurt, "And here I thought the wine was for me."

Nick's eyes met mine for a moment, and I could feel the heat rise between us. Oops.

"Want some pizza?" I asked, leading the way into the living room.

"Sure." Nick relaxed his tall frame into one of the distressed leather chairs, looking quite at home. Cat followed us and collapsed at Nick's feet, purring loudly. Apparently Nick had the Cat seal of approval.

"This is nice, Barbara," Nick said, glancing around. "Comfortable."

"Thanks," I said. And given that I couldn't remember the last time I'd vacuumed, it didn't look too bad. But I was more interested in the case than the state of my apartment.

"If the information on the mall collapse was there all the time, why did no one find it before?" I asked.

"Because they didn't know to look for it, I suspect. The discrepancy wasn't in any of the documents filed by the builders, it was between the first set of architects' drawings and the final engineering and builder's plans."

"And if Forrester hadn't died so conveniently, that would have come out."

"Uh huh."

"Can you link Rawlins to Forrester's murder?"

"I'd need more evidence, a clearer connection than I've got right now."

"Which brings us back to Jake."

"And Tony Rawlins."

"Who seems to have had motive and opportunity. If Jake was overdoing steroids, maybe he started waving his gun around."

"Giving Tony the means as well," Nick finished the thought for me, then did a double take. "Jake was doing steroids?"

"That's what the guy at the gym told me."

Nick shook his head. "Sounds like our friend Jake was on a pretty self-destructive path."

"Or he enjoyed the risk." I said. "Funny, when this thing started, I couldn't see why Jake had been murdered. With what I know now, it's only surprising he wasn't killed sooner. Now all we have to do is pin it on Tony."

"If it was Tony."

"Oh, I think it was. I've got a feeling about this one."

"Judge will need more than your feeling."

"Yeah, yeah, yeah. Tell me something I don't know," I said and grinned at him.

He grinned back. And I swear Cat grinned too.

I blinked, and focused on the case.

"We can probably put Tony at the scene of the crime," I said. "I've got a witness linking him with that stolen bike, and photos showing the bike outside Jake's. And the photo shows date and time. The financial records give probable motive. I just don't think it's going to be enough. He's too slippery."

"And he'll have top flight lawyers."

"There is that. Can we tie him into anything you might be able to pin on his father?"

Nick shook his head. "Wouldn't count on it. The timing is wrong. Andrea makes a much too likely suspect, and her trial starts too soon to rely on that connection. And we still don't have any direct links between Jake's murder and Forrester's. What about whatever is in the safety deposit box?"

"Forrester may have had the documents at his gym, but Chris removed them. So that wasn't what Jake was using to blackmail Tony."

"Unless either Forrester or Jake made copies."

It made sense. I shrugged. "Even if Jake did have something in that deposit box, we can't count on it being solid evidence. And Tony may have destroyed it. Besides, to get our hands on that box we'd need a warrant, and I'm not sure we can demonstrate probable cause."

"Don't worry about getting a warrant."

I kept forgetting who he was. "Thanks. But I'd feel a whole lot better if I had something firmer."

"Like Tony killing someone else."

"Well, maybe not that firm. No, like a witness, or a confession."

"You planning on getting young Tony to confess?"

Picturing "young Tony's" hard features and stony gaze, I shook my head.

"No. I don't know what I'm planning. But I have to do something, for Andrea's sake."

I must have sounded as dispirited as I felt, because the next thing I knew, Nick was putting down his wine glass and standing up.

"Look, it's late. I'd better go," he said, reaching down and kissing me. "I'll let myself out."

CHAPTER TWENTY-SEVEN

I didn't sleep well that night. My dreams were a confused mixture of conversations with Tony that went nowhere, Andrea's face as she said she was counting on me, long dark chases through alleys where whoever I was after was always just out of reach, and erotic segments with someone whose smile looked a lot like Nick's.

It didn't help that Cat joined me at some point, and crowded me off to the edge of the bed. I woke up feeling even more exhausted than when I'd turned in.

It wasn't till I was on my second cup of coffee that the pieces started to come together.

The next few hours were a blur. I made phone call after phone call, putting my plan together. For a while there, I wasn't sure I could make it fly, but by eleven a.m. I was sitting in the bar at Fiasco's, nursing a cup of coffee and waiting for Earl to show up. I had a proposition for him.

When Earl finally arrived, he was skeptical, wanting to know why he should put anything on the line. Until I explained what had happened to Jake, and why. Then I had his full cooperation.

As Earl saw it, Jake had been a financial genius, and his murderer deserved whatever he got. Which is what I had counted on him feeling. It pretty much matched how I felt about Tony, so I figured Earl and I would work well together.

As long as neither Jerry nor Nick figured out what I was up to until it was all over, everything should work out fine.

Earl had no problem with that, which didn't surprise me.

Mike Chalmers didn't have a problem with it either, which surprised me far more than it probably should have. For a lawyer, Mike was way too intrigued by the idea of playing detective.

Dave Jennings might have refused to cooperate, but that didn't matter since his role was unscripted.

By two o'clock that afternoon, my plan was in place. Now all we needed was Tony to play his part.

Which he did.

But then one of the things I'd finally recognized was that Tony Rawlins was a creature of habit. He strolled into Fiasco's around three and ordered a glass of Shiraz and a side of fries with gravy. No wonder his complexion was so bad.

I watched him from my viewpoint at the bar as he made himself comfortable at a window table, where he could see the action inside and out.

When it had finally occurred to me to ask the right questions, I'd discovered Tony first met Jake at Fiascos. I'd just assumed that Jake frequented Fiascos for the same reason Andrea did, because it was close. I'd been wrong, misled by the fact that Zeke didn't recognize Tony as a regular.

I finally learned that Zeke worked the late shift, and Tony was gone by then. But on Tuesday and Thursday afternoons, Fiasco's became the place for a group of motorcycle aficionados, including Tony.

Tony's wine had been served and he'd already drunk half of it by the time Mike strolled in and sat down at the window table behind him. Mike nodded to Tony in passing.

Then Earl came in and made his way to Mike's table. He also nodded at Tony as he passed him. Within minutes, Earl and Mike were deep in conversation. I couldn't hear them from where I sat, but their body language made it clear that theirs was an intense discussion.

Actually, I wasn't very interested in what they were saying, as I'd scripted both of them. I was more interested in Tony's reaction to the conversation he couldn't help overhearing.

It was worth watching.

As they talked, Tony's expression froze in place, and his normal slouch started to straighten out. And the longer they talked, the more frozen he looked.

He was taking the bait.

I didn't have to wait much longer. Tony stood up and strode towards the door, eyes intent. I watched him exit and turn left, towards Broadway. Good. I'd read him right.

I followed, winking at Earl and Mike as I went by.

Sprinting the half-block to Broadway, I slowed to a saunter as I turned the corner. No point blowing it at this stage.

Tony was easy to spot—half a block in front of me, walking east very fast.

I followed, matching his pace and staying a half block behind him. When he reached the lights, he stopped and waited for the walk signal, every line of his body screaming his impatience. He was headed for Andrea's place, all right.

I hung back, pretending interest in the display of handbags in a nearby window. When the light changed, I waited till Tony was well across, then sauntered in the same direction. I wanted to be very sure he was really arrogant enough to steal Jake's bike for a third time, and in broad daylight.

He was.

Racing for my car, which I'd parked just down from Andrea's in anticipation of exactly this outcome, I followed him. It was a ridiculously easy task, even given the way Tony wove in and out of the heavy traffic. Of course, I knew where he was going, which helped.

When I got to the Harley dealership, Tony was standing in the middle of the showroom, looking about him impatiently. He spotted Dave and headed straight for him. Even the fact that I was on the other side of the shop didn't keep me from hearing that greeting.

"Why didn't you tell me that Scott customized his bike?" he asked in a voice loud enough to stop every conversation in the place.

Dave tried to quiet Tony, a frantic expression on his face. But Tony wasn't listening. He was too angry to care about the consequences. And by the expression on his face, Dave knew it.

"I don't do business with people I don't trust," snarled Tony. "And it seems I can't trust you."

All the color drained out of Dave's face. He put a hand on Tony's arm, as though to usher him outside. Tony shook him off.

"I'm not going anywhere until I get some answers," he said, his voice rising with every word. "What did you do to that bike?"

While the two of them were occupied with each other, I moved closer, so I could hear both sides of the conversation.

"No—nothing" Dave was stammering. "Look, Tony, can't we go outside? We're attracting too much attention."

Tony glanced around, then turned his back on his fascinated audience. He did lower his voice, saying in a fierce undertone, "I don't believe you. And if you know what's good for you, you'd better come clean. You know what happens to people who mess with me. You don't want to end up like Scott, now do you?"

Dave looked sick and shook his head violently.

"Then show me that hiding place," Tony said, taking Dave's arm and propelling him towards the door.

By now, I was standing half-hidden behind a display of custom fenders and taillights. Tony and Dave passed me without even glancing my way. Through the plate glass windows, I watched as Tony marched Dave over to where Jake's bike was parked.

They stopped in front of the bike, and Tony made an abrupt gesture. Dave seemed to shrink into himself, but he was shaking his head, saying something.

Tony shoved him, insistent.

Dave was still shaking his head, pointing at something on the bike. Tony leaned forward for a closer look.

While they were both distracted I moved outside and stationed myself behind one of the concrete roof supports. Now I could hear them, but I couldn't see them.

"I knew Jake had the information. I knew I didn't find all of it," Tony was saying. "And I know now that you helped him install some hidden storage on his bike. Don't try to deny it. Jake's dead. There's no point keeping his secrets."

"I'm not keeping his secrets." Dave said. "I keep telling you, I don't know anything."

"You're good, I'll give you that," Tony said. "I went over that bike with a fine tooth comb, and I didn't find a thing. But good or not, I want that paper, and I want it now. And you're going to find it for me. Or it'll be the last thing you don't do."

There was absolute silence for a moment.

I stood listening, wishing I'd found a vantage point where I could see their expressions. Then there was a shuffling sound, and what sounded like a choked cry.

A frustrated Tony was getting violent. And doing so in front of an audience.

Only someone as self-involved as Tony would stage a confrontation in front of a showroom full of people and expect no reaction from them. That arrogance was what I'd been counting on.

And this little drama was unfolding exactly as I'd expected it to.

Out of the corner of my eye, I could see the squad car pulling up. In this neighborhood, you can usually rely on someone calling the police immediately when a situation looks like it's getting out of hand. Of course, I'd also put in a call to 911 on my cell. I wasn't taking any chances.

I moved out from behind the pillar until I could see Tony and Dave.

Tony hadn't seen the police yet. He was totally focused on Dave. His hands were around Dave's neck and his fingers were slowly tightening. And he was still yelling.

Dave, though turning an interesting shade of tomato red, was holding his own, thrusting at Tony's shoulders with considerable strength. I considered getting involved, but only briefly. Vancouver's finest do a good job all by themselves. They wouldn't need my help.

And they didn't, losing no time in arresting both Tony and Dave. I helpfully pointed out that I believed the bike had been stolen.

With that situation nicely under control, I moved some distance away so I wouldn't be overheard. Then I called Nick's office.

"Hi there," I said when he answered.

"Barbara? Where are you? I've been trying to reach you all day."

"I've been busy. Listen, young Tony has just been arrested. It would probably be a good idea if Rawlins senior were brought in for questioning today, so that he can't bail out his wonderful son quite so quickly."

"Tony's been arrested?" Nick said. "When did this happen? And what's he been charged with?"

"I don't think they've charged him yet. But when they do, I think it'll be theft and assault at the very least. He swiped Jake's bike again, and then he tried to strangle Dave Jennings."

"And you just happened to be there?"

I laughed. "It's a long story. I'll fill you in later, but right now I need to know if you're planning to arrest Rawlins."

"I hadn't planned on it today. But if Tony's in custody, then we're likely to get further if his father is too. And I've got enough now to make a charge stick, thanks to what we dug up."

"So you'll do it?"

"Yes. But I definitely want to hear that explanation."

"You'll get it. Later. I've got to run—there are a couple of things I still have to do."

I cut the connection before he could say anything.

Then I called Jerry, and for a change caught him on the first try.

"Hi, it's me. Jerry, one of your squads has just arrested Tony Rawlins for stealing Jake's bike and for assaulting a guy. You might want to suggest they question him about Jake Scott's death, too. Ask him if he has an alibi for that night. Oh, and you might want to talk to the other guy, too. Dave Jennings. Tony told him some pretty incriminating things, and I have a feeling he might be ready to talk."

I'd also been taping their little interchange, but I wasn't sure how clear the sound would be. And I didn't want Jerry to know exactly how involved I'd been in this.

It would be best all round if Dave told them everything himself.

"What are you up to, O'Grady?" Jerry was saying. "How do you know all this, and how is Tony Rawlins connected to Scott's murder?"

"Sorry, can't talk now. Just question Dave and Tony," I said, hanging up before he had time to ask me anything else. I'd said all I needed to.

Tony was in for a very uncomfortable session, which should prove illuminating. And if Dave was as angry as I expected he'd be, he'd be quite ready to tell them about the threats Tony had been making.

All told, it should be enough to put Tony behind bars for a good long time.

I liked that idea. A lot.

Smiling to myself, I walked back to my car and headed for Fiasco's. I'd promised to let my co-conspirators know how our plan had worked. Not surprisingly, they were most enthusiastic about the outcome.

We ordered pints of Okanagan Springs Amber Ale to celebrate and toasted our plan and each other. Earl was pleased to know that Jake's death would be avenged, and Mike was satisfied that Tony Rawlins would finally get what was coming to him.

"Daddy's money will have a hard time buying him out of this one," he said, raising his beer.

Especially if Daddy's up on charges of fraud and conspiracy to commit murder.

But I didn't say anything. They'd find out soon enough.

CHAPTER TWENTY-EIGHT

That evening I called Andrea.

"I don't think you have to worry about what to wear to court," I informed her in my most matter of fact tone.

"What to wear…" she began, and then she got it. "Barbara, you've solved it? You've caught the killer?"

"Well, the police have the suspect in custody, and they're checking his alibi," I said, deliberately cautious. "But yes, I found the killer. And I don't think there's any way he can get out of it."

"I don't believe it. I knew you'd find him. I knew I could count on you. How? Who? What happened?"

I grinned, and told her everything, exactly the way it had unfolded.

"You set him up? Barbara, that's brilliant."

"It seemed like the only way. I figured Tony Rawlins was stupid enough to fall for it, and arrogant enough to react the way he did."

"And you were right." She paused for a moment. "Barbara— thank you. I don't know what else to say, except I'm glad you're on my side."

"Anytime, Andrea. Just do me a favor?" It was a good thing she couldn't see my grin.

"What?"

"Don't get yourself arrested for murder again?"

She laughed. "I think I can safely promise that."

We talked a little longer, then rung off. There was one more person I needed to call.

"Matthews here."

"Doug, it's Barbara."

"Barbara? Barbara who?"

"I know, I know. I've been busy. But I've got something for you."

"Oh?" he said, his voice sharpening. I could picture him grabbing a pencil and one of his preferred yellow legal pads.

"About Jake Scott's murder? The police have arrested Tony Rawlins for stealing Scott's motorcycle, and I think they're about to find out he's the murderer."

Doug let out a low whistle. "Tony Rawlins, huh? How'd that come about?"

So I filled him in, leaving out Nick's role and the probable arrest of Kenneth Rawlins. I did mention that he might want to get a quote from Rawlins senior. Knowing Doug, he'd have the rest of the story in no time.

"So who killed Forrester?" he asked.

My guess was that Kenneth Rawlins had paid for it, but I didn't have anything to back that up. By the time he was done, Nick might, though.

"I don't know yet," I told Doug. "But I'm hoping the fallout from Tony's arrest will unravel that one a bit more."

"Nice work, Barbara. That's quite a jigsaw puzzle. And it's going to make a hell of a story. Well, I've got to go." And he disconnected.

I laughed to myself. Typical Doug. When he's on a story, everything else becomes irrelevant. Shaking my head, I dialed Chris's number, got him on the first ring.

"Yeah, hello?"

"Chris? It's Barbara O'Grady."

"Miss... I mean Barbara. Why are you calling? Do you have news?"

And finally, the answer was yes. "More like an update, Chris. But it's looking good."

"Tell me."

I grinned at the command in his voice. "Your Dad's drawings have surfaced, and Tony Rawlins has just been arrested on suspicion of murdering the man who had them."

"*Tony* Rawlins? Is he related to the guy who's been pestering my Mom?"

"His son."

There was a silence. I wished I could see Chris's expression as he digested this bit of news.

"I *knew* it! I just knew it! Rawlins, the father I mean, had my Dad killed, didn't he?"

"I think so. And Rawlins, Sr. is likely being arrested as we speak."

"For murder?"

"Not quite yet. But if I'm right about how it will play out, he'll be charged before the week is out."

Chris let out an explosive breath. Then there was silence.

"Chris?"

"So my Dad didn't commit suicide?"

"No. He didn't."

"And they'll clear his name?"

"I plan to keep working on this until they do."

"Thanks, Miss. . . Barbara. And I mean it. Thank you."

Sometimes I love my job.

"And I'll get your money to you as soon as the insurance company comes through."

I grinned again at the earnestness in his voice. Being paid by Chris was the least of my concerns. "Don't worry about it. Wait until your Dad's name is cleared. I know you're good for it."

I finished my wine, then put a pot of Dark Italian Roast coffee on to brew. Just as I was pouring a cup the phone rang.

"Barbara, what did you say to Mom?" my sister demanded.

"What do you mean, what did I say to her? We had tea."

"You must have had more than tea. And I want to know what you said."

"You told me to talk to her," I said.

"I told you to listen to her, find out what was wrong."

"I think she's bored with her life."

"Oh, great! Well, she's not bored any more."

"Susanna, what is going on?"

"That's what I want to know. And I hold you responsible."

This conversation was getting out of hand. "Responsible for what?"

"Do you know what our mother is planning to do?"

"No, Susanna, I have no idea what our mother is planning to do. Why don't you tell me."

"She's going to take parachuting lessons."

"She's what?"

"She's planning on jumping out of planes, Barbara. Small planes."

Well, I'll be. I didn't see that one coming. This was my mother we were talking about? "Good for her."

"Good for her? She could be killed. She's nearly sixty, Barbara. She's too old to be jumping out of planes."

Sixty was hardly old. "Not if that's what she wants to do."

"I don't care what she wants to do. She's past jumping out of planes."

"And that's exactly what was wrong with her. She thought she was past it, too."

"This is the last time I ask you to talk to her. And whatever you do, don't take her out for tea again." And she slammed down the phone.

I'd just disconnected, still grinning to myself, when the phone rang again.

"How did you do it, O'Grady?" Jerry demanded.

"Hi, Jerry. Does this mean you're charging Tony with Jake's death?"

"You know it does," he said, not sounding very happy about the whole thing. "So how did you know? And how did you arrange to have him arrested? I thought you'd agreed to stay out of police business."

Now I was riled. "I didn't agree to anything. Except to prove Andrea innocent. Which you and your colleagues had no interest in doing."

"Okay, okay. I'm sorry. I'm happy you've cleared Andrea. But I need to know what happened."

"Sorry, it's classified," I said. "I gather Tony confessed."

"Let's say he implicated himself. He was ranting when we brought him in, and once we had Jennings's story, Rawlins lost it altogether. Especially after he found out his father had been arrested."

There was a pause. "You didn't have anything to do with that, did you, O'Grady?" he said.

"Who, me?"

"Why are you always in the middle of things?"

"Did you want Andrea cleared or didn't you?"

"Of course I did." He stopped, and I could hear a confusion of noise in the background. "Are you ever going to tell me how this came about, O'Grady?"

"Do you need to know? Officially?"

"Officially, no."

"Then maybe I'll fill you in, someday. As a friend." And he had to be satisfied with that.

"Oh, and Jerry—Andrea's pen? You know, the one you guys found under the body, the one that was going to convict her of manslaughter? She'd been missing it since the night she went to Fiasco's with Jake to see if she could reason with him. Looks like he stole her favorite pen from her."

It didn't leave Jerry with a lot to say.

After he'd disconnected, I called Andrea, and told her that it was official. Tony had been charged with killing Jake.

I called Doug and let him know, too.

Then I called Nick and invited him for dinner. I was in the mood to celebrate, and at the moment, I couldn't think of anyone I'd rather celebrate with.

Besides, I owed him an explanation.

CHAPTER TWENTY-NINE

When Nick arrived at my place just after six, I met him at the door with a glass of wine. "I figured you could use this."

He accepted gratefully. I waved him towards the living room where he sank into the leather chair he'd occupied the last time. I switched on the fire then went and got my own wine. Returning, I collapsed into the chair opposite his and looked at him expectantly.

"Well?"

"Well what?"

"How'd it go with Rawlins, Sr.?"

Nick looked at me quizzically. "Exactly the way you expected it to go, I suspect. You can expect to hear the announcements shortly."

He lifted his glass in a silent toast. "I hear they've charged Tony with killing Scott. Congratulations on a job well done." And he grinned at me.

I smiled back. It was nice to be appreciated. "Thanks."

"But I'm curious. Last night you were stymied, today Tony's been arrested and Andrea goes free. So what was the missing piece?"

"There were two. Remember last night you said we didn't have a witness to the murder?"

He nodded.

"Well, I realized we did have a witness."

"We did?"

I nodded. "Tony himself."

"Explain. Please."

I laughed. "It was easy, once I put it together. In order to make sure Andrea was cleared, I needed firm evidence that someone else killed Jake. So I got Tony to talk."

"Well, that would work, all right. And it obviously has. But just how did you get him to talk?"

"That was the second piece. I'd started by assuming that Jake had provoked his own death because of his temper. Then, as I found out more about Tony, I assumed that he'd planned the murder. I woke up this morning with the realization that maybe it hadn't been planned, maybe Tony just lost his temper and shot Jake.

Tony may be skinny, but his complexion suggests steroid abuse. And he didn't have any trouble slinging those big bikes around. I talked to some of the people Tony hung out with and found out that our boy has developed a habit of losing his temper and becoming violent."

"So you set him up." Nick looked impressed.

I found I liked that look on him. A lot.

I grinned at him. "It wasn't difficult, once I realized that Tony and Dave Jennings must have worked together. And that Dave's fear when he heard about Jake's death was because he knew enough to suspect Tony. I gambled that Tony would go ballistic if he felt he'd been betrayed."

"And did he?"

"He did. When the police showed up, Tony was trying to strangle Dave, and threatening him with ending up like Jake. Dave was too afraid of what Tony might do to keep quiet."

Nick just shook his head. "I'm amazed Tony avoided prison as long as he did."

"It gets better. He lost his temper again when he reached the police station and realized he was being questioned about Jake's murder. And when he found out Daddy had been arrested, he started making all kinds of incriminating remarks."

"Way I heard it, a little birdie also suggested a certain safety deposit box be checked out," he said with a grin.

"Well, it was worth a try."

"Hmmm. Especially when it turned out that it contained a list of deficiencies on the building Forrester had been working on. Plus a copy of the revised drawings with notes on them in Rawlins senior's hand."

"I wasn't entirely sure Tony would have left them there."

"Any thoughts on how Jake got his hands on them?"

"Might be worth talking to Brant, the assistant manager at Hercules. He was Jake's dealer, so I suspect Jake could have black-mailed Brant into giving him access to Forrester's locker. It was pretty obvious, once I found out that Jake knew something funny was going on with the Walters."

"Well, it certainly helps out the case against Rawlins senior. Especially given that with his training, he can't deny knowledge that the revised plans were substandard. And with Jake Scott's finger-prints all over those plans, it doesn't make Tony look like any angel. But then, Tony seems to think he's immune from the laws that apply to the rest of us."

"Daddy has a lot of money."

"Money won't do either of them much good now."

"Except that kind of money can buy a lot of lawyers."

"True. There aren't any guarantees. But look at it this way. Tony's a lot more likely to do prison time today than he was yester-day. And Andrea has been cleared."

I nodded slowly. "All very true."

Raising my glass, I said, "Here's to us. We make a pretty good team."

Nick toasted me silently. Then he grinned. "But you never did go out with me."

"I invited you to dinner, didn't I?"

"This is a date?" he said. "If I'd known it was a date, I'd have brought wine. And flowers."

"In that case, I'll make sure you know next time. I'm very fond of flowers."

"Next time? I like the sound of that," he said, his voice deepening.

My knees went to mush at the sound. Ignoring them, I stood up. "Give me a hand with dinner?"

We drank our wine and chatted as we chopped salad and grilled steaks, then settled in to eat. Nick had a way of making me laugh, and the time passed effortlessly.

I'd bought a pecan pie for dessert, and Nick made the coffee. Later, sitting in front of the fire with more coffee and brandies, I looked up to see him watching me. There was a look in his eyes that was unmistakable.

And I didn't have to worry about Andrea any more.

Putting down my brandy, I stood up and moved towards him. He met me halfway.

To say that the rest of the night—and the following morning—was wonderful would be to seriously undervalue it.

ACKNOWLEDGMENTS

Many thanks to those who listened to the story and the process as it evolved, including (but not limited to) my first readers Carla Lewis, Sandy Constable, Roberta Rich, Kelly Morisseau, Marie Connell, Sharon Knapp, Bobbi Randall, Kayo Devcic, Sarah Rowse, Brad Rowse, Travis Rowse, Linda Roggeveen and Chris Petty. Thanks go to them for insightful comments on early drafts of the manuscript. Thanks also go to Sharon Knapp for research and suggestions on building deficiencies and to Linda Roggeveen for setting me straight on insurance legislation and issues. For the benefit of the story, I stretched the facts a little to allow Crestlife Insurance to sell both life and liability insurance. Many, many thanks also to Linda Roggeveen for her eagle eye on the copy edit. Any errors are, of course, mine.